'Dear me,' he drawled.

'What an unexpected pleasure.' His calm voice was at variance with the barely concealed hostility in his expression. 'How did you find me?'

'I didn't.' Mary was too shaken to feel any surprise at his question. She only knew that he was furious at their unexpected meeting. It hurt her almost more than she could bear. 'I wasn't looking for you. It was an accident.' She felt her hands begin to tremble and hid them in the folds of her skirt.

Justin Hawkridge smiled sardonically. 'A very convenient accident,' he observed.

Alice Thornton was born and brought up in the Sussex countryside. Her favourite subjects at school were English and History, and she has always made up stories for her own and others' amusement. She has a history degree from York University, and historical research is still what she enjoys most, next to writing. She works in London as a secretary in a large teaching hospital, and at present she has no children, pet or a husband!

AN UNSUITABLE MATCH ✓+

Alice Thornton

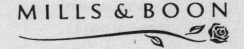

For the Doctors —
but you still have to buy your own copies!

*MILLS & BOON, the Rose Device and LEGACY OF LOVE
are trademarks of the publisher.
Harlequin Mills & Boon Limited,
Eton House, 18–24 Paradise Road, Richmond, Surrey TW9 1SR
This edition published by arrangement with
Harlequin Enterprises B.V.*

© Alice Thornton 1995

ISBN 0 263 79291 9

*Set in 11 on 12½ pt Linotron Times
04-9508-69908*

*Typeset in Great Britain by CentraCet, Cambridge
Printed in Great Britain by
BPC Paperbacks Ltd*

PROLOGUE
1819

'WHAT did he say?' Mary demanded tensely.

'He said, "Tell Mary it's over," ' Donald replied. ' "She was right, it would be a very unsuitable match, and. . ." '

'And what?' Mary prompted sharply as the large Scotsman's voice trailed away.

' "And a scandalous marriage," ' he finished unhappily.

Mary stared at him. Her grey eyes were wide and stormy with distress, but she didn't weep. Donald had never seen her weep, no matter how cruel life became—and life had been very cruel to Mary Drayton.

She bent her head abruptly, pressing tightly clenched fists against her mouth as if she was trying to hold back a cry of agony.

She was nineteen years old. A slight girl, slender-boned and apparently fragile. Her soft, tawny-brown hair should have ringed her face in a halo of curls, but it was currently dressed in a severe style which emphasised her slim neck and natural poise.

Her voice, which had sounded so harsh when she'd prompted Donald's reluctant revelation, was normally low and melodious. A testament to the

fact that she had been reared as a gentlewoman.
But her clothes were cheap and ill-fitting, uncompromising evidence of the hardship and impover-
ishment she had suffered for the last five years.

Yet, despite everything that had happened to
her, her skin was still beautiful and unblemished,
and so naturally fair that sometimes it seemed
almost translucent.

But now all the colour had been bleached out
of her face. She was as white as alabaster, and her
eyes were huge and very dark as she struggled to
come to terms with the grievous loss she had just
suffered.

Donald watched as she rocked silently back and
forth, her hands still pressed against her mouth.
He was powerless to comfort her.

'They say like always returns to like in the end,'
he said heavily.

'Did you give him my letter?' Mary asked, her
voice husky with unshed tears.

'Aye.'

'Did he read it? Does he know where I am?
Why didn't he come and tell me himself that he'd
changed his mind?' With each question she
sounded more and more overwrought.

'I don't know.' Donald shrugged helplessly.
'Maybe he didn't have the courage.'

'Of course he has the courage!' she snapped. 'I
dare say he wanted to save me pain. After all, he's
only told me what I've been telling him for the
past four months. It *would* have been a scandalous
marriage!'

Her voice cracked on the last few words and she turned away to stare blindly across the room.

'What are you going to do now, lass?' Donald asked awkwardly.

'I don't know.'

'Maybe you should——'

'*Not now*!' Suddenly Mary's composure broke.

She fled out of the parlour and up to her chamber, closed the door and turned the key in the lock. Old habits died hard, and she'd slept behind a locked door for the best part of five years.

Then her strength gave way and she fell on the floor, desolately sobbing out her grief and loss.

Outside there was a gale blowing, and it rattled the window-panes in their shrunken, rotting frames, but Mary didn't hear it. Nor did she hear the missel-thrush in the wind-tossed branches of the cherry tree, singing its heart out in the teeth of the winter storm.

She sat in a chair by the window, and listened to the inn sign creaking in the wind. It was past midnight. No doubt everyone else was asleep, but Mary was still awake. She was calmer now. The storm of tears had passed.

Though she had little energy for the task, she knew it was time to plan for her future. There was no one else to do it for her. Donald had been her loyal defender ever since he'd first entered her life nearly three years ago, but he always relied on her to make the decisions. He had provided the muscle and she had supplied the wits that had enabled them both to survive in St Giles. And St Giles was one of the most notorious thieves' kitchens in London.

Mary hadn't always lived in St Giles. Her father had been a rector and, as a child, she had lived a sheltered, happy life in a quiet rural parish in Sussex.

But her mother had died when she was twelve. And then, when she was fourteen, her father had also died—and she'd discovered that he had made no adequate provision for her. For nearly a week she'd thought that she would have to go and live with the squire, Sir Richard Moorcock, and his family—to be a poor companion to Sir Richard's daughters and an unpaid skivvy to his wife.

Then Mary's uncle, Alf, had appeared. Alf was her mother's brother. But, until his arrival, Mary had only been dimly aware of his existence. He had been disowned by his family over twenty years before, and she had disliked him from the first moment she met him.

But Sir Richard had been too grateful to be absolved of responsibility for her to ask any searching questions, and Alf had taken her. Mary had sometimes wondered whether, if Sir Richard had known *where* Alf was taking her, he would have been less sanguine about his decision.

Because Alf had kept a flash-house—a den of thieves, murderers and whores—in Church Lane in St Giles. He had also been a notorious fence, buying and selling stolen goods from all over London.

The shock of being thrown into such earthly purgatory had nearly killed Mary, but then she'd begun to wonder what Alf wanted with her. She'd soon discovered that he hoped to turn her innocence and quick intelligence to his advantage. A battle of wits and wills had ensued between them, which had ultimately ended in an uneasy truce.

Then, quite by chance, Mary had met Justin and they'd fallen in love. Despite all her protests that she wasn't a suitable match for him, he'd been determined to marry her.

The last time she had seen him, he had been about to visit an old friend in the north, but he had insisted on taking her into a jeweller's shop and having a wedding-ring engraved for her.

Then, only four days previously, while Justin was still away, Alf had been killed in a drunken brawl. Mary had seized her chance. With Donald's help, she had sold her uncle's alehouse to one of his competitors before the news of his death was widely known. Then she'd got out of Church Lane before anyone could retaliate.

She'd known that Justin would have no idea where she'd gone, so she'd sent Donald to tell him while she'd waited at a little inn several miles north of London. For three days she had been happy, not only because she'd escaped Church Lane, but because at last she had something more to offer Justin than her love. A dowry in the form of the profit she'd made selling the alehouse. Only now he wasn't coming. . .

She was abruptly recalled to her surroundings by a crash. She jumped, startled by the unexpected noise, then relaxed as she realised what had happened. The creaking from the inn sign had become increasingly distressed and at last the pole had broken and the sign had smashed to the ground.

Mary wasn't particularly surprised. The innkeeper was so lackadaisical about his responsibilities that he was bound to have ignored the rotten pole. She suspected his negligence was prompted by ill-health rather than sloth. Nevertheless, for three days her fingers had itched to do properly the tasks which he did carelessly and incompletely.

The sound of voices floated up from below as doors opened and people gathered around the fallen sign, but Mary paid no attention to them. She was sitting bolt upright, staring into space, as she suddenly realised how best she could invest her capital and preserve her independence.

'I'm buying the inn,' said Mary to Donald next morning. 'I've already settled the bargain with the landlord. I hope you'll be willing to stay and help me.'

'Aye,' Donald agreed stolidly, without further comment.

The Scotsman had survived twelve years in Wellington's army, but he only thought quickly in a fight—the rest of the time he was quite content to let Mary do his thinking for him. Indeed, there were times when it almost seemed as if he would be lost without her. Certainly she had provided him with both his conscience and his purpose in life for the past three years.

'And in the meantime,' Mary continued, 'I'd like you to go up to London and collect the wedding-ring Justin ordered for me before he went away.'

'*What*?' Donald exclaimed, startled. 'Why? I told you what he said.'

'I know. But I'm very young to be a landlady,' Mary replied calmly. 'And a widow is much more respectable than a spinster.'

Donald stared at her, chewing his lip uncertainly. 'Surely it would be better not to have a constant reminder of what's happened?' he protested.

'Perhaps, but I want that ring,' said Mary. She spoke quietly, but Donald had heard that tone in her voice before, and it was clear that she would brook no argument. 'I don't imagine Justin will have any use for it,' she continued. 'And if I'm going to be anyone's widow, I might as well be his. I'll never marry anyone else.'

to let Mary do his thinking for him. Indeed, there were times when it almost seemed as if he would be lost without her. Certainly she had provided him with both his conscience and his purpose in life for the past three years.

'And in the meantime', Mary continued, 'I'd like you to go up to London and collect the wedding-ring Justin ordered for me before he went away.'

'What?' Donald exclaimed, startled. 'Why? I told you what he said.'

'I know. But I'm very young to be a landlady', Mary replied calmly. 'And a widow is much more respectable than a spinster.'

Donald stared at her, chewing his lip uncertainly. 'Surely it would be better not to have a constant reminder of what's happened', he protested.

'Perhaps, but I want that ring', said Mary. She spoke quietly, but Donald had heard that tone in her voice before, and it was clear that she would brook no argument. 'I don't imagine Justin will have any use for it', she continued. 'And if I'm going to be anyone's widow, I might as well be his. I'll never marry anyone else.'

CHAPTER ONE
1826

THE November sun had already set when the carriage drew up outside the posting-house.

'We'll spend the night here,' Mr Penrose decided.

'Yes, sir.' Mary climbed down from the coach and cast a quick, professional glance over her surroundings. She had nothing to complain of in the speed with which the ostlers had responded to their arrival, but she would reserve final judgement until she had seen the state of the linen and tasted the supper that was laid before them.

'We'll eat in an hour when we've had time to recover from the journey,' said Mr Penrose.

'Yes, sir,' Mary agreed, and stood back to let him precede her into the inn.

Fifty-five minutes later she finished doing her hair, cast a shawl around her shoulders to protect her from the winter draughts, and went down to supper. But when she reached the foot of the stairs she hesitated. She had no idea which of the private parlours had been assigned to Mr Penrose.

She looked around for someone to ask but, although she could hear a mumur of voices coming from the taproom, there was no one in sight. She shrugged, and knocked lightly on the first door she came to. If it was't Mr Penrose who answered, she could always apologise and withdraw.

A familiar voice called for her to come in. She did so before she'd had time to think. Then she stopped short, as if she'd been hit with a mallet, staring in disbelieving shock at the man in front of her.

It hadn't been Mr Penrose's voice and it wasn't Mr Penrose pouring himself a glass of brandy, his back half turned to the door.

'What is it?' he asked, without troubling to look at her.

He was a tall, dark-haired man, dressed in the clothes of a gentleman. But, despite the elegance of his appearance, there was no disguising the innate power in his muscular body.

Although it was a cold evening he had discarded his coat, and his well-cut silk waistcoat emphasised the broad set of his shoulders and his lean waist. Even when he was performing the simple task of pouring brandy he moved with the contained, controlled power of a lazy tiger. And Mary knew that he was a fearless horseman and an excellent athlete.

He still had his back half turned towards her. But she knew that when he looked at her he would have strong, unforgettable features. A square jaw, slightly aquiline nose, and penetrating hazel eyes which were sometimes humorous, sometimes grave—and always capable of seeing more in two seconds than most men could see in a lifetime.

It was Justin!

The crazy beating of her heart seemed to thunder in her ears. She felt dizzy with shock. Unable to move or utter a single sound in response to his question.

'Well?' he demanded, swinging round impatiently when she didn't reply.

He stopped abruptly, the words dying on his lips, and she saw his eyes widen in surprise.

In the hallway behind her the shadows were dark but, though she didn't know it, she was standing in a circle of warm candlelight. Her fair skin was like porcelain, and her brown hair shone softly in the glowing light. She looked hardly older than when he'd last seen her.

She stared at him, her gaze locked on his face, her lips still slightly parted with surprise. He had changed, but at first she thought the differences were only superficial—then she met his eyes.

His gaze was hard and cynical. She could see no remains of affection, let alone love for her—only dawning anger in the fierce hazel eyes.

'Dear me,' he drawled, his calm voice at variance with the barely concealed hostility in his expression. 'What an unexpected pleasure. How did you find me?'

'I didn't.' Mary was too shaken to feel any surprise at his question. She only knew that he was furious at their unexpected meeting. It hurt her almost more than she could bear. 'I wasn't looking for you. It was an accident.' She felt her hands begin to tremble and hid them in the folds of her skirt.

Justin Hawkridge smiled sardonically. 'A very convenient accident,' he observed.

He strolled past her and closed the door. She felt her throat constrict as he brushed against her. She didn't know why he was so angry, but she knew him well enough to be acutely aware of the power in his large, lean body, and the effort it was costing him to appear calm.

She pressed her arms more closely against her sides, trying to make herself as small as possible. She was struggling desperately to maintain her own composure, but it didn't occur to her to leave. She had never walked out on Justin before, and somehow she couldn't bring herself to do so now.

He returned to the sideboard and poured out a second glass of brandy. 'How much do you want?' he asked harshly.

'What?' she repeated stupidly, staring at the brandy he was offering her in bewilderment. Nothing he said seemed to be making any sense.

'Let's not be coy about this, sweetheart,' he advised curtly. 'We're not children, and there's nothing more sordid than wrapping up a straight-forward bargain in mealy-mouthed euphemisms.'

Mary took the brandy automatically since that was clearly what he expected her to do. She still didn't know what he was talking about. If he had shown pleasure, or even indifference, at meeting her again she would have been better able to cope with the situation. But his undisguised hostility was undermining her confidence and her wits.

Only pride enabled her to keep her confusion and distress under any measure of control.

She struggled to understand what Justin meant while he watched her sardonically.

'You think I've come to ask you for money,' she said at last. 'Because I . . .because we. . . You think I've come to beg—or maybe even to blackmail you!'

Her voice rose in shocked realisation, and she stared at him in horror, seeing confirmation of her suspicion in his unyielding expression.

'Oh, you can't blackmail me, sweetheart,' he replied mockingly. 'It would be your reputation— or what's left of it—that would suffer, not mine. But I might be amenable to a little, no doubt charming persuasion.' His gaze flicked over her suggestively.

Mary closed her eyes, sickened and appalled by what he was insinuating. Yet she knew that, from his point of view, it was a reasonable assumption. There was an unmistakable aura of wealth about him, and she thought it likely that his intermittent differences with his family had been reconciled. It wasn't surprising if he thought she wanted to trade on her past association with him.

Nevertheless, now that the first shock of seeing him had passed, she was bitterly hurt and angry that he could accuse her of such a dreadful thing. She had done nothing to deserve it.

She met his gaze boldly, fierce, unconquerable pride in her stormy grey eyes.

'No, sir,' she said, her voice as cold and unyielding as his had been. 'I didn't know you were staying here until I opened the door and saw you. It was an honest mistake. I won't trouble you any further.'

She put down the brandy glass with an angry click and turned towards the door.

'*Mary*!'

She glanced back at him, startled by the urgency in his voice. But, before he had a chance to say anything else, there was an ingratiating knock at the door, and the landlord came in.

'Your dinner is nearly ready, my lord; I wondered if you——?' He broke off, staring at Mary in surprise.

'Ma'am! I didn't expect. . .'

'I came into the wrong room by mistake,' she explained. 'I couldn't remember which parlour you had assigned us. I was just leaving.'

'I do beg your pardon! Please, allow me to escort you. Your uncle is waiting for you in the rear parlour. My lord, please excuse me; I will be with you shortly.' The landlord divided an anxious bow between them.

Mary allowed herself to be ushered out of Justin's presence in a state of disquietude. She was deeply disturbed by their unexpected encounter but, even though she told herself that they had nothing more to say to each other, she was almost equally distressed that they had been interrupted. It was hateful to part with him on these terms.

She wondered why he had called her back, and then thought bitterly that it was probably to heap further accusations on her head. She wished she'd never met him again. She'd understood why he hadn't felt able to marry her, but it was agonisingly painful to be confronted with his cruel assumptions about her.

My lord, she thought, remembering what the landlord had said. That meant Justin's father was dead. He had finally acceded to his inheritance. No wonder he had such an air of prosperity. Donald had been right—like returned to like— and a baron's son would never completely forget what was due to his position.

It was very difficult to join Mr Penrose and talk calmly to him as if nothing untoward had happened. But Mary had had a great deal of practice at doing difficult things, and Mr Penrose was too preoccupied by his own troubles to notice if she seemed distracted.

'Uncle?' she asked, raising her eyebrows enquiringly, when the waiter had left them alone.

Mr Penrose flushed uncomfortably. He was a thin, rather stooped man in his late fifties, who seemed older because his manner was inclined to be both fussy and anxious. He had been a regular customer at Mary's inn for several years, and she was fond of him, but she couldn't help wondering what his reaction would be if he ever found out about her life before she'd become landlady of the Lazy Cat.

'I thought it would save you embarrassment,' he explained hurriedly. 'It's most unusual that we should be travelling alone together like this—and after what happened this morning. . .'

Mary suppressed a smile. That morning an impudent ostler had made a suggestive remark about old men and young women travelling together, and Mr Penrose had been brooding about it all day.

'Thank you,' she replied. 'But please don't feel badly on my account.'

'But I do,' he said earnestly. 'You have put yourself to so much trouble on my behalf, and I am involving you in a situation which promises to be most unpleasant—most unpleasant indeed.' He dabbed anxiously at his mouth with his napkin.

'I involved myself,' said Mary calmly. 'It may be that I'm mistaken. I hope I am.'

'Tell me again what you heard,' Mr Penrose begged. 'Perhaps there has been some mistake.'

'It was late one evening,' Mary began patiently, although she had told the story to Mr Penrose many times before. 'Your nephew Samuel was staying at the Lazy Cat on his way back to Bath after visiting you. He'd had half a bottle of brandy, and he was talking to his manservant, Phelps, when I overheard him. He said that you'd flatly refused to cover his debts, or allow him to draw on his own inheritance to do so.'

'It's true.' Mr Penrose nodded energetically. 'I thought if I forced him to face up to the consequences of his imprudence he would be more responsible in future. It was a most unpleasant interview. He used very violent language.'

Mary looked sympathetic, but she didn't comment directly on what Mr Penrose had said.

'Then he said that if he failed to repay his debt to one particular money-lender he might as well blow his brains out there and then because the man wouldn't wait another two years to get his money,' she continued.

'I always said it was foolish for my brother to leave his fortune in such a constrained way,' Mr Penrose remarked. 'I am to have control of it until Samuel is twenty-five—or until I feel he is sufficiently responsible to manage it himself.'

'I know, you told me,' said Mary drily. 'You also told me that if you died before Samuel was twenty-one another trustee would be appointed, but if you die after that time he can claim control of his fortune immediately. I think your brother must have had a very unusual way of managing his affairs.'

'He did,' said Mr Penrose unhappily. 'I suppose he thought that because I was so much younger than him the possibility of my death wouldn't arise—and he wouldn't have wanted to insult Samuel by appointing a trustee from outside the family.'

Once again Mary refrained from comment. She had never met the elder Mr Penrose, but she knew his son. If Mr Penrose senior had been anything like Samuel, it didn't seem impossible that he had deliberately engineered a situation which would lead to conflict among his surviving relatives.

'Please go on—I've been interrupting you,' said Mr Penrose.

'Well, then he talked about ways of getting hold of the money he needed,' Mary continued. 'He seemed to think he had two options. The first was to continue pursuing Miss Burleigh in Bath. . .'

'I believe she's a very considerable heiress,' said Mr Penrose. 'In normal circumstances I would say it was a highly suitable match——'

'The second possibility. . .'

'Yes, I know. He threatened to. . .to arrange a fatal accident for me.' Mr Penrose twisted his napkin nervously between his fingers. 'Perhaps you were right and I should have brought my lawyer with me—or my agent. But the *scandal* if anyone else found out about this. . .and perhaps it's all a mistake. . . Oh, my dear Mrs Drayton,' he added anxiously. 'I didn't mean to question your integrity—but perhaps he was only talking in his cups and didn't mean anything by it.'

'I hope that's all it is,' Mary said quietly.

'And I shouldn't have brought you,' Mr Penrose asserted, returning to his original theme. 'Exposing you to——'

'I made the charge against him,' said Mary firmly. 'It's only fair that I should be willing to attest to it when you confront him and, if necessary, apologise for my mistake.'

She also felt very strongly that, since it was her warning which had prompted Mr Penrose to confront his nephew, she had an obligation to ensure that no harm came to him as a result of doing so.

She would have felt happier if Mr Penrose had brought his lawyer or man-of-business with them, but despite her misgivings she was reasonably confident of her ability to handle the situation.

Besides, she was honest enough to admit to herself that, after seven years of respectable inn-keeping, she was beginning to feel bored and restless. She might wish she were going to Bath in less fraught circumstances, but she couldn't deny she was looking forward to the visit—or at least, she had been.

But that was before she'd met Justin. It was hard to concentrate on Mr Penrose's problems when Justin was only on the other side of the wall. His accusations had wounded her to the heart. But she didn't understand why he'd been so angry, and she kept wondering what he'd been going to say when the landlord had interrupted them.

'I beg your pardon?' She realised Mr Penrose had said something to her and she hadn't been paying attention.

'I was suggesting that we retire,' he said. 'We've travelled a long way today and you look tired. I am sorry to have caused you so much inconvenience. I shouldn't have brought you, but I really am grateful for your company.'

Mary summoned up a smile. 'I only hope that my presence can be of more practical benefit to you when we meet Samuel,' she said sincerely.

She didn't sleep at all that night. Her mind was full of Justin. Seeing him had vividly reminded her of the time when they had been lovers. Unlike many young noblemen, he hadn't ventured into St Giles on a wild spree, but because he was genuinely curious about all aspects of London.

The first time she'd seen him, he'd been sitting quietly in the corner of her uncle's alehouse. His clothes had been shabby, and he'd clearly had nothing of value on his person—a prudent precaution—but Mary had known immediately that he was in a different class from Alf's normal clientele. Even if his voice and manner hadn't betrayed him, his clean-limbed, active grace would have done so.

It had surprised Mary that no one bothered him. But both Alf and his customers had left Justin alone. She'd discovered later that his relative immunity to harm was caused by a combination of two things—his enviable ability to fade into the background when he wished to do so, and his equally notable ability to defend himself if anyone decided to dispute his right to remain unobtrusive. Since he wasn't doing any harm, and he wasn't an informer, it was easier to leave him alone.

And after his first visit Alf had even become quite proud of his noble customer, and let it be known that he would be extremely displeased if any harm came to Justin.

But Mary still hadn't been able to understand what he was doing in the flash-house until she'd seen his sketchbook. Many of the sketches had been done from memory—even Justin was wary

of getting out his sketchbook in the Blue Boar—
but all had been equally effective in capturing the
squalor and indignity of life in St Giles.

Despite his own privileged position Justin had
seemed to have an insight into the lives of those
less fortunate which was neither patronising nor
sentimental. After nearly five years among the
coarse, wretched, or dangerous inhabitants of
Church Lane, Mary had responded instinctively to
his pictures—and to the man who'd had the sensitivity to produce them. They'd fallen in love with
the sketchbook open beside them.

But that had been seven years ago. And when
Mary remembered the way he had spoken to her
last night, and the rich elegance of his fine clothes,
she began to wonder whether Justin Hawkridge
was the same man.

She got up early, and went out into the cold,
pallid morning light. A walk might clear her mind
and she strode briskly along the highway for over
a mile.

The sun was rising, illuminating half the sky
with a brilliant pink and silver sunrise, when she
retraced her steps. She paused to admire it, resting
her hands on top of a gate to look out across a
silver-turquoise meadow and the dark line of trees
beyond.

The wind caught a stray tendril of tawny hair
and whipped it into her face. She tucked it back
inside her bonnet with slender fingers, and shivered. She'd never been extragavant, and very few
of the clothes that were practical for her life at the

Lazy Cat were also suitable for a visit to Bath. She was wearing her best pelisse, which looked reasonably elegant but was nowhere near as warm as her everyday overcoat.

She rubbed her hands together to bring some warmth into them, and carried on walking. But when she returned to the inn, instead of going straight inside, she went to visit the stables. It was something she did every morning at the Lazy Cat and she was naturally curious to make comparisons.

A couple of stable-lads looked at her curiously, but no one approached her. She paused in front of a stall where a handsome chestnut snorted, tossing his head and eyeing her warily. She spoke to him softly and eventually he deigned to let her pat him.

She heard footsteps behind her, but she didn't look round.

A quiet voice said, 'Careful ma'am, 'e don't always take to strangers. Sometimes 'e can snap. Mind you,' the groom added, ''e seems to 'ave taken to you.'

Mary glanced at the man and smiled. 'Is he a high-stickler, or just bad tempered?' she asked, stroking the chestnut's nose. He snorted and nudged her hand.

'Just bad tempered, I reckon,' the groom replied.

Mary laughed, and the horse tossed his head at the unexpected sound. 'I'll bear that in mind,' she said.

The groom looked perplexed, and then embarrassed. 'I'm sorry, ma'am, I didn't mean you weren't. . .'

'I know,' she reassured him.

He was about twenty, she guessed, though his thin face looked older. He was short and slightly built, with narrow, stooping shoulders. He had probably been underfed for most of his childhood, but his eyes lit up when he looked at the horse. He wore the costume of a tiger—a gentleman's personal groom.

'What's his name?' Mary asked, nodding towards the chesnut.

'Barabbas,' the groom replied, always willing to talk about his charges.

'And that one?' Mary gestured to the next stall, where a perfectly matched chestnut mare stamped her forefoot in the straw.

'Mary. . .'

'A name with many associations,' said another, deeper voice behind her. 'So often it conjures up an image of saintliness—but it could just as easily describe a whore.'

Mary caught her breath. She hadn't heard Justin approach. She started to tremble, so she gripped the top of the wooden panel to hide it. Another hand appeared and lightly gripped the panel a few inches away from hers. He must be standing right behind her. She felt trapped.

'You startled me, sir,' she said, without turning round.

'My apologies.' But there was no apology in Lord Hawkridge's voice.

The tiger faded discreetly away and Mary was left alone with Justin. She knew she ought to turn and face him, but he was too close behind her— and she couldn't bear the possibility that he might still have that cold, hostile look in his eyes.

'Does this uncle treat you any better than the last one?' Justin asked mockingly in her ear.

'He's not. . .' she began instinctively, then bit her lip as she realised what Justin would inevitably think if she denied any relationship with Mr Penrose.

'I didn't think he was,' Justin murmured provocatively. 'I am reasonably well-acquainted with your family tree, sweetheart. Alf was your only surviving relative.'

She felt a light touch on her hair, then his fingers gently stroked the nape of her neck. She froze, startled by his caress. But as he continued to play with a tendril of her hair she was overwhelmed by a flood of sensations and remembered emotions. Her heart began to race and she was rooted to the spot, no longer capable of rational thought. He was very close behind her and she longed to turn towards him, to feel him take her in his arms, but she was afraid to move in case it broke the spell. This was only an interlude, it couldn't be real.

'I'll admit Penrose is wealthy,' said Justin softly, his breath ruffling Mary's hair, 'but couldn't you do better for yourself than a wizened old man?

There are plenty of younger, more exciting lovers to choose from.'

'He is *not* my lover!' Mary swung round indignantly, heedless of the consequences, and found herself almost breast to breast with Justin.

'Not a very satisfactory one if my lightest touch can hold you so mazed!' Justin taunted her. His face was in shadow; she couldn't see his expression.

She heaved in a deep, outraged breath, but before she could say anything his arms locked about her and his mouth closed on hers. She struggled to free herself, bracing her hands against his shoulders and pushing him away, but he was far too strong.

She wasn't afraid, but she'd seen too much violence to find any pleasure in an embrace that was forced upon her. She was on the point of kicking him—which would have been painful, since she was wearing wooden pattens—when his hold on her relaxed and, instead of being demanding, his lips became coaxing on hers.

All she had to do now was step back and she would be free—but she couldn't do it. He knew her too well and he was taking advantage of his knowledge.

It was cold in the stables, but his body was warm against hers. She could feel the power in his large frame, and now that his strength was no longer being used against her it excited her. She didn't remember if he'd made her feel like this in St Giles, but a flood of unfamiliar, stimulating sensations were washing over her. He teased her lips gently, persuasively, until they parted to allow him to explore her mouth more fully.

Mary couldn't resist. She had needed him and wanted him for so long that now she felt like a starving woman who'd been offered food. She had to take it, even though she knew the bread was poisoned. There was no future in this. They would never meet again. And, like all his kind, Justin Hawkridge was taking what he wanted, when he wanted it.

His kiss became more urgent, stirring dormant passions within Mary. Hardly knowing what she was doing, she pressed herself against him more closely, her hands beginning to slide up around his neck. . .

Then Barabbas snorted, his head only inches from theirs, and they were both startled. Mary sudenly realised what she was doing, and shoved Justin away from her, the violence of her reaction revealing how much his kiss had affected her.

'Dammit, Justin! You may be a lord but I'm not a common whore!' she insisted furiously, her churning emotions finding release in anger.

'There never was anything common about you,' he agreed sardonically. He was breathing rather rapidly, but otherwise he seemed completely in control of himself—and the situation. 'But I still say you could do better for yourself. Or is Penrose an indulgent companion? Does he allow you to see other men as well?'

Mary slapped Justin hard across the mouth. He

seized her wrist and held it in a vice-like grip. For a moment he loomed over her, but she was too angry to be afraid.

'You harpy!' he snarled. 'I ought to beat you for that!'

'The mark of a true gentleman!' Mary mocked, wrenching her arm out of his grasp. 'First you make unfounded, unspeakable accusations about me, then you want your revenge when I retaliate. You used to have more integrity.'

'*Integrity*. . .!' Justin exclaimed.

'Mr Penrose is not my lover,' Mary said through clenched teeth.

'He's not your uncle either.'

'He's my husband's uncle.'

They stared at each other in silence. A mail-coach pulled up in the courtyard outside, and the yard and stables were suddenly full of ostlers. Mary stepped aside to allow a string of glossy brown horses to be led past her, but apart from that neither she nor Justin paid any further attention to the activity all around them.

Justin caught her left hand in his, looking down at the ring on her third finger. 'I see,' he said, his voice suddenly expressionless. 'Have you been married long?'

'Four years.' Mary drew her hand away, hoping he couldn't hear the pounding of her heart. It was a lie, but it didn't matter. The only thing that mattered was that she couldn't let Justin outface her.

'Then it seems I must offer my belated congratulations.' He bowed ironically. 'Does he know about your life in the Blue Boar?'

Mary lifted her head proudly. 'Do you think I would marry anyone who didn't?' she asked coldly. 'Good day, sir.'

CHAPTER TWO

'I've made enquiries,' said Mr Penrose. 'Samuel has gone out of town on a visit for several days.'

'Do you know where he has gone? Is he expected to return?' Mary asked briskly.

'No. He doesn't seem to have been very informative about his destination,' Mr Penrose said, answering the first of her questions. 'But they certainly seem to expect him to come back,' he continued, 'and Miss Burleigh is still here. Do you think we should try to find him?'

'No,' said Mary firmly. 'It would be most uncomfortable to confront him with our suspicions under someone else's roof. We'll wait for him to return.'

'But I am keeping you away from your business for so long,' Mr Penrose protested.

'Donald will be able to manage things for a few days,' Mary said. 'And I have never been to Bath before. I assure you, sir, if you would do me the kindness of escorting me to the Pump Room tomorrow, I will feel well-repaid for the delay.'

'My dear Mrs Drayton, I would be honoured,' he said.

'The story of how Bath was founded always reminds me of the story of the Prodigal Son,' said

Mr Penrose as they made their way to the Pump Room next morning. 'The way Bladud became a swineherd when he was turned out of his father's household. But of course he had to leave because he had leprosy, not because he was greedy for material pleasures.'

Mr Penrose paused, a brooding look in his eyes. He was obviously thinking about another young man who was all too greedy for material pleasure.

'Tell me more about Bladud,' Mary prompted.

'Well, then the pigs began to develop sores on their skins!' Mr Penrose exclaimed. 'Think how dreadful the poor fellow must have felt—that even pigs weren't safe in his company. But then one day the swine plunged into a muddy quagmire after some acorns—and when they came out their skin had been cured! Then Bladud was able to go home, and later he returned and built a city on the site of his cure.'

'And people still drink the waters to this day,' Mary murmured. 'I wonder if anyone has tried it on pigs recently?'

'Mrs Drayton!' Mr Penrose looked shocked, then unexpectedly mischievous. 'Perhaps we won't enquire too deeply into that,' he suggested.

The Bath season was already underway, and the Pump Room was full of people. Some of them were there to take the waters, but most of them were more intent on seeing and being seen. They promenaded up and down under the watchful eye of Nash's statue, accompanied by discreet music from a small chamber orchestra.

Mary was fascinated. Since her childhood she had never had a chance to mix on equal terms with the gentry, let alone the aristocracy. Bath was no longer as fashionable as it had once been, but it still had its adherents. She watched them with interest.

'I think perhaps I'll take a glass of water,' said Mr Penrose. 'The last few days have been very trying; it would be a sensible precaution—don't you think?'

'It would indeed,' Mary agreed. She noticed that Mr Penrose seemed to be increasingly prone to ask her opinion, but he had good reason to feel anxious and in need of reassurance.

'Good gracious!' he exclaimed suddenly. 'I do believe that's my old friend Benjamin Knightley with his wife. I haven't seen him for years!'

Mr Penrose began to thread his way eagerly through the throng, leaving Mary with no choice but to follow.

'Penrose!' Mr Knightley shook his hand vigorously. 'You've been buried in Hertfordshire for so long I thought you were dead!'

'No, no!' Mr Penrose assured him, wincing slightly at the suggestion. 'How do you do, ma'am?' He shook Mrs Knightley's hand, then turned towards Mary. 'Allow me to introduce my niece, Mary Drayton. Mary, these are my old friends Benjamin and Isabella Knightley.'

'I'm very pleased to meet you,' Mary said courteously, although she couldn't help wondering about the wisdom of the introduction.

'Delighted, I'm sure,' Mr Knightley replied gruffly. 'You must be Abigail's girl. I must say, you don't look much like her. Didn't she marry a Campbell?'

'That's right,' said Mr Penrose quickly. 'I'm afraid Mary is a widow.'

'Oh, you poor thing!' Isabella exclaimed sympathetically. 'So young, too. Do join us.'

'You're very kind,' said Mary. She sat down, glancing briefly at Mr Penrose who was nodding and beaming in a most uncharacteristic fashion. It had never occurred to her that he would entangle her quite so deeply in his family matters, but he seemed happy with the result.

The next fifteen minutes provided Mary with equal parts amusements and bewilderment. She managed to field a number of questions about people she'd never heard of, before encouraging Mrs Knightley to expatiate on her own family. The subject which Mrs Knightley most enjoyed discussing was her grandchildren, and Mary was listening to a convoluted description of an incident in the nursery, when she glanced up and saw Justin approaching them.

He moved with the same powerful, easy grace which Mary remembered so well. The room was crowded, but he had no need to force a passage through the people. He smiled and exchanged greetings with the few acquaintances he had in the Pump Room, while strangers stepped instinctively out of his path, as if acknowledging that he had the right of way. Mary wondered confusedly how she could ever have imagined that he had a talent for fading into the background.

Mrs Knightley became aware that she no longer had Mary's full attention, and looked up to see what had distracted her.

'Good heavens!' she exclaimed. 'He seems to be heading straight for us. Benjamin! Do you know that man?'

Mr Knightley looked round, and almost goggled at the sight of Justin. 'It's Lord Hawkridge! He was pointed out to me in London, but I've never spoken to him. Penrose. . .?'

'No!' said Mr Penrose in a strangulated voice.

If Mary hadn't been so agitated, she would have found their reaction amusing, but as it was she could only stare at Justin with a considerable amount of apprehension. He was every inch the aristocrat in his bearing, but he had a dangerous gleam in his eyes.

He came to a halt in front of them, and bowed to Mary. 'Mrs Drayton,' he said suavely, 'I do hope you've recovered from the discomforts of your journey?'

'Yes, thank you, my lord,' she replied sedately. 'Please allow me to introduce you to my uncle, Mr Penrose, and his old friends, Mr and Mrs Knightley. Lord Hawkridge.'

She carried out the introductions without faltering, though inwardly she was seething with speculation about Justin's presence, and anxious about what he might say. She didn't miss the cold expression in his eyes as he acknowledged Mr Penrose with a brief nod.

'I had no idea you were acquainted with his lordship, my dear,' said Mr Penrose nervously.

'It was only a very fleeting meeting,' Mary explained hastily, her quick glance daring Justin to contradict her. 'I accidentally went into the wrong parlour by mistake, one night at an inn when we were on our way to Bath. It hardly seemed worth mentioning.'

'Not worth mentioning!' Mr Knightley croaked. 'My lord, it's an honour to meet you! I'm a great admirer of yours.'

'You flatter me, sir,' Justin replied drily. 'Mrs Drayton, perhaps you would care to take a stroll around the room with me—unless you have any objection—sir?' The last few words were directed at Mr Penrose, and there was a cold, almost contemptuous expression in Justin's eyes as he said them.

'No—oh, no,' said Mr Penrose. 'No, indeed.'

'Are you here for the sake of your health, my lord?' Mary asked, accepting the support of Justin's arm without obvious enthusiasm. 'My uncle was telling me only this morning how efficacious the water once proved in the curing of swine.'

Justin's cold, haughty expression relaxed slightly.

'You've just shocked your fish-faced companion out of what little wits he appears to have,' he said sardonically as they walked away. 'Don't you have any understanding of the respect due to my position?'

'No,' said Mary flatly. 'Do you have any understanding of how much you've just embarrassed me?'

'Oh, I think I have a very fine appreciation of that—Mrs Drayton,' Justin retorted. 'Your paramour is very keen to show you off to his friends, is he not?'

'He is *not*——' Mary began through gritted teeth, then broke off as another couple came too close.

'But he isn't your husband's uncle—because you don't have a husband,' Justin pointed out. 'And this——' he laid his hand over hers, his fingers lightly touching her wedding-ring '—is a prop to provide you with added respectability.'

Mary tried to draw her hand away, but his grasp tightened and she desisted. She was beginning to feel extremely disturbed. It was bad enough to have to walk side by side with Justin, pretending that they were no more than chance acquaintances, without the added distraction of his hand on hers. His touch filled her with conflict, because her heart and body still remembered when they had been lovers, even though she was currently furious with him—and confused by his angry response to her.

'I should have used another name,' she said bitterly. 'But it never occurred to me I'd need to. As I keep telling you, there's a perfectly innocent explanation for the whole thing, though why I should have to explain anything to you I can't imagine.'

'You have very flexible principles,' said Justin savagely. 'I expect you find them useful in your profession. But you really ought to change your name for your father's sake.'

'My *father*!' Mary exclaimed.

'I dare say that, as a man of God, he would be most disappointed in the path your life has taken.'

Mary jerked her hand away from him. 'As a man of God he should have made more provision——' She broke off, catching her lower lip between her teeth. Her face was rigidly expressionless, but her grey eyes were stormy.

'You're drawing attention to us, sweetheart,' Justin murmured, and drew her hand through his arm again.

Mary saw that they were indeed the centre of attention, and forced herself to appear composed, 'You are a bastard, Justin,' she muttered through grimly smiling lips.

'You may be right,' he conceded.

'What?' Mary's eyes flew to his face.

'That last comment was below the belt. Strike it from the record—but I don't retract anything else I've said.'

Mary caught her breath, more shaken by his oblique apology than she had been by his accusations. It was almost frightening to realise how well he knew her—all the weak spots in the armour she had built around herself. No one else could have wounded her so unerringly—and no one else could have recognised so quickly what they'd done.

'Is that Nash?' she asked, speaking at random, looking up at the statue in an alcove at one end of the room.

'Yes.'

'Well, now I've seen the Pump Room,' she said. 'It's turned out to be far less remarkable than I'd supposed. I'd like to return to the others.'

'As you wish.' Justin inclined his head ironically. 'I'm sure you'll find their company less stimulating than mine.'

'I certainly hope so,' Mary retorted. 'Are you staying in Bath long, my lord?'

'That depends.'

'On what?'

Justin smiled blandly.

'Ah, allow me to return your niece to you,' he said as they rejoined Mr Penrose and the Knightleys. 'I'm afraid she's not impressed by the unfortunate Beau, but then I understand that he himself often had a rather cavalier way with visitors to his domain. Good day to you all.'

He nodded briefly and strode away.

'Well, what a very unusual man,' said Mrs Knightley in the silence that followed his departure.

'He's a very rude man,' said Mary forthrightly. 'He seems to delight in setting people's backs up.'

'My dear! What did he say to you?' Mrs Knightley breathed.

'Nothing of consequence,' said Mary crisply.

'But the tone of his conversation showed neither kindness nor consideration for others. I cannot abide a man who shows no charitable feelings towards those less fortunate than himself.'

She caught herself up as she saw that the Knightleys were staring at her in open-mouthed astonishment, while Mr Penrose was listening almost proudly to her outburst.

'Well, never mind Lord Hawkridge,' she said more temperately. 'Mrs Knightley, you were telling me about what happened to Jemima the day the squirrel got into the nursery.'

It was late afternoon when Mary slipped out, unaccompanied, to make her way to Barton Fields. She had no idea if Justin would respond to her hastily scribbled message, but she wasn't prepared to risk another meeting in front of other people. And when she'd made discreet enquiries about possible meeting-places, the open space of the common-land had seemed ideal.

It was a bleak November day. Grey clouds scudded overhead, threatening rain, and a bitter wind cut through Mary's clothes. She shivered, but she was grateful for the weather. No one was likely to be out on such a day unless they had business of their own to attend to—and that made it much less likely that they would pay attention to her business.

Mary reached the Fields and looked around. She had a moment of panic that Justin wouldn't come, or that if he did come they wouldn't be able to find each other—and then she saw him.

He was striding towards her, apparently indifferent to the knife-like wind. But since he was wearing a heavy, caped greatcoat he had good reason to be warmer than Mary. She was still wearing her Sunday-best pelisse, and she was very cold.

'You summoned me?' said Justin ironically, by way of greeting.

'I asked you to meet me,' Mary corrected him. She hesitated. Now that he was here, in front of her, she didn't quite know how to begin.

'Why?' Justin raised his dark eyebrows. 'Are you looking for a new protector?'

'No, I'm not!' she retorted forcefully. She might have known he'd put the worst possible interpretation on her actions.

'You mean you're satisfied with the one you've got?' Justin asked disbelievingly. 'But sweetheart, he doesn't even dress you very well.' His sharp eyes had seen the way she hunched against the cold in her thin pelisse.

'He doesn't dress me at all!' Mary snapped.

'Ah, you mean he's more interested in *undressing* you,' Justin said. 'Well, I can understand that ambition—although I don't imagine he achieves it with any style.'

'For God's sake, Justin!' Mary exploded. 'I've told you I'm not his mistress. Why can't you believe me?'

'Because I know you,' he replied tautly, his

expression both mocking and angry. 'I can remember how you told me once you'd do anything to survive—even if it meant sharing the bed of a cracksman. I don't suppose you shed one tear when he was transported, did you?'

For a moment Mary stood very still. It was true that she'd once been forced to become a thief's mistress in return for his protection, but she'd never hidden the fact from Justin. She'd never had any secrets from him. She could hardly believe how brutally he'd flung her degradation in her face.

Her fair skin was as pale as porcelain as she met his scornful gaze, and she looked nearly as fragile. It was almost possible to imagine that the November wind would blow her slender body away like last summer's dried flowers—except for the fierce, proud expression in her stormy grey eyes.

'I didn't weep for Bill. Why should I?' She lifted her chin defiantly. 'He protected me before Donald came, during that brief time when Alf turned completely against me—but he didn't do badly out of the bargain. And I will not bow my head in shame before you or anyone else. I did not steal. I did not lie. And I did not trangress any law made by man.'

She was breathing quickly when she finished speaking, but her gaze was locked with steadfast intensity on Justin's face, heedless of the freezing wind tugging at her clothes.

Justin looked down at her. His expression was

no longer mocking. She couldn't quite tell what he was thinking. He lifted his hand and touched her cold cheek with his warm fingers.

'I wonder what the righteous would say if they knew what the lilies of the field have to sacrifice to be arrayed in cheap broadcloth?' he said quietly.

Mary bent her head. She could deal with Justin's anger, but his kindness nearly destroyed her defences. She could feel tears threatening, but she was determined not to give way to them in front of him.

She took a step backwards.

'That's all in the past,' she said, trying to sound brisk and practical. 'I'm more interested in the present. I can understand why you were suspicious of my motives the first time we met—but I told you it was an accident. And I *don't* understand why you've continued to be so hostile—or why you tried to embarrass me today. I came to ask you to leave me alone.' Her voice faltered slightly on the last few words, but she managed not to look away.

'Very good, sweetheart,' he said sardonically. The momentary tenderness in his manner had disappeared. 'You must have been practising. Your technique is excellent. If I didn't know better I might truly believe you're an innocent wronged.'

'*Stop it!*' Mary cried, pushed almost beyond endurance by his continued antagonism. She pressed her hands against her cheeks, heedless of the way the wind whipped her skirts against her legs. 'Justin, you were the one who decided we weren't a suitable match. *Of course* you were right, but you don't have to go on and on demonstrating how very unsuitable I was.'

'*What*?' For a moment Justin stared at her, disbelief and doubt in his eyes, then he seized her shoulders. 'What the devil are you talking about? You *disappeared*!'

He shook her roughly, and her bonnet fell back from her head, hanging by its ribbons around her neck. Mary gazed at him, stunned by the violence of his reaction to her words.

'I had to disappear. Alf was dead,' she said jerkily. 'But I sent you a letter.'

'What letter? I never received a letter.' Justin's fingers dug into her shoulders. A few drops of rain had started to fall, but neither of them noticed.

Mary stared at him, trying to understand what was happening. It would be easy to accuse him of lying, but Justin was too proud and confident to hide behind deception. If he said he hadn't seen her letter, then he hadn't seen it — and that didn't make sense.

Her eyes lost their focus as she looked back over seven years to the moment Donald had stood in front of her and told her Justin didn't want her. Donald had never liked or trusted the young nobleman. Perhaps he'd been jealous of what Justin meant to Mary. With slow, horrifying certainty, she realised that Donald had lied.

She felt cold then, in a way which had nothing to do with the November wind. Until that moment she had trusted the Scotsman, but now it seemed that even he had betrayed her. It wasn't safe to depend on anyone.

'Tell me!' Justin demanded insistently.

Mary focused on his face: hard, suspicious, questioning.

'I gave the letter to Donald,' she said simply. 'He came back and told me you'd decided we weren't suited after all.'

'And you believed him!' Justin exclaimed incredulously.

'Why not? He was right,' Mary replied bleakly.

'That wasn't his decision to make,' Justin said harshly. 'What happened to you? How did you survive? Who looked after you?'

'No one! I didn't need anyone to look after me!' Mary snapped furiously, insulted by his ready assumption that she couldn't manage on her own.

'How?' Justin demanded. 'Those years in Church Lane only left you fit for one thing. You could hardly have found genteel employment as a governess or a lady's maid after that.'

Mary wrenched herself out of his grip, staring at him in appalled understanding.

'That's how you think of me, isn't it?' she cried. 'That's why you flung Bill Crawford in my face just now. Is that how you've always thought of me? Fit only to be a common whore?'

Justin opened his mouth to say something, but she swept on, paying no attention to him.

'Did you pretend you wanted to marry me so that I'd agree to be your mistress? Well, you needn't have put yourself to the trouble. I would have been your mistress then, willingly—but not now. I wouldn't be any man's mistress now!'

She turned to go, but he seized her arm and swung her round to face him.

'What about Penrose?'

'I've told you!' she spat at him. 'There's a perfectly innocent explanation for why we travelled together.'

'Then tell me what it is.'

'*No!*' She was too angry to explain anything to Justin, and too hurt that he still didn't trust her word. Besides, Mr Penrose wouldn't like it if his family business was discussed with anyone else.

It was raining harder now, slanting icy spears of water into her face. She shivered, and pulled her bonnet back on to her head. Somehow the rain seemed to have doused the heat of their argument. There was nothing left to say, yet Mary couldn't quite bring herself to walk away.

She held out her hand to him.

'I'm sorry you thought I'd run away,' she said steadily. 'I'm sorry that you never received my letter. But it's over now, and it ended for the best for both of us. Please, let's leave it there.'

He took her hand in his, and she felt his virile warmth encircle her cold, slender fingers.

'You should buy a muff,' he said. 'Shall I escort you back to your hotel?'

'No, thank you.' Mary wasn't going back to the hotel, but she had no intention of telling Justin that. 'If we meet again, please don't continue to snipe at me, my lord. It doesn't do justice to either of us.'

She turned and walked away, knowing that he was watching her, almost disappointed that he'd let her go so easily. But there wasn't anything left to say. If she was honest she knew that their love had never really had a chance. The only possible role she could ever play in Justin's life was as his mistress—and she was never again going to gamble her security and independence on someone else's good intentions.

The icy wind nearly blinded her, but it was only when she reached up to brush a hand across her eyes that she realised hot tears were mingling with the rain on her cheeks.

'My dear, are you sure you don't mind that we are no longer staying at the hotel?' Mr Penrose asked anxiously after dinner that evening.

'Of course not,' Mary assured him. 'This is a beautiful house. I've never stayed anywhere so elegant.'

'I suppose it is rather pleasant,' said Mr Penrose, looking around as though that particular aspect of the situation had hitherto escaped him. 'But when Knightley told me of the possibility of hiring it I immediately thought of the greater privacy it would afford us—I mean for our interview with Samuel,' he added hastily, in case Mary had mistaken his meaning.

'I quite understand,' said Mary.

'Also, I can never feel entirely at home in a

public hotel. One can never be sure that the linen is properly aired, or that things will be done exactly to one's taste,' Mr Penrose continued. 'Not that I mean to imply that things aren't done handsomely at the Lazy Cat, of course.'

Mary smiled. 'I know that,' she said. 'I'm not unhappy with the situation. I know we're in Bath in rather distressing circumstances. All the same, you are providing me with an opportunity to do several things I've never done before. I'm very grateful to you, sir.'

Mr Penrose flushed. 'You're too kind, too kind,' he muttered. 'Um, did you never have a chance to visit here with your husband? I suppose you could never leave the inn?'

'My husband died before I bought the Lazy Cat,' said Mary. She twisted her wedding-ring absent-mindedly. It wasn't an uncommon gesture for her.

'It must have been dreadful to be left alone so young,' said Mr Penrose sympathetically. 'But I dare say Donald was a great support and comfort to you. He has always seemed a most loyal servant.'

'Yes.' For a moment a rather cold look crept into Mary's eyes. 'Yes, he's devoted to me. Mr Penrose. . .' she roused herself '. . .it occurs to me that while we're waiting for your nephew to return it might be worthwhile making Miss Burleigh's acquaintance.'

'Miss Burleigh?'

'To see if we can discover how advanced their courtship is,' Mary explained.

'Oh, I see. But I don't know the Burleighs,' Mr Penrose protested, looking worried. 'I wonder if the Knightleys do? Perhaps they would be able to provide us with an introduction.'

'Even if they don't, I don't foresee any problem,' Mary replied. 'Miss Burleigh and her mother were at the Pump Room today; I enquired. All we need to do is approach them, tell them how highly Samuel has spoken of Miss Burleigh, and presume upon our relationship with him to introduce ourselves to them. It should be quite easy. Would you like another cup of tea, sir?'

Mr Penrose regarded her with something like awe.

'Are you never at a loss, ma'am?' he asked.

Mary smiled. To tell the truth, after all the years of being deferential to her customers, she was feeling slightly nervous about introducing herself so brashly to the heiress. But she had no intention of letting Mr Penrose know that.

'Very frequently,' she replied. 'But I've discovered that, to be a successful landlady, it pays never to let your guests know when they've disconcerted you.'

CHAPTER THREE

'THERE has been a delivery for you, ma'am,' said the butler austerely. 'From Madam Eustacia, the dressmaker.'

'For me!' Mary exclaimed. 'Are you sure there hasn't been any mistake?'

'No, ma'am. The direction on the attached note is most clear.' He offered her the letter on a silver tray.

Mary glanced down at it and recognised Justin's handwriting. Her heart immediately began to beat faster, but she gave no outward sign of her agitation.

'Thank you, Grigson,' she said calmly, picking up the letter. 'Would you have it taken up to my chamber, please?'

'Certainly, ma'am.' He bowed and went out of the drawing-room.

Mr Penrose had hired the servants with the house while the owner, a retired merchant who'd fallen on hard times, was away. Mary was sure the household was already seething with gossip about its temporary tenants. This incident wasn't going to do anything to discourage speculation, but there was nothing she could do about it.

She broke open the seal with a trembling hand

and read the note. It was very brief. 'Armour comes in many guises.'

It was signed with a single, unadorned H. Mary had seen the same initial on Justin's finished sketches. She let her hand fall into her lap, tears of relief pricking at the back of her eyes. Her first thought was that their friendship wasn't going to end on a note of bitterness after all. She glanced at the clock. She was due to go to the Pump Room with Mr Penrose very shortly, but she still had a few minutes in hand.

She ran upstairs and opened the package from the dressmaker. She wasn't surprised to discover that it contained a pelisse, beautiful, fashionable — and warm. There was also a cosy muff. She touched the rich cloth gently, caught in a rush of conflicting emotions.

She could hardly accept the gift when she was trying so hard to distance herself from Justin — and when he had accused her of such dreadful things. But it was typical of him that he should have responded to a practical need. He had never been content simply to sketch the pinched and hungry faces in St Giles, though Mary doubted if anyone else knew of his philanthropy.

She could have been insulted by the implicit suggestion that she could be seduced by a warm coat. But she was far more moved by the fact that he'd noticed she was cold. No one else ever noticed when she was cold or uncomfortable. Even Mr Penrose, who'd spent three days travelling with her, hadn't noticed how cold she'd been in her thin pelisse. Justin might think of her as little better than a common street-walker, but at least he cared enough about her not to let her go cold.

Perhaps the gift was a sign that he believed her explanation of what had happened. Perhaps he'd forgiven her for disappearing without telling him where she was. It didn't fully assuage her hurt at the way he'd flung her dishonourable past in her face, but it softened her grief.

She heard a sound from the doorway and looked up. A maid was standing there, a milliner's box in her hands.

'This just came for you, ma'am,' she said eagerly.

'Thank you.' Mary opened it.

'It's beautiful!' the maid exclaimed. She touched the pleated silk which lined the bonnet almost reverently. The merchant was a widower, and very little female finery ever came into the house. 'Look how it brings out the colour of your eyes,' she continued. 'You must wear it to the Pump Room this morning. Did you order it when you went out yesterday afternoon?'

Mary alllowed the assumption to go by without correcting it. Almost without realising she'd done so, she'd decided to accept the pelisse. If Justin intended it to be the first step in her seduction she would correct his misapprehension. But if it was intended as an olive-branch she could do no less than accept it.

* * *

'My dear, you look splendid this morning,' said Mr Penrose as they made their way to the Pump Room. 'You see what a difference even one glass of the water can make. Oh, but you didn't take any.' He paused, looking puzzled.

'It must be the Bath air,' said Mary calmly. 'It's very invigorating, is it not?'

'That must be it.' Mr Penrose's expression cleared. 'Oh, dear, I do hope that the Knightleys know Miss Burleigh—and that they're here.'

'Never mind,' said Mary. 'If they aren't, I shall impersonate the kind of gushing, impulsive female who simply *cannot* wait for a formal invitation to meet someone she's heard such fine things of. After all, sir, Miss Burleigh may be an heiress, but you're hardly lacking in consequence yourself.'

Mr Penrose puffed up slightly at her praise, then deflated equally quickly.

'My father made his fortune in India,' he said. 'We didn't exactly come over with the conqueror. Of course, Martlesham House is one of the most elegant residences in Wiltshire, but even so. . .'

'How is it you come to live in Hertfordshire when your family home is in Wiltshire?' Mary asked.

Mr Penrose flushed.

'My brother resented the fact that, apart from the house, my father divided his fortune equally between us,' he replied. 'He was most unpleasant to me. I found it more comfortable to move away—and my late wife came from St Albans.'

'I hadn't realised you were a widower!' Mary exclaimed.

'Oh, yes,' said Mr Penrose sadly. 'She died giving birth to our first child. It was stillborn.'

'I'm so sorry,' Mary said gently. 'How dreadful for you.'

Mr Penrose glanced at her.

'It was nearly thirty years ago,' he said. 'If it wasn't for her portrait in the drawing-room I think I might almost believe it never happened. She was such a beautiful, loving creature,' he added wistfully. 'You see, we are alike in having lost our partners young.'

Mary looked down, unable to think of anything to say.

The Pump Room was crowded as ever, but the Knightleys were nowhere to be seen, and Mr Penrose did not number any of the other people present among his acquaintances. It was a long time since he'd been to Bath.

'Never mind,' said Mary. 'There's Miss Burleigh and her mama over there. All you need to do is remember that you're a man of consequence, and that in introducing ourselves to them it is we who are doing them the favour.'

'I'll do my best,' said Mr Penrose meekly. 'I surely believe that they should be honoured to meet you, my dear.'

Mary glanced at him, rather startled by the warmth in his tone, but by then they'd reached the Burleighs.

It wasn't, in fact, very difficult to ingratiate

themselves with them. As far as Bath was concerned, Samuel Penrose was a very personable young man who was also heir to a considerable fortune. The terms of his father's will—and his own profligacy—were not generally known.

'This is my daughter, Lucinda. And this is my cousin, Miss Emma Lewisham,' Mrs Burleigh concluded the introductions. 'Unfortunately, my husband died several years ago, but Miss Lewisham has been a great support to me.'

Miss Lewisham produced a smile which managed to convey both her gratification at Mrs Burleigh's compliment and her humble belief in her unfitness to receive them. It set Mary's teeth on edge, but nothing in her demeanour revealed her true feelings.

'I'm very glad to meet you all,' she said warmly, but without any hint of unbecoming boldness. The charming manners she'd learnt so long ago at the rectory still stood her in good stead. No one could have guessed how unusual such a situation was for her. 'It's my first visit to Bath, and we don't have many acquaintances here,' she continued, 'but it's so pleasant to meet new people, isn't it?'

Mrs Burleigh smiled. 'I'm sure you'll soon have many friends here,' she said. 'Won't you join us for a while?'

'Thank you.' Mary's smile lit up her eyes and she sat down beside Lucinda, hoping that Mr Penrose would have the good sense to entertain the two older ladies.

'I believe you reside in Bath permanently,' she said to Lucinda. 'You must know it very well.'

'I suppose I do,' Lucinda replied hesitantly.

She was by no means an unattractive girl, but she was shy and a little awkward in her manner. And at the moment she was also nervous because she didn't know Mary and she didn't know what to talk about. Mary could easily see how she might have been dazzled by the attentions of a dashing young man—if that was what had happened.

'I must admit, I still feel a little strange and out of place here,' Mary confessed. 'We only arrived two days ago. And I've led a very retired life for the past few years. Perhaps you could point out some of the Bath notables to me?'

'I'd be delighted to,' Lucinda said, much more sure of herself now that Mary had given her an opening.

The next few minutes were occupied by an increasingly lively and confidential conversation between the two young ladies which left Mary with a mischievous sparkle in her grey eyes and Lucinda giggling behind her fan.

Despite the fact that Mary had an ulterior motive for gaining Lucinda's confidence, there was nothing contrived about the way in which she drew the younger woman out. She liked people, she enjoyed meeting new acquaintances, and she easily found herself warming to Lucinda. It was a long time since she herself had looked at the world with such innocent yet hopeful eyes.

'You must be very fond of your cousin,' Lucinda

said at last, blushing slightly. 'He is a very fine young man, isn't he?'

'I'm afraid I don't know him very well,' Mary replied apologetically.

'Oh, but surely——?'

'I grew up in Scotland, and my marriage kept me in the north,' Mary explained. She found it very difficult to lie to Lucinda, but she didn't have much choice. 'It's only recently I've come south. Samuel spoke very highly of you, but I must rely on *you* to learn more about *him*.'

Lucinda blushed even rosier. 'He's very charming,' she said, stammering slightly. 'He waltzed with me at Mrs Carling's ball. I'm not very good at dancing,' she added naïvely, 'but he assured me I would improve with practice.'

Mary didn't feel the slightest desire to smile. She could recall all too clearly the contempt with which Samuel had spoken about Lucinda Burleigh. His threats about terminating Mr Penrose's life might or might not have substance to them, but he represented a very real danger to Lucinda's future happiness.

'Forgive me, Miss Burleigh, but how old are you?' she asked quietly.

'I will be twenty-one next May,' Lucinda replied, almost as if she were confessing to a crime. 'Papa died just before I was due to come out,' she added in an undertone. 'And since then Mama hasn't felt up to the rigours of a London season.'

'No, I see.' Mary glanced at Mrs Burleigh, who

was busily chatting to Mr Penrose, and quite complacent about the growing friendship between her daughter and his putative niece.

At twenty-six—although of course Mrs Burleigh didn't know her precise age—Mary was too old to be considered competition for Lucinda. She was also Samuel Penrose's cousin—Samuel had made a very good impression on Mrs Burleigh—and Mr Penrose's niece. Almost as importantly, she was very prettily behaved, charming and warm-hearted. All in all, just the kind of friend Mrs Burleigh would have chosen for her daughter.

'I've never had a London season myself,' said Mary, who would have been quite startled by the trend of Mrs Burleigh's thoughts if she'd known them. 'I've often thought that, once the first excitement wears off, it must become very tiring. And if you don't have many acquaintances you always have the worry that there won't be anyone you can talk to.'

'Oh, yes!' said Lucinda eagerly. 'You understand perfectly. There's nothing worse than sitting out every dance with Mama or Cousin Emma.'

'But surely here in Bath you have acquaintances?' Mary protested.

'But they don't want to dance with me,' said Lucinda simply. 'Besides, we've only lived here since Papa died. It's not quite the same as people you've grown up with. And Mama says I must be very careful not to be taken in by people who are more interested in my fortune than in me,' she concluded, with the air of one who was quoting a much repeated warning.

'Do you have a fortune?' Mary asked delicately.

'I will have.' Lucinda sighed. 'That's what makes it so difficult,' she confided. 'I know I'm not very elegant or. . .or lively. So it does seem much more likely that people would be interested in me for my money rather than myself, don't you think?'

'No!' said Mary emphatically. 'Miss Burleigh, if you give them the chance I am sure you will find many people who will like you for yourself.'

'But how am I to distinguish them?' Lucinda asked. 'That's why I was pleased when Mr Penrose. . . That is, Mama says he is very wealthy too. So he cannot be interested in my fortune, can he?' There was a measure of doubt in her voice. She wasn't as foolish as she first appeared, or perhaps she just wasn't used to the notion that anyone could find her attractive.

It was a tricky question for Mary to answer. She didn't want to tell Lucinda of her suspicions about Samuel, but nor did she want to encourage her friendship with him.

'I don't believe anyone could fail to enjoy your company,' she said, choosing her words very carefully. 'But rich men, as well as poor men, can sometimes have a distressingly material view of life.'

Lucinda stared at Mary, a question forming in her eyes, but before she had a chance to voice it Mr Penrose interrupted them.

'My dear Mary, isn't that Lord Hawkridge approaching us?' he said suddenly.

Mary looked around. 'Yes, it is,' she said. Her heart skipped a beat. She wasn't sure whether she was pleased to see him or not; she only wished she didn't have to confront him before so many curious eyes.

'Good gracious! Are you acquainted with him?' Miss Lewisham gasped. 'My sister lives in South Audley Street, and she sends me all the society gossip. Apparently he's a dreadful rake! He keeps mistresses on all the main post roads the way some men keep horses!'

'*Emma*!' Mrs Burleigh exclaimed, outraged.

'Good heavens!' Lucinda stared at Justin wide-eyed, while Mr Penrose gave him another, far more penetrating glance.

'I'm very sure he doesn't,' said Mary drily, just as he reached them.

Justin gave no indication that he'd heard her comment, but acknowledged her and Mr Penrose with a somewhat curt greeting. Mary's temper began to rise. He had no business to single her out, then treat her in such a cavalier manner. But she kept her face expressionless as, once again, she was forced to introduce him to her companions.

Once she'd finished her introductions, she withdrew from the conversation, and waited to see what would happen next. It was a curious situation. The Burleighs, like Mr Penrose's father, had made their money in trade, and they showed a distressing tendency to be overawed by Justin's title—not to mention his rather formidable presence.

'I don't believe we've seen you in Bath before, my lord,' said Miss Lewisham breathlessly, before anyone else could speak. 'I hope you'll find the city to your liking.'

'Thank you, ma'am. It has already provided me with a great deal of entertainment,' Justin replied rather coldly. 'I had forgotten how quickly scandal spreads here. Perhaps it's carried in the water which everyone drinks so assiduously.'

Miss Lewisham went a dull red and deflated into her unbecoming purple gown. Justin raised his eyebrows very slightly, then turned his attention to Lucinda.

'I went for a stroll this morning,' he said to her, smiling with far more warmth than before, 'and I confess, I was impressed. I'd forgotten how fine some of the architecture is here. But it must seem commonplace to you, since you see it every day.'

'Y-yes—I mean no,' she stammered. 'The view from Beechen Cliff is very nice.'

'I must make a point of going there before I leave,' said Justin, without a hint of condescension in his voice. 'Mrs Drayton, may I persuade you to take a brief promenade with me? Please excuse us.'

'What are you trying to do? Destroy all my credibility?' Mary demanded when they were out of earshot. It wasn't what she'd meant to say, and as soon as the words left her mouth she caught herself up, miserably aware of what his probable response would be.

'No,' Justin replied mildly.

'Oh,' she said.

She was disturbingly aware that, despite all their bitter words, there was still a strong emotional bond between them. More than that, she could feel the undisciplined spark of excitement that flared in her every time he came near her—and every time he touched her. Even now, in the crowded Pump Room, she was acutely conscious of the warmth and strength of his arm beneath her hand.

'Why did you send me the pelisse?' she asked abruptly.

'Because you were cold,' he replied.

'Is that the only reason?' she challenged him, turning to face him.

He smiled. 'You may interpret it as an invitation to share my bed if you wish,' he said softly. 'But there's no obligation.'

'And which post road did you intend I should adorn?' Mary flashed before she could stop herself.

His smile broadened, and she saw a gleam of amusement in his hazel eyes.

'I'm afraid the stories of my amorous adventures have been greatly exaggerated,' he murmured, so low that only she could hear. 'Even if they were only half true I doubt if I'd have the energy to crawl out of bed in the morning—let alone walk across this room to procure you a glass of water.'

'I don't want any water,' Mary protested. What she wanted to do was find out exactly how much truth there was in the rumours about his mistresses, but she couldn't quite bring herself to ask him. She told herself it didn't matter.

'My dear girl, of course you do,' he corrected her solemnly, guiding her through the throng of people. 'You can't come to Bath without tasting the water. I trust my small gift didn't cause you any embarrassment with Penrose?' he added.

'He didn't notice,' said Mary. 'Besides, despite your repeated insinuations, it's none of his business. I came to Bath to help him out of a fix, and I'd hate to cause him distress—but I'm no more answerable to him for my behaviour than I am to you, my lord!'

'What fix?' Justin asked a few minutes later as she was sipping her water.

'That's none of your business, Justin.' She lifted her head and met his gaze squarely, a determined, almost steely look in her grey eyes. 'The only reason I accepted the pelisse was to save myself embarrassment,' she said steadily. 'It will make no difference to my relations with you.'

Justin looked down at her. Mary couldn't read the expression in his eyes, yet there was something strangely intimate about the moment.

'How did such an indomitable spirit come to be housed in such a fragile vessel?' Justin asked at last, very softly. 'I never thought of you as a common whore. I know you did what you did out of grim, uncompromising necessity.'

His words warmed Mary more than she could ever have believed possible. But then she saw his hand start to lift towards her, and she was jerked horribly back to the reality of her surroundings.

'Don't touch me!' she snapped, stepping back.

'Ah, of course, I'm not supposed to do anything which will provide fuel for Miss Lewisham and all her soul-mates here today,' Justin remarked in his normal voice, although there was a slight flush on his swarthy cheek. 'I shall endeavour to live up to your exacting requirements. May I take that glass from you? What fix?'

'I told you, that's none of your business,' said Mary, still shaken by what had just nearly happened. 'And how did you know where to have the pelisse and bonnet sent? Did you follow me last night?'

'Hardly. Since you'd picked such an out-of-the-way spot for our assignation I was more or less forced to follow the same route back into town that you did,' Justin said drily. 'You can't blame me for being curious when you turned off at Queen Square. You must admit, it's a rather irregular arrangement.'

Mary bit her lip as she heard the sardonic tone creep back into Justin's voice. 'Mr Penrose doesn't trust the linen in public hotels,' she explained, aware that it sounded a rather lame excuse.

Justin raised his eyebrows. 'That must cause him considerable inconvenience,' he said blandly. 'Why are you cultivating the gauche Miss Burleigh?'

Mary blinked. She'd expected him to reiterate his earlier suspicions about Mr Penrose, but instead he'd completely changed the subject.

'She's not gauche, she's just a little unsure of herself,' she said, adjusting to the new turn that the conversation had taken. 'Don't alarm her, Justin. It's not fair.'

'I didn't alarm her,' he pointed out calmly. 'I made an innocuous, not to say boring remark about the architecture of Bath. You can't get much less alarming than that!'

'You seem to have an ability to alarm people just by saying good morning,' said Mary roundly. 'I can't think why they're all so in awe of you!'

'It's certainly not a trait you share,' Justin replied drily. 'How did you care for the water?'

'I've tasted worse,' she said. 'I'd like to go back to the others now, please.'

'Surely you use the word "like" inappropriately?' Justin murmured provocatively, but he did escort her back to Mrs Burleigh's party.

'You've been trying our water,' said Miss Lewisham, leaving Mary in no doubt that she and Justin had been under observation for the whole time they'd been away. 'I'm sure that's a wise precaution. Did you not wish to try some, my lord?'

'My doctor informs me that water in all its guises is poison to my system,' Justin replied austerely. 'It's a great inconvenience to me, but one must abide by expert advice.'

'Indeed one must.' Miss Lewisham nodded

energetically. 'I drink very little water myself. Do
you care for tea, my lord?'

'Unfortunately not. It's made with boiling
water, you see.'

'Oh, dear me. Yes. Of course. So it is,' Miss
Lewisham agreed. 'But surely——' she looked
perplexed '—you cannot be confined to drinking
nothing but *intoxicating* liquids?'

'No. Vinegar,' said Justin heavily.

'Vinegar!' Miss Lewisham exclaimed. 'Oh, yes,
yes, I quite see that that would be an *excellent*
solution to the problem!'

There was a muffled gasp from Lucinda, and
then she hid her face behind her fan. Mrs Burleigh
looked slightly uncomfortable, and Mr Penrose
disapproving.

'Mary, my dear,' he said, pointedly ignoring
Lord Hawkridge, 'Mrs Burleigh has been kind
enough to invite us to a small party she is having
tonight for Miss Lucinda. I said that we would be
pleased to accept.'

'Of course we would,' said Mary warmly,
although her first thought was that she hadn't got
anything suitable to wear. But she could deal with
that problem later.

'Lord Hawkridge,' said Mrs Burleigh diffidently, 'would you care to join us? It won't be
anything grand, I'm afraid, but we'd be honoured
by your presence.'

'Thank you, ma'am, I would be delighted to
accept.' Justin bowed slightly and took his leave
of them.

'He certainly is a very handsome figure of a man,' said Miss Lewisham as he walked away. 'And one has to forgive the aristocracy a certain laxity of moral standards.'

'Emma!' said Mrs Burleigh despairingly.

'My dear, I can't help noticing. . . That is to say. . . Oh, dear. . .' Mr Penrose's voice trailed away unhappily.

They were sitting in the drawing-room of the house in Queen Square.

'What is it, sir?' Mary asked courteously, although she thought she knew what Mr Penrose wanted to say.

'Please forgive me, Mrs Drayton,' he assured her earnestly. 'I don't mean to be in any way impertinent, and I am deeply aware of how much you are putting yourself out for me. . .'

'You are concerned about the attention Lord Hawkridge seems to be paying me,' said Mary equably, when once again Mr Penrose proved unable to complete his sentence.

'I know it's not my concern, and I'd never wish to be thought interfering,' said Mr Penrose anxiously. 'But a man of his ilk really isn't to be trusted.'

'I think he is amusing himself,' said Mary calmly. 'Please don't disturb yourself, sir. I am very well able to take care of myself.'

Mr Penrose looked at her uncertainly, his thin face even more creased with anxiety than usual.

'It wouldn't do, you know, even if you were my

niece,' he said. 'And if his lordship ever found out that you're really an innkeeper——' He broke off, dabbing his lips with his handkerchief. 'Forgive me, my dear, I did not mean to imply. . . That is to say, I often feel you were more truly born a lady than I was born a gentleman.'

Mary smiled. 'My father was rector of a large Sussex parish,' she said. 'I used to play with the squire's daughters. But that was a very long time ago.'

'The hurly-burly of life in a public house must have come as a great shock to you after such a childhood,' said Mr Penrose tentatively. He was clearly dying to know the whole story, but was too polite, or timid, to ask.

'It did take me a little while to get used to the change in my circumstances,' Mary acknowledged. She stood up. 'Excuse me, sir. I must go out.'

'Why?' Mr Penrose demanded, with uncharacteristic bluntness. Then he flushed uncomfortably.

Mary felt a flicker of annoyance. She was getting tired of having her every action questioned, first by Justin and now by Mr Penrose. But she knew Mr Penrose had her best interests at heart—that he was probably anxious in case she had an assignation with Lord Hawkridge—so she bit back a sharp retort.

'I must buy a new dress,' she said. 'I have nothing to wear to Miss Burleigh's party.'

Mr Penrose stared at her in consternation. 'Oh, my dear Mrs Drayton, I had no idea that in accepting Mrs Burleigh's invitation I would be putting you to such expense. How thoughtless of me. Please, you must let me reimburse you.'

'That's quite unnecessary,' Mary replied stiffly.

'No, I insist,' he said. 'I cannot allow you to be out of pocket on my behalf. It's unthinkable!'

Mary hesitated. But she was a practical woman, and it seemed to her that, in the circumstances, Mr Penrose's offer was quite fair.

'Thank you, sir,' she said, accepting it.

CHAPTER FOUR

MARY was hesitating outside a dressmaker's establishment on Milsom Street when she heard a light footstep behind her. Her breath caught in her throat, and she didn't need to turn round to know who it was.

'I found Madam Eustacia very helpful this morning,' said Justin in her ear.

'Which is a very good reason for me not to visit her this afternoon!' Mary retorted, swinging round to face him. 'Especially dressed like this!'

'Your ineffectual cavalier set you a problem when he accepted Mrs Burleigh's invitation, didn't he?' said Justin, amusement in his voice. 'I saw it in your expression at the time. The everlasting cry of womanhood: "But I haven't got a thing to wear!"'

'I haven't, but I will have,' said Mary through gritted teeth. 'Go away, Justin. People are looking at us.'

'You will be the envy of other, less favoured damsels,' he assured her infuriatingly.

Her eyes flashed dangerously. 'I doubt it,' she said curtly.

He raised his eyebrows.

'Perhaps I should come in with you?' he suggested. 'I could offer my advice—I have an excellent eye for colour—and then I could carry your purchases home for you afterwards.'

Mary took a step backwards.

'No,' she said. 'Definitely not.'

'Why? Would Penrose object?'

'*I* would object,' said Mary, but a faint colour stained her fair cheeks at his question. It followed so pat upon Mr Penrose's warning.

'He's cautioned you against me!' Justin exclaimed. 'For what reason?' The humour had vanished from his face and now there was a dangerous gleam in his hazel eyes.

'Because men of your ilk are not to be trusted!' Mary flashed. 'He suspects you of harbouring improper thoughts towards me!'

'Something he would know nothing about?' Justin said derisively.

'No, he doesn't!' Mary exclaimed indignantly, as much offended on Mr Penrose's behalf as she was on her own. 'He's never treated me with anything other than respect.'

'Then he has water in his veins, not blood,' said Justin harshly. 'You should look elsewhere for company, sweetheart. You have too much fire to be satisfied by such an arrangement.'

'Are you suggesting I become *your* mistress?' Mary demanded, too angry to be circumspect. 'You must be out of your mind!'

There was a moment's silence. Justin looked at her, his mouth set in a hard, unyielding line, an angry flame in his eyes.

'At least the dressmaker would come to your

door,' he drawled cuttingly. 'And I would do my best to ensure that your other needs were adequately catered for.'

His gaze flickered over her, the hard yet intimate gleam in his eyes leaving her in no doubt as to his meaning.

Mary caught her breath in horror. She felt as naked and wounded as if he had stripped her clothes from her back. Whatever his protestations that he didn't see her as a common whore, he had made his opinion of her plain enough.

'No,' she said in a low, throbbing voice. 'No, never!'

She turned and went into the dressmaker's.

'Oh, ma'am, you do look lovely,' said Hetty, the maid who was helping her dress.

'Thank you.' Mary glanced at herself in the mirror.

It seemed to her that the beauty of her clothes was not matched by the woman wearing them. She felt tired and plain. But perhaps her superficial finery would be enough to deceive others as effectively as it seemed to have done Hetty.

She had spent far more on the dress than she had intended to, and certainly more than Mr Penrose had given her. But, even though she knew that her extravagance had been inspired by the desire to show Justin that she didn't need him, she didn't regret it.

Besides, this was probably the only fashionable

party she would ever go to, and she meant to make the most of it.

She had chosen a simple yet elegant dress, in a deep rich blue, which complemented the delicate translucence of her skin and the changing lights in her grey eyes. It had a wide skirt adorned only by a single trim, large puffed sleeves which reached to her elbows, and a low neckline, cut straight across from slightly dropped shoulders, which emphasised her slender neck and excellent carriage.

Her hair was arranged in loose curls, dressed with a ribbon. To complete the ensemble she wore long white gloves, silk pumps, and a simple gold locket which was the only ornament she had to remind her of her mother. Somehow she had managed to preserve the trinket through all the vicissitudes of her life in St Giles.

'You really do look beautiful,' said Hetty, almost reverentially.

She was so sincere in her flattery that Mary started to feel better. A hint of pretty colour crept into her pale cheeks, and the merest suggestion of a sparkle illuminated her eyes.

'You must be looking forward to tonight,' Hetty added.

'Yes, I am,' Mary admitted.

It was true. She was feeling nervous and on edge, but she had never been to such a party before, she would never have the opportunity to do so again, and she was determined to enjoy it.

And more than anything she wanted Justin to

see her in her beautiful gown and know that she needed neither him nor his charity.

'You'll be the belle of the ball,' said the maid enthusiastically. 'You'll dazzle all the gentlemen, ma'am.'

'I'm hardly in the first blush of youth,' Mary protested, smiling ruefully.

'You don't look a day over twenty, ma'am,' said Hetty stoutly.

Mary shook her head in laughing disbelief, flattered but not convinced, though Hetty's championship had done a great deal for her morale.

But when she caught a glimpse of herself in the mirror she thought that perhaps there was some truth in what Hetty said. Despite the hardships she had endured, the years had been kind to her. Her eyes still had the capacity to sparkle with mischief when she was amused, her tawny-brown hair shone warmly in the candlelight and her fair skin remained as pure and unblemished as it had been the day she'd left the rectory for the last time.

In fact, apart from the depth of experience in her fine grey eyes, she really might have been a débutante about to attend her first party.

For tonight she would pretend that it was so.

'Perhaps you'll catch the eye of Lord Hawkridge,' said the maid, innocently throwing Mary's emotions into turmoil.

'What do you mean?' she asked carefully.

'He'll be there too, won't he?' Hetty prattled on, unaware of Mary's reaction to her comment.

'A very fine gentleman by all accounts, though a bit odd.'

'In what way?' Mary asked curiously, relaxing slightly as she realised that the girl was only repeating gossip.

'Well, my cousin Annie works up at the hotel,' the maid began confidentially, 'and she was busy cleaning out the hearth in the coffee-room yesterday morning, ready to make up the new fire, when she heard someone behind her. So naturally she turned round to see who it was, and there was his lordship, bold as brass, *drawing* her!'

The maid paused dramatically, her eyes sparkling with excitement.

'Good gracious!' said Mary encouragingly, since a response seemed to be called for. 'What did she do then?'

'Well, she's got a bit of a temper, has Annie,' the maid continued. 'So she asked, sharp, like, what he thought he was doing, and he showed her. She said there were little pictures all over the page, all higgledy-piggledy, without any rhyme or reason to them. Little pictures of her cleaning the hearth, and a chairman outside the Pump Room rubbing his hands to keep them warm, and a skinny lady drinking the waters like she thought they were poison. . .' Hetty ran out of breath.

'I see,' said Mary. 'Did she find that reassuring?'

'She said he was a proper gentleman,' the maid replied. 'He told her he'd been in the coffee-room since before she'd come in—he must have been up early, or perhaps he never went to bed—and she was such a picture of diligence he couldn't help drawing her. He said he was sorry he'd startled her, and hoped he hadn't put her out — and then he gave her half a crown. She said he was a proper gentleman, not at all stand-offish, but not familiar either, if you take my meaning.'

'Yes, I do,' said Mary, smiling faintly. She could just imagine the scene.

She wondered what the awestruck Knightleys, or even Miss Lewisham, would say if they heard the story. It seemed that, for all the occasional grandeur of his manner, Justin still retained the ability to see everyone he met as an individual. In fact, he'd probably liked Annie better than Miss Lewisham. He'd never been able to abide humbug.

Her eyes fell and she gripped her hands tightly in her lap. If only things could have been different. But even if the years in St Giles had never happened it wouldn't have made any difference. The rector's daughter could never be a suitable match for the baron.

'It must be nice to have your picture drawn,' said the maid wistfully. 'Not when you're cleaning out the hearth, of course — but in your best dress and bonnet.' She caught sight of Mary in the mirror and smiled excitedly. 'Perhaps he'll draw you, ma'am,' she suggested. 'That would be something, wouldn't it?'

'I'm not sure I want my likeness taken,' said Mary sharply, then she saw the maid's crestfallen expression and relented. 'Yes,' she said, 'it would be something.'

'My dear!' Mr Penrose stood up as she came into the drawing-room, staring at her as though he'd never seen her before. 'You look exquisite!'

'Thank you, sir,' Mary replied.

Then, as he continued to stare at her, she began to feel slightly uncomfortable. She had denied to Justin that Mr Penrose had any romantic interest in her, but she was no longer entirely sure. Not that she suspected he was going to invite her to become his mistress! But she could sense that his regard for her was growing warmer. She hoped it would never become any more than that.

'Would you care for a glass of sherry before we leave?' Mr Penrose asked after a moment.

'Yes, thank you,' Mary said. She smiled ruefully. 'I confess, I am a little nervous.'

'But you have no reason to be,' he assured her. 'I will be the envy of every other gentleman present—at having such a lovely niece, I mean.'

'You are very kind, sir.' She sipped her sherry, very conscious of the anxious tension in her companion, and the steady ticking of the clock on the mantelpiece.

She put her glass down. 'Shall we go? We wouldn't want to be late.'

To her own surprise, Mary turned out to be a great success at Lucinda's party. For this, three things were partially responsible. Firstly, she was new to Bath. Secondly, she was believed to be the niece of a wealthy man. And thirdly, gossip about the way Lord Hawkridge had twice singled her out in the Pump Room had already reached nearly every guest present. Naturally everyone was curious about her.

But the main reason why she was a success owed nothing to such vulgar factors. She had come to the party determined to enjoy herself, and her pleasure in her surroundings was infectious. She had charm and warmth and, although she would never have believed it, an air of innate good breeding.

To some extent, of course, she was acting a role. She was certainly aware of the irony when she heard herself described as a 'pretty-mannered, modest young woman' by old Mrs Melville. But on another level she was only being herself, for this genteel society—or something like it—was where she had begun, and where she might have ended if her father had made better provision for her.

'I'm so glad you could come, Mrs Drayton,' said Lucinda eagerly, when all the introductions were over and she had time to speak confidentially to Mary.

'It was very kind of you to invite us at such short notice,' Mary replied warmly, 'especially as we are little more than strangers.'

'It doesn't seem so,' Lucinda assured her. 'How easily you make friends,' she added almost enviously. 'I never know what to say to people—

apart from the most mundane remarks that nobody could be interested in.'

'I think you underestimate yourself,' Mary said, smiling. 'And overestimate the wit and intellect of everyone else! Most conversation is pretty mundane if you ever really listen to it.'

'I suppose so,' said Lucinda doubtfully. 'I dare say you've had a lot of experience of meeting people,' she added, diffidently anxious to learn more about her new friend.

'I've travelled quite a bit,' Mary replied. It wasn't exactly true, but she'd met a lot of travellers, which, in the present context, seemed to come to the same thing. 'You soon discover that most people are too busy working out what they're going to say when it's their turn to pay full attention to what you're saying.'

Lucinda gasped. 'I thought I was the only one who did that!' she exclaimed.

'Don't you believe it!' Mary said mischievously, smiling at the girl.

But despite her calm exterior Mary was still feeling very edgy. So far Justin hadn't appeared. It was possible that he'd decided to cut the party, or that he'd deliberately chosen to be late in order to make a grand entrance. Mary knew it would be better if he didn't come, but she desperately wanted him to do so.

She wanted him to see her in her beautiful gown and know that she didn't need him to survive. She wanted him to see her mixing with these people, to see how well-liked she was and how comfortable she was in this setting. And most of all she wanted him to see that there was more to her than the wretched, frightened girl who had once purchased crude protection for herself by becoming a thief's moll.

She caught herself up as she realised that she'd just glanced nervously at the doorway for a third time, and tried to concentrate on what her companion was saying.

'It's Lord Hawkridge!' Lucinda exclaimed.

Mary looked up, and there he was, bowing to his hostess.

'Oh, dear, he's coming over here,' said Lucinda.

A pulse began to beat in Mary's throat. 'Of course he is,' she said in a voice she didn't quite recognise as her own. 'It's your party.'

He acknowledged both ladies courteously, his gaze resting briefly on Mary before he turned his attention back to Lucinda.

'Miss Burleigh, I would apologise for my tardiness, except that the blame rests entirely with you,' he said, a twinkle in his hazel eyes.

'With me?' Lucinda squeaked, staring at him in agitated alarm.

'You advised me to see the view from Beechen Cliff, did you not?' Justin reminded her, sitting down beside her. 'You were quite right—it is very impressive.'

'Oh, I see,' said Lucinda, understanding dawning in her expression. 'But I had no idea. . . That is, I did not mean for you. . . It was so windy today.'

'It was a trifle draughty,' Justin acknowledged. 'But I turned my collar up, and I was able to make several sketches before the light failed.'

Apart from that first, quick glance, he hadn't paid any further attention to Mary.

She gripped her fan tightly in her hands. Was he ignoring her to punish her for refusing to be his mistress? Or did he simply think there was nothing left to say between them? A great weight settled on her chest. She could not believe how agonising his indifference was. His anger had been preferable.

'Sketches? Of course!' Lucinda exclaimed, a combination of awe and nervous eagerness in her eyes. 'Cousin Emma says you are famous for your paintings, my lord.'

'Miss Lewisham exaggerates,' said Justin, smiling. 'If I have a talent at all, it is for pen-and-ink sketches, not for great, sweeping landscapes—or even for formal portraits.'

'You must have visited many exhibitions,' said Lucinda wistfully. 'I have often wished. . . But Mama has no liking for London, and I could never persuade her to go to Rome.'

'Perhaps you will have an opportunity to do so one day,' Justin said. 'Do you paint yourself?'

'I did a water-colour from Beechen Cliff,' Lucinda admitted shyly. 'Mama liked it and showed it to all her friends, but I didn't think it was very good. It was too dark, and some of the washes were muddy. Sometimes I think there is not enough colour in the world!'

'You would appreciate Turner, I think,' said Justin.

Mary listened, making no effort to take part in the conversation. Why should she? Lucinda had clearly forgotten her new friend in her natural excitement at discovering that she shared an interest with Lord Hawkridge. And Justin. . .well, Mary had always known she wasn't fit to be anything but his whore.

All around her people were talking, laughing and flirting, while beside her Justin and Lucinda talked about old masters, but Mary sat as poised and unmoving as a marble statue. Mrs Burleigh's well-appointed drawing-room faded away, and she saw the horror and filth of St Giles as vividly as if it were there in front of her. She could smell the stench of Church Lane, and feel the disgust that had overwhelmed her when her uncle's leering customers had reached out with groping hands to touch her.

She'd spent a year resisting Alf's determined efforts to turn her into a genteel thief. Her uncle had had so many plans for her—but she'd thwarted them all. She'd been proud of herself. But then he'd withdrawn his protection from her, in the hope that desperation would finally break her spirit.

So, in anger and fear, she'd struck her bargain with Bill Crawford. She'd agreed to be the crackman's mistress in the hope that he'd protect her from others even worse than he was. And he had. Until he'd been caught cracking a house in

Berkeley Square and been rewarded with trans-portation for his bad luck.

She'd never made the same bargain again. Donald's arrival in Church Lane, and his instant, unquestioning, unswerving loyalty, had ensured that.

But once was enough. Nothing would ever change the fact that she'd knowingly sacrifice everything she'd been taught to hold dear. Nothing would ever wash away the stains of that bargain. No honest man could ever be expected to marry her.

She had told Justin so, seven years ago, and he had refused to accept it. No one could blame him if he had finally come to see the truth of her words.

'Mrs Drayton!'

Mary jumped. Mrs Burleigh's crowded drawing-room once more slid into view, and she saw Lucinda staring at her anxiously.

'Is something wrong?' Lucinda asked, forgetting to be diffident in her concern.

'No. Oh, no,' Mary said uncertainly. She tried to smile, but the attempt faltered. The horrors she'd seen still lurked at the back of her grey eyes. For a moment the crowded, brightly lit room seemed less real than her memories of St Giles.

'It is very warm in here,' said Justin quietly. 'It wouldn't be surprising if Mrs Drayton felt faint. Perhaps you could procure her a glass of lemon-ade, Miss Burleigh?'

'Of course.' Lucinda got up immediately, not at all put out by the request.

'I am not faint,' Mary protested, struggling to regain her self-possession.

'I know,' said Justin gently. 'But it was better than telling her that for a few minutes you weren't at her party at all—she might have asked where you'd gone.'

'How did you know?' Mary whispered, shaken anew by the understanding in his eyes. Sh'd been so sure that he no longer had any interest in her.

'It wasn't difficult,' he said softly. 'Whatever's happened to you in the last seven years, I doubt if anything has hurt you more than that.'

Mary caught her lip between her teeth, trying not to give way to tears. Just when she was feeling most lonely and abandoned, he had reached out to her with kindness. She should have known that he would at least show her that courtesy.

He laid his hand on her gloved forearm, just above her wrist. She felt the warmth and reassurance in his touch, and suddenly all she wanted to do was throw herself into his comforting embrace. She wanted to feel his strong arms soothing her and his deep voice telling her that everything was all right—that he'd forgiven her the sins she'd been forced to commit to save herself.

But that was a dream that could never come true. Oh, yes! If she weakened she might one day lie in his arms. She might even hear him tell her that she'd only done what she'd had to do. But there would never be true forgiveness for what had happened in St Giles. How could there be?

She looked at him, her eyes sparkling with

unshed tears, and her lips twisted into a crooked smile.

'Let us call a truce, sweetheart,' he said very quietly. 'At least for tonight. I won't ask questions you cannot—or will not—answer. And you can stop treating me as if I'm a cross between Casanova and Bluebeard.'

He stood up before Mary could reply, and she felt bereft as he took his hand away from her arm. Then she saw that Lucinda was approaching with a glass of lemonade.

'Perhaps you will do me the honour of allowing me to take you down to supper later, Mrs Drayton?' he said. 'Miss Burleigh.' He acknowledged Lucinda courteously and strolled away.

'Do you feel better?' Lucinda asked solicitously.

'Very much, thank you.' Mary smiled at her. 'I'm so sorry to have made such a spectacle of myself. I'm not normally vapourish.'

'I don't think anyone else noticed,' Lucinda reassured her. 'I didn't myself at first, but then Lord Hawkridge saw that you were unwell and he indicated that I should speak to you. I think he was afraid that you might be startled if he did so.'

'That was very—considerate—of him,' said Mary. Her throat was choked with unshed tears, but she took a small sip of lemonade, forcing herself to swallow it.

'I think he is a nice man,' said Lucinda. 'He did not seem at all bored to be talking to me about art. He told me all about the great pictures he's seen in Italy, and. . .'

She prattled on, repeating almost verbatim much of what Justin had said to her, offering no cues signalling the need of a reply. Such loquacity was so uncharacteristic that Mary was sure that Lucinda was merely trying to provide her with an opportunity to recover her composure. She was very grateful for the girl's tact and kindness. And by the time Mr Penrose approached them she was more determined than ever that Lucinda shouldn't be hurt by Samuel.

'My dear, you look a little pale. Are you quite well?' Mr Penrose asked anxiously.

'Oh, yes,' Mary replied brightly. 'I did feel a trifle faint a few minutes ago, but Miss Burleigh kindly brought me some lemonade and now I'm quite refreshed.'

'I saw Lord Hawkridge conversing with you,' said Mr Penrose, looking put out. 'What can he possibly have had to say at such length?'

'He was talking to me,' said Lucinda, surprisingly. 'He was telling me about a tour he made of Italy.'

'I see.' Mr Penrose gave the appearance of a man who had a great deal to say, but who had unfortunately just had a gag shoved in his mouth.

Lucinda glanced from Mr Penrose to Mary. 'Excuse me,' she said. 'I think Mama is beckoning to me.'

'What a very thoughtful girl she is,' Mary said warmly. 'Have you had any private conversation with Mrs Burleigh, sir? Does it seem to you that there is any substance to the idea that Samuel is trying to fix his interest with Lucinda?'

Mr Penrose had been about to make a further comment on Lord Hawkridge, but instead he frowned, looking even more anxious and wizened than normal.

'I fear so,' he said heavily. 'Apparently Mrs Burleigh was in daily expectation of receiving a formal visit from him before he suddenly went out of town. But perhaps——' he brightened '—that means he has thought better of the scheme.'

'Or perhaps he was simply trying to pique Miss Burleigh's interest. Or perhaps he had some other business that he urgently had to attend to,' said Mary drily. 'Mr Penrose, don't you think it might be advisable to give Mrs Burleigh some hint that he won't have control of his inheritance for another two years?'

'No!' Mr Penrose exclaimed emphatically.

'But if Lucinda is truly considering marrying him, that is something they have a right to know,' said Mary reasonably. 'I'm not suggesting that you should mention our other suspicions. But when the marriage settlements are drawn up the constraints on his inheritance will become common knowledge. They might as well know sooner rather than later.'

Mr Penrose shook his head obstinately. 'It may not be necessary for them to ever know,' he said. 'And I cannot feel comfortable discussing Samuel's affairs with strangers before I have first discussed them with Samuel.'

Mary pressed her lips together, but she didn't pursue her point. Around them, couples were beginning to go down to supper, and she saw Justin walking towards them. So did Mr Penrose. She heard him give a muffled exclamation of annoyance, then Justin was bowing before her.

'Mrs Drayton,' he said, 'may I escort you down to supper?'

'Thank you, my lord,' Mr Penrose intervened stiffly before Mary could speak, 'but that will not be necessary. I will escort my niece myself.'

Justin raised his eyebrows haughtily. 'I believe Mrs Drayton is already promised to me, sir,' he said coldly. 'Is that not so, ma'am?'

'Mary!' Mr Penrose exclaimed, too put out to show his normal, anxious awe of Lord Hawkridge. 'Is that true?'

Mary hesitated, glancing from Justin's arrogant, unyielding expression to Mr Penrose's unbecomingly flushed and indignant face. She had no doubt of what the outcome would be if Mr Penrose refused to back down, and she had no desire to be the centre of an unpleasant scene. She laid her hand lightly on his arm.

'Forgive me, Uncle,' she said, 'but I believe I did promise Lord Hawkridge I would go down with him. I'm sure Miss Lewisham would be delighted to go down with you.'

For a moment Mr Penrose looked obstinate. Then she saw the acquiescence in his eyes, and felt a flicker of relief. She stood up and allowed Justin to escort her out of the room.

CHAPTER FIVE

'How can you tolerate him?' Justin demanded as
they walked downstairs.

'He is a *little* trying,' Mary conceded. 'But he's
very worried at the moment.'

She was on tenterhooks as to what Justin might
say to her, yet at the same time she felt almost
exhilarated. Whatever happened in the future, she
was with Justin now. And he had spoken kindly to
her. If this was to be the last time they met, at
least they could part on friendly terms, without
bitterness. She knew that was the best she could
ever hope for.

There was a cold supper laid out in the dining-
room. Justin went to fetch Mary something to eat
and a glass of champagne. The moment she was
alone she found herself the centre of a small group
of young people. She had enjoyed a lively conversation with them earlier in the evening, but now
she felt almost frustrated by their friendliness. She
wanted to be with Justin.

'Mrs Drayton, do you care for riding?' asked a
young but extremely dashing young man in a
heavily embroidered waistcoat.

'Very much,' Mary replied, trying hard not to
follow Justin with her eyes.

'I was sure you must!' he exclaimed. 'Caroline

and I——' he nodded towards his sister '—are planning to set up an expedition to ride over to Norton St Philip tomorrow. We're going to have luncheon at the George. Would you care to make up one of our party?'

A quick smile lit up Mary's eyes. Riding had been her one extravagance during her years at the Lazy Cat, though she'd always been careful to do nothing to draw undesirable attention to herself. Her love of speed had been indulged only very early in the morning, when there was no one to see her galloping flat out across the fields behind the inn.

'I'd love to do so,' she said. 'Unfortunately, I can foresee at least two problems. I haven't got a horse and, since I didn't expect to be riding when I came to Bath, I didn't bring a riding habit.'

'Oh, that's easily solved,' Caroline said quickly. 'You can borrow a habit from me, and Peter will arrange to hire a hack for you. Do say you'll come.'

'Well. . .' Mary hesitated.

She had no doubt that she would enjoy the expedition, but she'd never intended to become so caught up in the social whirl of Bath. Besides, although it was flattering to be included so generously in the activities of her new acquaintants, she couldn't help wondering how they'd react if they found out she wasn't Mr Penrose's niece.

'I did promise my uncle I'd go to the Pump Room with him tomorrow morning,' she said, glancing across to where Mr Penrose was staring darkly at his fellow guests. 'Thank you, my lord,' she added as she accepted the champagne and the plate of elegant patties that Justin offered her.

A slight constraint fell upon the group at Justin's presence. The young people were somewhat in awe of him, and not quite sure what to say to him. It was Caroline who broke the silence. She was too ebullient to remain overawed for long.

'Lord Hawkridge, don't you think a ride would be better for Mrs Drayton than a glass of water in the stuffy Pump Room?' she demanded.

He smiled. 'You sound like a woman after my own heart, Miss. . .?' He paused, raising his eyebrows enquiringly.

'King,' she supplied. 'Caroline King. This is my brother, Peter. And this is Adam Hastings.'

'How do you do?'

There was a round of mutual acknowledgements, then Peter King said shyly, 'Would you like to accompany us, my lord? Of course, if you have another engagement. . .' His voice trailed away as if he was amazed at his own presumption.

'I'd be delighted to do so,' Justin replied immediately. 'And I'm sure, between us, we can persuade Mrs Drayton that a ride in the fresh air is just what she needs.'

'I'll have my best habit sent round to you first thing,' said Caroline eagerly. 'And we'll call for you at ten o'clock. And Peter will hire a horse for you.'

'Let me take care of that,' said Justin smoothly.

'I will have to procure a mount for myself, and I can just as easily do so for Mrs Drayton as well.'

'It seems that all my objections have been overruled,' said Mary, smiling.

Her frustration at having her brief interlude with Justin interrupted had been ameliorated by the prospect of riding with him. They wouldn't be alone together, of course, but that was probably a good thing. She wanted the solace of his company, but she knew that for both their sakes she had to continue to keep him at a distance.

Then she glanced across the room towards Lucinda. Despite the fact that the party was in Lucinda's honour, she was sitting talking to her mother and Mrs Knightley. She looked both sad and uncomfortable. Mary didn't say anything, but her lips pressed together in a firm line. A faint smile illuminated Justin's eyes as he followed the direction of her glance, but he didn't say anything either.

'But she probably won't want to come,' Caroline protested, quickly divining Mary's thoughts. 'Mrs Burleigh will say it's too hazardous, and Lucinda never does anything even remotely adventurous. Besides, she hasn't got a horse either.'

'Not an insurmountable problem,' Justin said. 'I would be happy to deal with it.'

'It is her party, Caroline,' her brother pointed out. 'My lord,' he appealed to Justin, 'perhaps if *you* asked Mrs Burleigh would be more willing to agree.'

'Miss King?' said Justin quietly.

Caroline pouted for a moment, then she smiled ruefully.

'I didn't mean to be ungracious,' she said. 'It's just that I've never really felt I know Lucinda. Perhaps if she comes for a ride with us it will be different.'

'In that case I will execute my commission without delay,' Justin declared.

Mary watched Lucinda's face light up as Justin spoke to Mrs Burleigh. Then she glanced across the room to where Mr Penrose was virtually ignoring Miss Lewisham in his efforts to keep an eye on Lord Hawkridge. She wondered what he would say when she told him about the riding trip—but it really wasn't any of his business.

After supper there was an impromptu dance. Mary looked on, outwardly calm, but inwardly apprehensive, as the preparations were made. She had learnt to waltz over a decade ago with Sir Richard's daughters, romping round the nursery at the manor-house while her father played chess with Sir Richard, but since then she had never had an opportunity to practise.

She had just decided that she wouldn't dance, when Justin appeared at her side, pre-empting Peter King by seconds.

'Dance with me?' he asked.

'I don't think so,' said Mary, although suddenly the prospect of waltzing had become extremely enticing. 'I haven't danced since I was fourteen,' she explained. 'I'm not sure I remember how.'

'In that case it's essential that you dance with me first,' said Justin reasonably. 'You can practise on me, and I'll promise not to tell anyone how many times you step on me.'

Mary was surprised into laughter.

'What a gallant offer!' she exclaimed.

'It is, isn't it?' he agreed.

He took her hand, and even through her gloves she felt the warm, compelling pressure of his fingers. As he drew her on to the dance-floor, and circled her waist with his other hand, she suddenly wondered if this was a good idea. He was too close to her, and she was too intimately aware of his every move. She could feel the warmth of his hand through the thin fabric of her dress, and her heart began to race.

She knew she was blushing, and she didn't dare look up at him. She couldn't remember ever feeling this fierce excitement in his presence when she'd first known him. But in those days she had almost deliberately closed her mind to the physical attraction between them.

Seven years ago, the sordid bargain she had struck with Bill Crawford—when she had sold herself to the thief in return for his protection— had still been a very recent memory. And it had severely numbed her capacity to experience sensual pleasure. She had loved Justin deeply. But it had been for his compassion, his humour and his insight—not for the burning desire that his touch aroused in her.

But in the years since they'd last met something

had changed. Now she was acutely aware of every aspect of his physical presence. She was almost shamefully conscious of the latent power within his large frame, and the confident assurance with which he guided her around the floor.

She remembered the way he'd swept her into his arms in the stables three days ago, and how difficult it had been for her to resist. If he kissed her again she would be even less able to withstand the aching yearning that he ignited in her.

But she had to resist him because otherwise she was doomed to become his mistress—and that would destroy her.

'I could keep the time for you,' Justin murmured in her ear. 'One, two, three, one, two, three. . .'

'Be quiet!' Mary whispered fiercely. 'I've got to concentrate!'

'I'd noticed!'

Mary gasped indignantly, and put all her effort into minding her feet. In fact she concentrated so hard that she almost forgot it was Justin she was dancing with, and it was only later that she wondered if that was what he'd intended. Had he realised how disturbed she was becoming and deliberately tried to distract her?

For a brief instant she almost panicked, but then she reassured herself that he couldn't possibly have known the cause of her agitation. He was simply being kind to her because he knew she was feeling unsure of herself in unfamiliar surroundings.

The music was beguiling and the room was full of colour and light. Almost in spite of herself Mary began to relax, giving herself up to the enjoyment of the dance. It was an innocent pleasure, and her joy in it was as pure and untarnished as a soap bubble, floating up in the sunlight.

But her happiness was as fragile as the bubble — and inevitably the music came to an end.

She danced the next waltz with Peter King.

'How excellently you dance!' he exclaimed. 'But I dare say you've had a great deal of practice. Lucinda Burleigh was telling me earlier that you've travelled. I expect Bath seems very tame in comparison to some of the places you've seen!'

'Not at all!' Mary replied quickly. 'In fact, I can hardly remember when I last had such an entertaining time. Everyone has made me feel so welcome!'

'You make it very easy for us to do so,' Peter complimented her.

'Thank you, sir,' she said, more gratified by his flattery than she cared to admit to herself. After so many years of providing unobtrusive service to her customers, it was unbelievably comforting to be noticed as a woman in her own right. When this adventure was over, she would go back to her old life at the Lazy Cat, but at least she would take some happy memories with her — as well as painful ones.

She sat out one dance with Lucinda.

'It's your doing that I've been invited tomorrow, isn't it?' the younger girl asked.

'Oh, no—Mr and Miss King arranged everything,' Mary replied lightly.

'But I'm sure Caroline wouldn't have asked me if you hadn't suggested it,' said Lucinda. 'I know she thinks I'm dull. I once heard her describe me as a mouse without a squeak!'

'She's certainly a very outspoken young lady,' Mary said drily. 'No doubt she'll learn to be more circumspect in time. Are you happy to come with us?'

'You mean, do I feel offended because I've only been invited at your prompting? And by someone who has such a. . .a *diminishing* opinion of me?' Lucinda asked quietly.

Mary glanced at her, a quick, almost rueful smile in her grey eyes.

'Yes, that's what I meant,' she said.

'No.' Lucinda sighed. 'I don't blame them for thinking I'm boring,' she added. 'But I would like Caroline to like me. Does that sound stupid?'

'No,' said Mary gently. 'I can remember times when I've felt the same way.'

'Peter King danced with me earlier,' Lucinda continued, more brightly. 'He does so sometimes; I think he feels sorry for me.'

'Perhaps he likes you,' Mary suggested.

'I don't know.' Lucinda began to pleat her handkerchief nervously. 'Excuse me, ma'am, but does Mr Penrose disapprove of Lord Hawkridge paying attention to you?' she asked in a rush.

'I'm not sure that he is paying any special attention to me,' Mary replied calmly, although her heart began to beat a little faster.

'I didn't mean to be impertinent; it's just—it's just that I think you should know that Cousin Emma often speaks a great deal of foolishness!' Lucinda blurted, her words tumbling over each other in her haste to say them. 'I think Lord Hawkridge is a very kind man, even if he did make fun of her this morning—which she quite deserved for being so toadying to him.'

'Thank you,' said Mary. She smiled at Lucinda. 'You are very considerate.'

'Then you aren't offended?' Lucinda asked, relieved.

'Of course not.' Mary looked away, watching the dancers twirl around the floor. Candlelight reflected from the softly shining silk dresses. She knew it was a sight she would remember for a long time.

'In return for your kindness, may I also risk being impertinent?' she asked abruptly, turning back to Lucinda.

The girl nodded, although she looked slightly apprehensive.

'Are you very attached to Samuel?' Mary asked bluntly.

Lucinda began to pleat her handkerchief again, not meeting Mary's eyes.

'I think he is a very handsome and charming gentleman,' she said in a low voice. 'I was so thrilled when he singled me out—and he was kind to me. . . Do I sound very foolish?' She looked up suddenly.

'No.'

'But I think. . .' Lucinda took a deep breath, as if she was trying to keep up her courage '. . .I think you were warning me against him this morning in the Pump Room, and now I'm not sure. I think. . .perhaps it was too good to be true that anyone could be interested in me for myself. After all, even a rich man who wanted to improve his estate might think it was worthwhile marrying me to do so, mightn't he?'

She tried to smile bravely, but she had to catch her lower lip between her teeth to stop it trembling.

'My dear, it wasn't your desirability I was calling into question,' said Mary quietly. 'I'm sure that somewhere in the world, possibly even in this room, there is a man who would marry you even if you didn't have a penny to your name.'

'I did wonder why Samuel went away so suddenly,' Lucinda told her. 'If he'd truly cared about me he would have told me why—or perhaps he wouldn't have gone. Or maybe he saw that I was getting too attached to him and he thought it was better to leave.'

It seemed to Mary that Lucinda was taking her own inadequacy for granted. According to Lucinda's interpretation, either Samuel was only interested in her for her fortune, or he wasn't interested in her at all, and had left her to prove it.

It was very difficult to think of anything to say

which might help. It certainly wasn't going to do much for Lucinda's self-esteem to discover that Samuel's only motive for courting her was to pay off his debts.

'Can I be very odious and give you some unsolicited advice?' Mary asked, trying to find a way out of the dilemma.

Lucinda nodded.

'Supposing we forget about Samuel for a moment and imagine that a hypothetical Prince Charming is just about to walk through the drawing-room door,' said Mary. 'And he is an honourable, noble and worthy man. And suppose he sees you, and you see him, and you both fall instantly in love—the rest of us would be green with envy.'

Lucinda smiled wanly at the fantasy.

'But if at that moment he carried you away across his saddlebow to live the rest of your life in an enchanted kingdom, you would never learn any more about the world you left behind than you know right now,' Mary continued. 'You might never get to see for yourself the paintings and statues in Rome—or even get another chance to paint the view from Beechen Cliff without muddying the washes.'

Lucinda acknowledged the last few words with a distracted smile, but for the most part she watched Mary's face intently.

'Are you telling me I shouldn't fall in love with Samuel?' she asked, still painfully absorbed by her immediate anxieties.

'I'm telling you that when you gamble with

something as important as the rest of your life you should be very clear of what you stand to win or lose,' said Mary. 'Believe me, I know what I'm talking about!'

'You do look dashing, ma'am,' said Hetty approvingly, next morning.

Mary laughed, taking one last glance at herself in the mirror.

The riding habit Caroline King had sent round was a vibrant cherry-red, with a neat bodice and huge flowing skirts. It was trimmed with braid almost up to the elbows, and there was more braid on the bodice and skirt. The costume was completed by a tall hat, which had a filmy veil attached to its crown. Mary knew the veil would flutter provocatively at the slightest breeze, and it amused her to think how much Caroline must enjoy wearing it.

'I think Miss King is the dashing one,' she said to Hetty. 'It was kind of her to lend it to me.'

'I'm sure you'll have a wonderful time, ma'am,' said Hetty. 'It's a beautiful, fine morning, and there isn't much wind either.'

'Thank you.' Mary smiled at her, and then went down to face Mr Penrose.

He looked up disapprovingly as she entered the drawing-room.

'A most unsuitable costume,' he grumbled. 'I cannot think how you came to agree to such an expedition. Have you forgotten why we came to Bath?'

'No, I haven't,' said Mary calmly, laying her hat down on the table. 'You came to Bath to confront Samuel with your suspicions, and I came to support you. But I have always been as concerned for Miss Burleigh's sake as I am for yours.'

'That's no reason to go riding with Lord Hawkridge!' Mr Penrose protested.

'I'm not—or only incidentally,' Mary retorted. 'I'm going riding with Lucinda Burleigh and her friends. Mr Penrose,' she continued blandly, 'you won't allow me to mention our suspicions to Mrs Burleigh, and it may be that you are right to do so. But it cannot do any harm to encourage Lucinda to take a more active part in Bath life. If she has more friends, it may be that she won't be so susceptible to the flattery of your nephew and we won't need to take any further steps on her behalf.'

Mr Penrose stared at her, chewing his lips nervously. Then his expression cleared a little.

'I'm sorry, my dear,' he said heavily. 'I did not mean to seem critical. I dare say you may be right about Miss Burleigh. But I cannot help being concerned about you. Miss Lewisham was telling me such things about Lord Hawkridge last night. . .'

'I expect she was,' said Mary briskly. 'Scandal appears to be her only interest. *Our* concern should be Samuel. From what Lucinda tells me, he seems to have left Bath only the day before he came to demand money from you. Something must have prompted his hurried departure—a communication from the money-lender perhaps. But he hasn't been back to Bath since, though that was certainly his intention when I overheard him talking to Phelps.'

'Perhaps he's thought better of his wild words,' said Mr Penrose hopefully. 'Or perhaps he's hiding from the money-lender.'

'That could be possible,' said Mary thoughtfully, tapping her gloves against her hand. 'From the sound of him, he employs extremely violent collection methods. But I'm not convinced. What do you intend to say to Samuel when we do see him?'

'I don't know,' Mr Penrose admitted anxiously. 'I suppose I must let him have enough money to pay off this debt—and then warn him against such behaviour in future.'

'I think you should give him complete control of his fortune immediately—if that's possible,' said Mary frankly. 'And also make it clear to him that he is not—and never will be—a beneficiary under your own will.'

'But I am supposed to hold his inheritance in trust for him until he can deal with it responsibly!' Mr Penrose protested. 'It is not responsible to hand it over to money-lenders, or fritter it away on wild living. And as to my will—he is my only close relative.'

'I know,' said Mary drily. 'That's precisely my point, sir. There is nothing you can do about his extravagance. He will undoubtedly dissipate his fortune as soon as he gains control of it. It makes no difference if he does so now or in two years' time.

'And as far as your own property is concerned,' she continued after a pause, 'leave it to your old school, the local foundling home, the Royal Society, the Church. . .it doesn't matter. But make sure Samuel knows your death will never be of any benefit to him. Then we can all sleep more comfortably at night.'

Mr Penrose stared at her, horror dawning in his face at the forcefulness of her advice, and the deadly serious manner in which she spoke.

'You really do think I'm in danger,' he said, the depth of his shock audible in his voice. 'I didn't know. . . I thought it was just that he was talking wildly in his cups. I thought. . .just scandal. Perhaps he would try to take advantage of Miss Burleigh, but. . .' He gazed at her, kneading his hands together in distress. 'Oh, dear! Oh, dear! Whatever am I going to do?'

Mary crossed quickly to his side, sitting down beside him.

'There is no reason to be so alarmed, sir,' she reassured him. 'If you do as I suggest, he will have no motive to hurt you. Can you break the terms of your brother's will?'

'Yes. Once Samuel had reached twenty-one, it was left at my discretion as to when I gave control to him,' said Mr Penrose miserably. 'That's why he is so angry with me. Are you really sure?'

'I have heard men make threats before,' said Mary quietly. 'It may be that he was speaking idly, but I don't believe he was.'

'Why didn't you tell me what you feared

before?' Mr Penrose asked fretfully, but then he answered for her, before she could speak. 'You did, I just didn't understand how seriously you meant it. I will do as you suggest. This very morning I shall go into Bath and have a new will drawn up. And I shall set in train the arrangements for handing over control of his inheritance to Samuel. Oh, I do hope these precautions aren't necessary.'

'So do I,' said Mary. 'But they cannot hurt. And when you've done that I think we should perhaps make further enquiries about Samuel's whereabouts. We cannot let this matter drift forever.'

'No,' said Mr Penrose. He looked at her with something that was almost a smile on his thin, nervous face. 'You seem to be far less daunted by all this than I am, my dear.'

'That's because I'm not directly involved,' Mary replied. 'It's always easier to give advice when it's not your problem.'

She glanced round as the door opened, and stood up as the butler came into the room.

'Lord Hawkridge and his friends have arrived, ma'am,' he announced.

'Thank you. I will be with them directly.' She caught up the long train of her skirt in her hand and went to pick up her hat. Then she looked at Mr Penrose and smiled. 'I'll see you later, sir. Please don't worry too much. I'm sure we can sort things out satisfactorily.'

CHAPTER SIX

'You ride very well,' Justin said. There was genuine appreciation in his voice, and Mary blushed rosily at the compliment. Praise from Justin meant so much more to her than from any other man.

'Thank you!' she replied, a sparkle of pleasure in her eyes.

Their party had separated quite naturally into three couples, with Caroline King and Adam Hastings leading, Lucinda and Peter King next, and Justin and Mary bringing up the rear. Occasionally Mary would hear a ripple of laughter carried back on the wind from Caroline, and she knew that the ebullient Miss King was enjoying a lively flirtation with her companion.

Lucinda was more subdued, both because she was shy and because she was far less at home in the saddle than Caroline. But Mary noticed that Peter was taking good care that nothing should alarm either Lucinda or her horse.

'I should have guessed you'd be an excellent horsewoman,' said Justin. 'But we've never had an opportunity to ride together before. Did your father teach you?'

'No. One of Sir Richard's grooms.' Mary smiled reminiscently, looking back over the years to her childhood. She glanced at Justin, a mischievous

108

twinkle in her grey eyes. 'We used to gallop over the Downs as if the devil himself were after us,' she confessed. 'Thomas used to say, "Now, Miss Mary, now, Miss Liz, remember you're *ladies*," but it never used to stop us.'

'I don't suppose it did!' said Justin, grinning. I can't think of a better incitement to go faster. I dare say you got into all sorts of scrapes.'

'Oh, yes!' Mary laughed. 'Elizabeth was always slightly more restrained than I was. I always wanted to go farther and faster. I came off in a ditch once, when Thomas had already warned me not to tackle it. I was very young then. I let go of the reins and Daphne cantered off home. Thomas made me walk back through the village in my muddy habit to punish me for my wilfulness—I was so humiliated!'

Justin laughed. 'I wish I'd seen that,' he said.

'If you'd seen it my folly would have been immortalised on the pages of your sketchbook and I'd never have lived it down!' Mary retorted.

'Possibly.' He grinned. 'On the other hand, I'm only four years older than you, so if you were very young at the time. . .'

'I was ten,' said Mary.

'Ah, well, in that case I would certainly have sketched you,' said Justin. 'I was quite a competent draughtsman by the time I was fourteen—and even more inclined to sketch everything I saw in those days than I am now.'

'Lucky for me you didn't see me, then,' said Mary.

'Perhaps. Have you had much opportunity to ride recently?' He asked the question casually, as if it were of no importance, but Mary suddenly realised that he was waiting alertly for her answer.

She caught her breath. She had been enjoying her memories of the uncomplicated happiness she had known as a child, but now she had to deal once more with the difficulties and uncertainties of the present.

'I do ride,' she said cautiously, 'but not often on such a fine mare as this one.' She leant forward and patted the grey appreciatively on the neck. The mare tossed her head, snorting, demonstrating her quality, and Mary laughed. 'I was expecting a tired hack. Where did you get her?'

'I borrowed her from a friend of mine,' Justin replied. From the gleam in his eyes, Mary knew he was aware that she'd evaded his question, but for the moment it seemed he wasn't going to press it. 'For a price,' he added.

'What price?' Mary asked, intrigued by the amusement in his voice.

'He wants me to paint a portrait for him,' Justin explained.

'Oh.' Mary looked at him suspiciously. His expression was grave, as befitted a man who had undertaken a serious commission from a friend, but Mary knew him too well to be deceived. 'Whose portrait?' she demanded.

'Fanny Matilda's.'

'And who——?'

'His prize sow.'

Mary was startled into a choke of laughter. The mare's ears twitched responsively to the unexpected sound, and Justin grinned.

The winter sunlight was clear and bright, and a warm glow of happiness had brought pretty colour to Mary's cheeks. The soft tawny curls which peeped out beneath her tall hat shone in the light and her veil fluttered in the breeze.

'You'll enjoy that!' she exclaimed, glancing instinctively towards Justin, expecting to see an answering gleam of humour in his expression.

Instead she found herself gazing straight into his eyes. He was no longer laughing. He was looking at her with an intensity which made her pulse race. Both horses came to a standstill, as if they were aware of their riders' preoccupation.

Justin's neat chestnut crowded the mare. The grey flicked her ears irritably, but she made no other protest. Then Justin slipped an arm around Mary's shoulders and leant over to kiss her.

His lips were warm and persuasive on hers. She felt his tongue, gently probing and coaxing her still closed mouth, and her lips parted instinctively.

The world spun away. She had no power to protest. She turned towards him, leaning into the kiss, one hand loosely holding the reins. Her other hand, still grasping her riding crop, lifted to clutch at his collar.

The kiss deepened as he began to explore her mouth, taking his time, slowly and insistently arousing her, matching his actions to her responses. Last night she had nearly lost herself in his arms when they'd danced together and he had gently reminded her of their surroundings. Today he made it impossible for her to be aware of anything but his caresses.

Excitement and pleasure coursed through her. She forgot her good intentions to keep him at a distance, and clung to his collar like a drowning man clinging to a rope. Last time he had kissed her she had been angry and insulted by his unfounded accusations. This time she had already been in sympathy with him and it was easy to surrender herself to his kiss.

He could sense her willingness, and her desire, and his arm tightened around her shoulders. She was leaning far over into his embrace, supported partly by his arms and partly by the side-saddle. It was a precarious cradle, yet she felt quite secure.

At last he lifted his head. She opened her eyes, a soft, instinctive sound of protest in her throat. He was breathing quickly, his hazel eyes—only inches from hers—dark with passion, but he smiled crookedly.

'If we pursue this much further we may both end up in an indignified heap on the grass,' he murmured.

Mary gasped, suddenly remembering where they were—and what had happened. She straightened up hurriedly, feeling the cool breeze on her burning cheeks. She glanced ahead; Lucinda and Peter were almost out of sight. She could only hope that neither of them had looked behind. She gathered up the reins.

'We must catch up,' she said hurriedly, feeling confused and embarrassed and unsure of herself.

'Not yet.' Justin caught her arm before she could urge the mare forward.

Mary looked at him, her bewilderment and uncertainty evident in her eyes. She had been trying to convince herself that a few hours in Justin's company would be enough to compensate her for all the lonely years ahead. But now he had confronted her not only with his desire for her but also her desire for him.

She was afraid. It would be so easy to give in to him. And then she would lose everything. Her self-respect, her independence, her security. She couldn't let Justin, of all men, do that to her.

'What are you afraid of?' he asked softly.

'*Nothing*!' Mary denied, more vehemently than she'd intended.

'Then why won't you talk to me?' he demanded. 'You used to talk to me, for God's sake! You used to tell me whatever you were thinking.'

'That was a long time ago,' said Mary tautly.

'I know that!' He bit off the hastily uttered words, staring at her in exasperation. 'What have you been doing these last seven years?' he asked more temperately.

'Managing,' Mary replied, her eyes briefly losing their focus as she remembered the loneliness that lay behind her.

'*How*?'

Mary glanced back at him. It hurt her that he couldn't let that question rest. That he couldn't trust her when she'd told him that she'd lived a respectable life.

'How do you think?' she asked bitterly. 'I've done very well. I don't need your help, or anyone else's, my lord.'

'You never did,' said Justin, an icy note creeping into his voice.

Mary heard the coldness and a wave of despair swept over her. She stretched one hand impulsively towards him.

'Please don't!' she begged, her pain visible in her eyes. 'I'll be leaving Bath soon. I couldn't bear it if we parted on terms of bitterness after we've already——' She broke off, no longer trusting her voice to remain steady.

'After we've already what?' Justin asked, taking her hand. His eyes were hard and searching on her face, but he held her hand in a warm and comforting clasp. Mary wanted to cry, but she swallowed back her tears and smiled bravely.

'All this time you've thought I deserted you and I've believed you no longer wanted me,' she said. 'Isn't it enough to know that neither of us betrayed the other? We've moved on since then. You've come into your inheritance, I've. . .made a new life for myself. We can't go back.'

'If you're trying to tell me you no longer feel anything for me, I don't believe you,' said Justin harshly. 'We don't have to go back, we can go forward—if only you would allow us to do so.'

'No!' Mary dragged her hand out of his grasp. Any minute now he would renew his offer to make her his mistress and she didn't want to hear it. She didn't want to be reminded of the only role she was fit to play in his life—and she was afraid she wouldn't have the strength to refuse him.

She put her heel to the mare's side. The grey bounded forward, eager to stretch her legs, and the chestnut matched her instantly. Mary leant forward, urging the grey into a gallop. The wind whipped at her skirts and tugged at her hat. Normally she would have gloried in the power of the mare's smooth stride, but today she was simply trying to escape. She wanted to gallop through the fresh winter morning forever, until her past was left so far behind that she could no longer see it or remember it.

The horses' hooves drummed on the ground, echoing the pounding of her heart. Trees flashed past her, blurred and indistinguishable from each other. Faces of men long dead or gone from her life flashed upon her inner eye with far more clarity. Her father, her uncle, Bill Crawford, even Donald. She had trusted them all once, and they had all betrayed her. She wished she could forget them, erase them from her memory—but she couldn't. They would be part of her forever.

Ahead of them she could see Lucinda and Peter. They had turned to look back. Beside her she could see Justin out of the corner of her eye.

'Mary!' he shouted over the thunder of hoofbeats.

She ignored him. She wondered if he would try to grab her reins. She was so overwrought that if he had done so she would have slashed at him with her crop.

But he didn't. The chestnut dropped back to a canter as they approached the others, and the grey slowed instinctively. A bitter smile twisted Mary's lips. It happened every time. At the very moment when she thought Justin was going to impose his will on her—force her to accede to his wishes—he drew back, and left her free to make her own decision.

It was one of the reasons why she loved him. She had never thought his forbearance sprang from weakness. It was a measure of his confidence in himself that he was prepared to give her so much room. But it made it so much harder to walk away from him.

For a brief instant she wondered what it would be like to be his mistress. Would he accord her the same freedom of choice in those circumstances? Perhaps there could be a future for them. Perhaps he would understand her need to preserve her independence. She could keep the Lazy Cat, maybe get someone in to help Donald run it when she was away. . .

The vision of a life which included Justin floated tantalisingly before her eyes. Then it faded. It was a compromise which could only bring unhappiness. She could not bear to live a life of such subterfuge—and she couldn't tolerate the fact that any children she bore would have no right to their father's name. She had sacrificed her own good name, but she could not inflict a similar shame on any innocent soul she brought into the world.

'I wish I could ride like you,' said Lucinda enviously, breaking into Mary's thoughts.

'It's only practice,' Mary replied, speaking with a lightness she didn't feel. 'I try to ride most mornings.'

She saw Justin glance at her sharply, and realised she'd inadvertently partially answered his earlier question, while at the same time arousing his curiosity.

'I hope you live somewhere you can indulge your taste for speed,' he said humorously, but with an intent expression in his eyes. 'It would never do to gallop like that down the Row.'

Despite herself, Mary smiled.

'It would certainly cause a stir,' she agreed. 'Perhaps I should try it one day when I'm feeling bored.'

'I'd like to be there to see you do it,' he said, an answering gleam in his eyes. 'With my sketchbook close to hand—to catch all the startled reactions.'

Peter laughed, but Lucinda turned eagerly towards Justin.

'Is it true you agreed to paint a pig in exchange for borrowing these horses?' she asked.

'Yes, Miss Burleigh.' He bowed slightly in her direction.

She stared at him incredulously.

'I thought Pete—Mr King—was teasing me!' she exclaimed. 'Are you sure you want to? A *pig*!'

'Not just any pig,' Justin said gravely. 'Fanny Matilda is a matriarch of substance—with several prizes to prove it. She also has a countenance full of character and dignity. I will enjoy the commission.'

Mary glanced at him, hearing the sincerity in his voice. She knew he was speaking the truth. Justin could find beauty and interest in the most unlikely subjects.

'You've already met the *grande dame*, then?' she said teasingly.

'Oh, yes. Henderson was very anxious for me to make her acquaintance.'

'But how will you set about it?' Lucinda asked, genuinely interested.

In a few moments a lively discussion ensued on the merits of oil or water-colour for the commission, the need for preliminary sketches, and exactly how the model was going to be posed.

Mary dropped back, and found Peter riding beside her.

'I hope Miss Burleigh is enjoying herself,' he said.

'She certainly seems to be doing so,' Mary replied, smiling.

She was grateful for the distraction of conversation. It would have been so easy to lose herself in contemplation of Justin and her own problems, but she was conscious that she still had to present an unexceptional manner to her other companions.

'Perhaps we should have made more of an effort

to include her in our diversions before,' Peter conceded contritely. 'But she has always been so retiring, and I was. . .that is, we were anxious not to seem as if we were only pursuing her friendship because she's an heiress.'

'Your sensitivity does you credit,' said Mary drily.

He flushed. 'You think I should have made more of an effort, ma'am?' he asked awkwardly. 'But Caroline——' He broke off, obviously not wishing to repeat his sister's opinions on the subject.

'You were in a difficult situation,' Mary said more kindly.

'I did start to pay more attention to her,' Peter insisted eagerly. 'But then Penrose appeared and she seemed so taken with him. Of course, he's rich. I could hardly compete——' He broke off again, looking vexed with himself for his indiscretion.

'Do you really think Miss Burleigh is more interested in a man's possessions than in his character?' Mary asked quietly.

'Of course not!' he exclaimed indignantly.

'Well, then.'

'But my prospects are in no way comparable to Penrose's. Though there is something about him I cannot quite like. . .' He caught himself up, his eyes flying to Mary's face in consternation. 'I'm sorry,' he said stiffly. 'I had forgotten he was your cousin.'

'Please don't apologise,' said Mary calmly. 'If

we are to be entirely honest, I must confess that I also find there is something about him that I cannot quite like—but I beg you will never repeat that to anyone.'

He met her eyes steadily for a moment. She was increasingly coming to the opinion that there was more to him than his flamboyant waistcoats suggested, and she wasn't disappointed.

'You have my word,' he said seriously but without over-emphasis. 'Thank you, ma'am.' He urged his horse forward to overtake Lucinda and Lord Hawkridge, and a moment later Justin fell back beside Mary.

'*Where* do you manage to ride most mornings?' he asked immediately.

'Justin——'

'No,' he interrupted her without apology. 'If you think I'm going to let you disappear without any idea of your whereabouts, you are much mistaken. You did it once—you're not doing it again.'

'I *didn't*——' Mary broke off, biting her lip. She looked up and met Justin's eyes.

'So you say,' he said drily. 'Does Penrose have some kind of hold over you? Is that why you're so reluctant to trust me?'

'No!' Mary insisted.

'It does seem unlikely,' Justin conceded, a faint smile on his lips as he saw her outraged expression. 'You have a far stronger personality than he has. But you might be using him to protect you from someone else—the way you once used Bill Crawford.'

'*No*!' This time anger throbbed in Mary's voice. 'I don't need his protection or anyone else's. I can look after myself.'

'Then what is so terrible about your life these past seven years that you can't tell me about it?' Justin demanded fiercely. 'Do you have so little faith in my ability to understand?'

'I don't want you to understand!' Mary retorted wildly. 'I want you to leave me alone! Why can't you believe me when I tell you I managed by myself? I have done nothing to be ashamed of—nothing.'

'I didn't say you had any reason to be ashamed,' said Justin tightly. 'But it's hard to believe your life is entirely—to your choosing, shall we say?—when you're so adamant in refusing to tell me about it. Don't you think I have any right to know what's become of you?'

'Right?' Mary spat furiously.

Too much had been said already, and she was still wound up from Justin's kiss. She was far too upset to realise that she was making him the target for all the accumulated anger and pain of her life.

'I don't think anyone has any rights left in me, my lord—not even you!' She lifted her chin proudly; her veil fluttered defiantly in the breeze. 'Hasn't it occurred to you that I might not have told you where I live simply because I don't want you to follow me?' she demanded.

Justin stared at her, tight-lipped. Once again

the horses had come to a halt, but this time the gulf that had widened between them seemed almost unbridgeable.

'Why?' he demanded.

'Because I never want to see you again,' she flung at him.

There was a moment's silence. The mare tossed her head restlessly, and Mary shortened the reins instinctively.

'I don't believe you,' said Justin harshly, a muscle twitching in his rigid cheek.

'Of course you don't!' Mary exclaimed recklessly. 'You don't believe anything I say! But if I'd told you I was Mr Penrose's mistress, or that I'd been living in a brothel all these years, you'd have believed that!'

'*Mary*!'

'Don't touch me!' The grey mare danced uneasily aside as she saw Justin reach out towards her. 'I was happy!' she said bitterly. 'My life was ordered and comfortable. Then you just appear and think you can turn it all upside-down—but I'm not going to let you. No one's ever going to do that to me again.'

She swung the mare round and cantered after the others.

They ate a hearty luncheon at the George. It was an inn which, Peter cheerfully informed Mary, was famous for, among other things, providing shelter for the Duke of Monmouth during his ill-fated rebellion against James II.

'Apparently someone took a shot at him through the window. Missed him, of course, otherwise there'd have been no battle of Sedgemoor.'

'You know a great deal about local history,' said Lucinda shyly.

'I've lived in Bath all my life,' Peter replied gruffly, but he looked gratified.

Mary might have been pleased at the tentative friendship which was building between them, but she felt too disturbed to show more than a superficial interest in her companions. She needed time alone and she needed time to think, to come to terms with what had just happened—but she didn't have either. She wondered painfully if perhaps it was impossible for her to reach a comfortable understanding with Justin. Their feelings ran too deep and too strong. They must be lovers—or forever be at war with each other.

'Don't you think, Mrs Drayton?' said Lucinda, and Mary suddenly realised that she hadn't been paying any attention to the conversation.

'I beg your pardon?' She summoned up a smile and from then on forced herself to show an interest in her companions. Though she couldn't bring herself to look at Justin.

They lingered over the meal, and it was only towards the end that Mary discovered that Justin had been as remote from the others as she had.

'My lord! You've been sketching us!' Lucinda exclaimed suddenly.

Mary glanced round quickly. He wasn't even sitting at the table. He'd withdrawn slightly, just as he had used to do in the Blue Boar, when he'd wanted to observe without himself being observed. And they had all been so engrossed in their conversation that they hadn't noticed.

'Please, may I see?' Lucinda asked eagerly.

He hesitated fractionally, then handed her the sketchbook. They were seated informally, with Mary on Lucinda's right and Peter on her left, Caroline and Adam on the opposite side of the table with Justin.

Lucinda looked down at the picture, then she held it silently for Mary to see. On her other side, Peter craned his neck to get a better view.

The sketch had originally been intended to show all three of them, but Lucinda and Peter had been blocked in only roughly. All the artist's attention had been devoted to Mary. He had depicted her with her head turned towards Lucinda and Peter, apparently listening to her companions, yet she was clearly isolated from them.

Her pride, her pain and her loneliness were there for all to see, unrelentingly pinned to the cruel white page—but so was Justin's response. If he hadn't spared her, he hadn't spared himself either. And she saw more clearly than if he had spoken that he was as wounded as she was by everything that had happened between them.

She turned her head away, unable to look at the image any longer.

'May I see?' Caroline reached out imperatively to take the sketchbook. Then, when Lucinda did not immediately give it to her, she stood up, clearly intending to go and look over Lucinda's shoulder.

Lucinda turned the page quickly.

'I don't think you've flattered me, my lord,' she said, sounding almost vexed. 'I'm sure my nose isn't so long—and I'm positive you've made my eyes too small.'

'I didn't notice. . .but why don't you take your revenge, Miss Burleigh?' Peter said eagerly.

He reached over and picked up Justin's travelling ink-well, putting it down beside Lucinda.

'Oh, I couldn't!' she protested instinctively.

A warm smile dawned in Justin's eyes.

'Of course you can, Miss Burleigh,' he said. 'See, I will even sharpen your weapon for you.' And he picked up his knife and reshaped the pen nib for her.

'Well, if you're sure,' she said doubtfully.

'Go on, Lucinda!' Caroline urged her. 'I've never seen anything you've drawn. It will be fun.'

Lucinda glanced at Caroline, possibly recognising that she was being treated rather like a sideshow. Then she looked back at Justin. For a long moment she did nothing but study him, and Caroline stirred restlessly. Then Lucinda dipped the pen in the ink and began to draw with far more confidence than might have been expected in the circumstances.

Adam went to stand beside Caroline. They were all engrossed in what Lucinda was doing. Mary stood up and went quietly out of the room.

* * *

'Mrs Drayton.'

Peter found Mary standing in the churchyard. She was looking towards the church. Her veil was blowing jauntily behind her, but her expression was bleak and unfocused, and he didn't think she was aware of her surroundings.

'Mrs Drayton?' he said again.

She turned towards him. For a moment her eyes remained blank, then her familiar smile illuminated them.

'You shouldn't let considerations of wealth stand in the way of what you want,' she said, as if they were continuing a conversation. 'There are so many other, far more insurmountable barriers. Are we ready to go now?'

'Yes, ma'am.' He offered her his arm. 'We promised Mrs Burleigh we would bring Lucinda back in good time. She drew a very nice picture of Lord Hawkridge,' he added with satisfaction. 'I think it surprised Caroline.'

'I'm so glad,' said Mary warmly.

CHAPTER SEVEN

'MARY?' said Justin.

She glanced at him but she didn't answer. Once again they were riding in couples, in the same pairings and order that they had ridden out.

'Unless you want to break up what appear to be two extremely satisfactory flirtations—at least, from the point of view of those enjoying them— you have to ride with me,' he went on, an edge of humorous resignation in his voice. 'You might as well talk to me.'

'There isn't. . . I don't think there is anything left to say,' Mary replied almost wearily.

'Don't you?' said Justin. 'I think there will always be something left to say between us.'

There was a note of deep sincerity beneath his light tones, and Mary glanced at him swiftly. Her grey eyes were wide and hurt. It was almost as if she was looking to him for reassurance.

He swore softly under his breath.

'Every time I try to talk to you, we end up fighting,' he said. 'All I want——' He broke off. 'Why are you so afraid I'm going to turn your life upside-down?' he asked gently.

Unexpected tears filled Mary's eyes and she turned her head away. She didn't want Justin to be kind to her—not now. It wasn't fair.

'Mary?'

'Because you're a lord. And I am. . .what I am,' she said painfully, without looking at him. 'I won't be your mistress, Justin. And if you won't be my friend there isn't much left, is there?'

He didn't immediately reply, and the bitter core of despair within her began to grow till it threatened to engulf her. It seemed to her that his silence was answer enough. She listened to the muffled thud of hooves on the turf and wondered if he would ever speak again.

'There was once,' he said at last.

'But we were a lot younger and far more foolish then,' Mary retorted, dashing a tear from her cheek and finding relief in brisk practicality. 'Besides, I don't suppose your father would have permitted the match.'

'I didn't always do what my father wished,' said Justin mildly. 'Very rarely, in fact. It was one of the main reasons why we couldn't spend more than half an hour in the same room without coming to cuffs.'

'On trivial matters,' Mary persisted impatiently. 'But marriage is important. You couldn't marry to bring disgrace and scandal into your family.'

'I've heard you say so many times,' he said slowly. 'Is that still what you think?'

'Of course it is!' she exclaimed. She glanced at him quickly, then equally quickly turned away again. 'How could I think anything else? But I'm not prepared to be your mistress. Not now. I. . .' Her voice faltered and she didn't try to continue.

It was colder than it had been in the morning. The wind cut more chillingly through her riding habit, and clouds were appearing on the horizon. If they didn't make haste it would rain before they reached Bath.

'We must catch up with the others,' she said. 'Mrs Burleigh won't like it if Lucinda gets soaked through. I don't think Mr King would like it either—although I suppose if she catches a chill it will at least make it more difficult for Samuel to pursue her—though of course I'd never wish her to be ill. . .' She was talking for the sake of it, hardly aware of what she was saying. She simply wanted to bring the conversation back to less immediately painful topics.

'I don't know what you're talking about,' said Justin, interrupting her without ceremony. 'And at the moment I don't particularly care. Look at me. Just. . .look at me.'

She turned her head reluctantly, unwilling to meet his eyes, but unable to resist the deep tone in his voice.

'You've told me several times you won't be my mistress,' he said steadily. 'Now I'm telling you that I will never again make you such an offer.' His lips twisted in an unamused, almost self-mocking smile. 'You may trust me on this,' he added. 'Even my father never doubted my word.'

Mary looked down, her heart pounding. Her first feeling was not one of relief, but of loss. Yet he'd only given her what she'd asked for. How could she be so fickle? Because she wanted so much more. But at least she could be as gracious in accepting his promise as he had been in making it.

She lifted her eyes to meet his steady gaze. She knew his features so well. His hazel eyes which always saw more than she expected. His firm yet sensitive mouth. His strong jawline, and that air of casual authority he wore, as if he had no need to raise his voice to be heard.

Was she saying goodbye to him now? Would she ever see him again?

'Thank you, my lord,' she said formally. 'Will you. . .can we still be friends?'

A smile illuminated his face, flecks of gold dancing warmly in his hazel eyes. It was a smile of affection—if not love.

There was a time when he'd always looked at Mary like that, before all the misunderstandings and bitterness had come between them. It reminded her of the past so forcefully that she could hardly believe this might be the last time they met.

Surely she would wake up and find it was all a dream? That her uncle and Bill Crawford were only figments of her imagination—no greater impediment to her happiness than pantomime demons?

But if there had been no Alf she would never have been to St Giles—and she would never have met Justin. She could not change the past. Only live with it.

'Is that what you want?' Justin asked. 'To be friends?'

'Yes.' Mary did not trust herself to say anything more than the single word.

Justin drew the chestnut to a halt and stretched out his right hand to her.

'Then we will be friends,' he said.

She hesitated, then put her right hand in his, feeling the firm pressure of his fingers as they shook on their agreement. She would never again know the touch of his hands—except, perhaps, in the formal gestures of greeting and parting. There was a bitter taste in her mouth and her throat was full, as if it was choked with all the tears she had struggled not to shed.

'Now we really must catch up with the others,' she said, taking up her reins again and trying to sound businesslike, though she felt as if she'd been mortally wounded.

'But not so quickly that you don't have time to tell me why we've been cultivating Miss Burleigh so assiduously over the past two days,' said Justin as they urged their horses into a gentle trot. 'And also, now I come to think of it, where Samuel fits in. Who *is* Samuel?'

Mary glanced at him doubtfully. He sounded so normal it was hard to believe everything that had gone before.

'Mr Penrose's nephew,' she revealed cautiously. 'And I didn't know we were cultivating Miss Burleigh.'

'Well, you certainly are,' said Justin judiciously.

'I'm just along for the ride—so to speak. But I haven't been backward in drawing her out—in so far as Peter King has given me an opportunity to do so. I just wish I knew what all this effort was in aid of. Friends do talk to each other,' he added as she hesitated.

'Yes, I know. But it's not my secret. And Mr Penrose is *so* anxious to avoid scandal,' Mary replied uncertainly.

She could think of nothing better than to confide her worries about Samuel to Justin, but she knew that Mr Penrose would hate it.

'I don't claim to be Penrose's friend,' Justin said drily, 'but as *your* friend I will engage not to create a scandal.'

'I know that.' Mary threw him a quick smile.

It was becoming easier to speak naturally to him by the second. All that was left of what she had lost was a dull ache beneath her breast. But she told herself that it was better to hold the comforting light of a candle in her hand than cry forever after the unattainable moon.

'It's a trifle complicated,' she said slowly.

'I'm moderately intelligent.'

'To explain, I meant,' she retorted. 'I think the best place to begin is with the fact that Mr Penrose's brother—whose name escapes me at the moment—left his fortune to his son, Samuel, in a particularly contentious way.'

She went on to describe the threats she'd overheard Samuel make, and her instinctive decision to warn Mr Penrose.

'Where did you hear these drunken ravings?' Justin asked, frowning.

'In perfectly unexceptional circumstances,' Mary replied quickly, a challenge in her eyes.

Justin glanced at her shrewdly, but he didn't pursue the matter. 'And then you went to warn Penrose,' he said. 'Why did he believe you? Did he know you? Did he already have doubts about the nephew?'

'I've been distantly acquainted with him for years. But as to whether he believed me, I'm not entirely sure that he did,' said Mary frankly. 'At least, not until this morning, when I told him he should change his will.'

'Why did you do that?' Justin asked sharply.

'Because I don't think there's any action we can take against Samuel unless, God forbid, he does something to warrant it,' Mary explained thoughtfully, unaware of the frown in Justin's eyes. 'The best protection for Mr Penrose is to hand over control of Samuel's fortune immediately, and make sure he can never get his hands on Mr Penrose's. And the best protection for Lucinda. . .'

'Is Peter King,' Justin said.

'Not necessarily,' Mary replied quickly. 'I was going to say friends. If she doesn't feel lonely and excluded, she's less likely to be susceptible to a fortune-hunter's charm.'

'Is Samuel charming?' Justin asked, a curious expression in his eyes.

'He has never seemed so to me,' Mary said

honestly. 'Arrogant, rude and potentially cruel, I would have said. But they seem to like him well enough in Bath.'

'And how have you been in a position to make such an assessment of his character?' Justin asked conversationally.

Mary looked up and met his eyes.

'I know,' he replied for her. 'In perfectly unexceptional circumstances. Are you aware that friends often reveal more to each other than simply their names and their immediate concerns?'

'But we can only be friends while I'm in Bath,' said Mary flatly. 'We hardly inhabit the same social circle, my lord.'

'I have many friends,' Justin replied equably. 'They don't all frequent Almack's. My friend Henderson, for example, is a large-hearted farmer with three sturdy sons and a prize pig he is extremely fond of. He doesn't seem to have any inflated notion of my consequence. He was quite adamant that I couldn't borrow that mare unless I agreed to paint Fanny Matilda.'

'But he doesn't have. . .' Mary caught herself up, biting her lip.

'It's true he doesn't have such a dubious past,' Justin agreed cheerfully. 'At least not to my knowledge. But who knows what skeletons might not come bouncing out of his cupboards if we rattled the doors long enough? Do you really think Samuel meant his threats?' he added more seriously.

'Yes,' said Mary simply. The colour which had

flamed in her cheeks at Justin's casual mention of her past slowly cooled. How could he be so light-hearted about something which had wounded her so badly?

'Then why did Penrose make you come to Bath with him?' Justin demanded. 'Surely he knew he was exposing you to an unpleasant scene at best—and personal risk at worst?'

'He didn't make me come—I chose to do so,' Mary said quickly. 'I'd made the accusation; it seemed to me I had a duty to stand by it. And I was worried about Mr Penrose. I wasn't sure if he'd be able to handle Samuel. Besides. . .'

'Besides what?'

'I was getting bored,' she admitted, almost defiantly. 'Perhaps I wasn't born to lead an entirely respectable life after all.'

Justin smiled, but his expression was distracted.

'There are degrees of excitement,' he said. 'Go home, Mary. I think you've already provided Miss Burleigh with all the protection she needs—and I will undertake to provide whatever help Penrose needs. There's no reason for you to be involved in this business any longer.'

'You'll look after Mr Penrose?' Mary said, staring at him in astonishment. 'But you don't even like him!'

'No, I don't,' Justin agreed. 'But friends often perform unpleasant tasks for each other—so I'm told. And I don't like the idea of you having anything more to do with a man like Samuel Penrose.'

'I can take care of myself,' Mary protested, torn between gratification at his concern for her welfare and irritation that he should so readily assume that he needed her help.

'I dare say you can,' said Justin austerely. 'But that doesn't mean you have to put yourself at risk to take care of every ineffectual nincompoop you meet!'

'Mr Penrose is not a nincompoop! He's. . . he's. . .' Mary's sense of humour got the better of her and she started to giggle as she remembered some of Mr Penrose's more exasperating characteristics.

Justin's expression relaxed. There was a hint of relief in his eyes, although Mary didn't see it.

'Oh, it's not fair to make fun of him,' she gasped after a moment. 'It's not his fault he's inclined to be a little. . .a little over-concerned about things. And he has good reason to be anxious at the moment.'

'I might feel warmer towards him if he'd shown more concern for *your* safety,' Justin retorted. 'And if he hadn't been so keen to adopt you as his niece.'

'Oh, that was for my sake,' Mary assured him, a humorous light in her eyes. 'The first night on the way to Bath he was particularly fussy. The kind of guest you want to throttle. First he sent the supper back twice, then he complained about his sheets—and there was nothing wrong with either. I was quite surprised. He'd never been so difficult when he came. . . But of course he was very agitated. The next morning one of the ostlers made a lewd remark about us—and then it was Mr Penrose's turn to be embarrassed.'

'And that accounts for transforming you into his niece?' said Justin, raising his eyebrows. 'But why did he persist with it when you came to Bath and met people he already knew?'

'I don't know,' said Mary honestly. 'I mean, obviously the same basic situation still applied, but I was never so surprised as when he introduced me to the Knightleys as his niece. I've been on tenterhooks ever since that someone who actually knows his sister and her family will appear. That *would* create a scandal.'

'If he's so concerned with appearances, why the house in Queen Square?' Justin asked, a not entirely friendly expression in his eyes.

'I told you,' Mary replied calmly, although she was aware of the chill in Justin's question. 'He doesn't trust the linen in hotels—and he was very ill at ease in those surroundings. He's very nervous about confronting Samuel. He wants it to be in private.'

'More fool him,' said Justin drily.

'That's what I thought,' Mary agreed. She sighed. 'Perhaps I should have made more of an effort before to impress upon him the possible danger, but. . . Oh, Justin, he's old enough to be my father, but he seems to have no more genuine understanding of the evil that can exist in the world than——'

'I've always wished I could have met your father,' said Justin quietly as she broke off.

'You would have liked him,' said Mary, unsurprised that he had followed the trend of her thoughts so easily. 'He had no affectations. He was always himself. And he was so friendly and kind and—good.'

Justin didn't say anything, and when she glanced at him she saw that his lips were pressed together and the line of his jaw was very pronounced in the pale afternoon light.

'I would favour a little less virtue and a little more foresight—wouldn't you?' he demanded bluntly, meeting her gaze.

'You know I would,' she replied, sighing. 'But he's still my father and it's better if I remember the good things—— Oh, what's the point of talking about it? It's all in the past now, anyway.'

'Will you go home and leave me to deal with Penrose?' Justin asked after a moment.

'No, I won't,' said Mary flatly. 'Mr Penrose would hate it if he knew I'd been discussing his affairs with you. And Samuel isn't even in Bath. I don't know what we'll do if he doesn't turn up soon. I can't stay here indefinitely.'

'Of course not, you have a business to run,' said Justin smoothly. 'I expect Donald's been a great help to you. Is he still with you?'

'Yes, he——' Mary broke off, staring at Justin.

'Too many clues, sweetheart,' he murmured provocatively, just as they were about to catch up with Lucinda and Peter. 'In what—unexceptional—circumstances could you overhear Samuel make such threats? Have experience of the kind of guest you want to throttle? And be surprised that Mr Penrose could prove such a difficult guest? Besides, I've just remembered a rumour I didn't pay much attention to when I first heard it—that you stung Seb Collins for a very fair price for the Blue Boar before you left Church Lane. If that rumour was right, you'd have had all the capital you needed.'

Mary drew in her breath indignantly.

'If you've always known I sold the Blue Boar, why the devil did you accuse me of selling myself to a richer man?' she demanded in a furious undertone.

'Because it was only one of many rumours,' Justin replied. 'And I knew Seb Collins. I couldn't imagine anyone pulling such a trick on him. Not even Alf. You must have been very lucky.'

'I wasn't lucky,' said Mary categorically, her eyes blazing. 'I held my own against Alf for five years! Did you really think I wasn't a match for Seb?'

She was outraged by his easy assumption that it was more likely that she would have become another man's mistress than that she could have outwitted one of the most notorious bosses in St Giles. Justin had known the truth all these years and he hadn't been able to credit it! Even he had preferred to think the worst of her!

By this time they were riding alongside Lucinda

and Peter King and Mary quite deliberately turned
her back on Justin and smiled at the others.

It seemed, in any case, that Peter wanted to talk
to her, because he allowed his horse to fall back,
leaving Lucinda to ride on with Justin. Mary
observed the manoeuvre with a certain amount of
amusement.

'Your friendship with Miss Burleigh seems to
be flourishing,' she said blandly. 'As does your
sister's with Mr Hastings,' she added, glancing
ahead to where Caroline rode with Adam, their
conversation apparently still as lively now as it had
been several hours ago.

Peter looked at her, but he refrained from
comment.

'Quite,' Mary said, a rueful expression in her
grey eyes. 'You're very tactful, sir.'

'You look happier, ma'am,' he ventured. 'I was
afraid, earlier. . . Have you known Lord
Hawkridge long?'

'We met on the road to Bath, a few days ago,'
Mary replied. She sighed. 'Yes, I knew him several years ago,' she admitted, 'but that isn't——'

'I'm not prone to gossip,' he assured her
quickly. 'Was that before——?' He broke off,
flushing. 'I'm sorry, I didn't mean to pry,' he said
awkwardly.

'It was before I was married,' said Mary quietly.
'A long time ago. Now, what can I do for you,
sir?' she added more briskly. 'And does it have
anything to do with Miss Lewisham?'

Peter stared at her in blank amazement. 'Are you a witch, ma'am?' he demanded.

Mary laughed. 'No,' she said. 'But if I were you the problem of Miss Lewisham would be looming quite large in my mind. If you call on Miss Burleigh at Lansdown Crescent, Miss Lewisham will undoubtedly hang on your every word, and then comment *sotto voce* on your handsome figure and elegant waistcoats as soon as she thinks you're out of earshot. And if you try to arrange an assignation with Lucinda anywhere else, Miss Lewisham will probably chaperon her—and a similar situation will ensue. Yes, if I were you I would certainly be giving some thought to the problem of Miss Lewisham.'

Peter grinned uncomfortably.

'I wasn't expecting you to sum up the situation so. . .so. . .'

'Bluntly?' Mary supplied helpfully. 'Or tactlessly? I would be very concerned if I thought you were trying to take advantage of Miss Burleigh's innocence, or her good nature——'

'I assure you——' Peter began.

'But I don't think that is the case,' Mary continued, ignoring his interruption. 'Have you mentioned your reservations about Miss Lewisham to Lucinda?'

'I didn't quite like to,' he admitted. 'It seemed so calculating, and not quite. . .' He paused, clearly unable to find the words to express his unease with the situation.

'Calculating is only another term for foresight,'

said Mary, 'and I'm all for exercising that. How would it be if I asked Lucinda to come shopping with me tomorrow morning? I'm sure I could do with another bonnet, or a new pair of gloves. And no one could fault you if you met us by chance on Milsom Street?'

'Thank you, ma'am,' he said gratefully.

'Don't thank me until we see if she'll accept my invitation,' said Mary.

'Miss Lewisham,' said Justin a few minutes later as they once more fell back behind the others.

'Did Lucinda say anything about her to you?' Mary asked curiously. She was still very angry with him, but she was holding her irritation at bay. She'd had enough of recriminations and arguments for one day.

'Not exactly,' said Justin. 'We had a very round-about conversation in which she managed to make it plain to me that she didn't think the worse of me for making fun of the old trout in the Pump Room yesterday morning. She also expressed the view that it was a pity elderly people so often feel it necessary to usurp the conversation of their younger relations. She didn't phrase it quite like that.'

'I don't suppose she did,' said Mary. 'But Miss Lewisham is an awful cross for anyone to bear. She terrifies the life out of me.'

'Why?'

'Justin! Think what would happen if she ever found out the truth about me!' she exclaimed.

'But you won't be staying in Bath,' said Justin

reasonably. 'And why should you care what a vicious-minded tattle-tale thinks about you?'

'I don't,' said Mary. 'But I care what other people think about me.' She looked ahead towards Lucinda and Peter.

'She won't find out,' said Justin calmly. 'The worse thing she can discover is that you're not really Penrose's niece.'

'That's bad enough!' Mary protested.

'Not necessarily,' he said. 'As far as I can tell, there are only two people in Bath whose opinion you really care about. And I doubt if either of them would think the worse of you if they knew the reason for your unintentional masquerade.' He smiled crookedly. 'Judging by the way Lucinda covered up your picture at the George, she has your best interests at heart,' he added. 'And Peter King seems to think highly of your opinion.'

Mary closed her eyes briefly, remembering the distress she had suffered earlier in the day, and grateful that Lucinda had so effectively hidden the sketch from the others.

'I'm sorry,' Justin said quietly. 'I didn't mean to do that to you. It started off as a sketch of all three of you. But. . .you were the subject I was interested in. Not that I think Caroline or Hastings would have seen anything in it. They don't strike me as having that kind of insight.'

'They do say the pen is mightier than the sword,' said Mary shakily, trying to smile. 'It's not easy to be confronted with yourself in such circumstances.

Much worse than unexpectedly catching sight of yourself in a mirror.'

'I know.' Justin brought the chestnut to a halt, reached into a large pocket and pulled out his sketchbook. He tore out the page with her picture on it and offered it to her. 'Keep it or destroy it,' he said. 'It's yours.'

Mary took it, hardly able to bring herself to look at it, but unbelievably moved by his action. Now she need never fear the strangers who might one day look through his sketchbooks—as she had once done—asking questions and possibly even commenting on her picture. And wondering what she meant to the artist.

'May I see the sketch Lucinda did of you?' she asked on impulse.

'Of course.' He handed her the sketchbook.

She looked down at it and smiled. Lucinda's style was less polished than Justin's. The proportions were not quite right, and she lacked his minute powers of observation and insight into his subject. But the likeness was very good. It had amused him to be sketched, and Lucinda had captured his quizzical expression beautifully. Mary had seen him wear just that look many times.

'Do you want it?' she asked abruptly.

Justin leant over without comment and took the sketchbook out of her hand. Then he tore out that page also and gave it to her.

'I'm sure Miss Burleigh would be flattered that you like it,' he said, almost flippantly.

Mary glanced at him, startled, but she couldn't read his expression.

'Thank you,' she said. She folded the two sketches neatly together and tucked them carefully inside the bodice of her habit. 'I think we'll beat the rain back,' she said. 'I hope so, or Mrs Burleigh may not allow Lucinda to come shopping with me tomorrow morning!'

AN UNSUITABLE MATCH 145

Mary glanced at him, startled, but she couldn't read his expression.

'Thank you,' she said. She rolled the two sketches neatly together and put them carefully inside the bodice of her habit. 'I think we'll best

CHAPTER EIGHT

'GOOD morning, Mrs Drayton, I am so pleased to see you again,' said Mrs Burleigh warmly. 'Please sit down. Lucinda's just getting ready. She hasn't been able to stop talking about her outing yesterday.'

'Thank you.' Mary smiled. 'I'm glad she enjoyed it,' she said. 'I think we all did. It was a beautiful day for a ride.'

'Riding over to Norton St Philip must have seemed very slow to Lord Hawkridge after his London entertainments,' said Miss Lewisham. She spoke with a little tinkling laugh, her sharp eyes on Mary's face. 'But I dare say Bath seems very dull to you also, Mrs Drayton—since you have seen so much of the world.'

'Oh, no,' Mary replied serenely, although Miss Lewisham's manner set her teeth on edge. 'I have received such a warm welcome from everybody that I could not possibly find Bath dull.'

'It was kind of you to ask Lucinda to go shopping with you,' said Mrs Burleigh with dignity. 'I find I get very weary on such expeditions, but I'm sure Lucinda should go out more.'

'On the contrary, it's I who am grateful,' said Mary. 'Lucinda has a very good eye for colour; I shall be glad of her advice.'

'Mrs Knightley has often said I have excellent taste,' said Miss Lewisham. 'I would be happy to come with you, Mrs Drayton. Lucinda is rather young to be entirely depended upon not to make a mistake.'

'I'm sure Mrs Drayton appreciates your offer, Emma,' said Mrs Burleigh before Mary could speak, 'but I would like you to come to the Pump Room with me this morning.'

She glanced up and smiled as her daughter came into the drawing-room.

'I'm so sorry to have kept you waiting, ma'am,' Lucinda exclaimed, looking flustered.

'That's quite all right,' said Mary, smiling. 'I have no urgent commissions to execute.' She stood up and turned to Mrs Burleigh. 'Good morning, ma'am. Thank you for letting Lucinda come out with me.'

'I was in terror that Cousin Emma would insist on joining us,' Lucinda confided a few minutes later when they were safely out of the house. 'She's been hinting that she wanted to do so ever since she found out you'd invited me.'

'I don't think your mother would have agreed to that,' Mary said, glancing curiously at Lucinda. She wasn't sure whether her young friend knew that Peter King intended to meet them later, or whether it was just that Lucinda didn't particularly like her cousin.

'She will say things that make me blush for her,' said Lucinda, unaware of Mary's scrutiny. 'And for me! Oh, Mrs Drayton, it was a lovely day yesterday, wasn't it?'

'I was afraid you might find it rather tiring,' Mary said mildly. 'Since you aren't used to riding so far.'

'Oh, no!' Lucinda protested vehemently. 'Well, actually,' she admitted, with a rueful gleam in her eye, 'I am a little stiff this morning, but I wouldn't tell Mama for anything! Did. . .did *you* enjoy yourself, ma'am?'

'Yes, I did, thank you,' Mary replied. 'I'm used to taking my rides alone. It was very pleasant to have company for a change.'

For a moment Lucinda looked as if she wanted to pursue the subject. But, if she did, she thought better of it. They walked a few paces in silence, then Lucinda asked brightly, 'What kind of bonnet did you have in mind, ma'am?'

'Good gracious! Isn't. . .isn't that Mr King coming towards us—with Lord Hawkridge?' Lucinda exclaimed as they were walking along Milsom Street. She was clearly trying to appear unconcerned, but the rosy colour tinging her cheeks gave her away.

'I do believe it is,' said Mary gravely. 'What a coincidence.'

Lucinda threw her a startled glance, not unmixed with suspicion, but she didn't have time to say anything before the gentlemen greeted them.

'Good morning, ladies,' said Justin courteously.

'I hope you're none the worse for your ride,' Peter said eagerly to Lucinda.

'Oh, no!' she exclaimed. 'I enjoyed it immensely.' Then she blushed, clearly wondering if she'd shown too much unbecoming enthusiasm.

There was a few seconds' silence as the young people gazed at each other, neither quite sure what to say next.

Mary felt a considerable amount of sympathy for Lucinda. She herself hadn't expected Justin to be with Peter, and she was feeling foolishly nervous and tongue-tied. She never wanted him to know how long she had sat looking at the picture Lucinda had drawn of him, hours after she should have been asleep.

'Perhaps, ladies, if you're not in a hurry, you might care for a stroll in Sydney Gardens?' said Justin eventually, only the faintest gleam in his eyes indicating that he found the situation amusing.

'By Jove, yes, sir! What a good idea!' Peter exclaimed. 'Miss Burleigh, do say yes. It's far too beautiful a morning to waste shopping.'

There was no doubt what Lucinda wanted to reply. Nevertheless, she glanced questioningly at Mary.

'I'll have many opportunities to purchase a new bonnet,' Mary said instantly. 'But I haven't been to Sydney Gardens yet—and I really ought to do so before I leave Bath.'

'What an accommodating chaperon you are,' Justin said softly a few minutes later, when Lucinda and Peter were walking a few paces ahead of them.

'It is all right, isn't it?' Mary asked, suddenly anxious. 'I mean. . .'

'You were so clearly determined to throw them

together yesterday, I thought I'd better make some enquiries,' said Justin, an edge of laughter in his voice. 'Respectable family. Not wealthy, but completely acceptable. Caroline's generally regarded as a bit fast, and Peter's waistcoats inspired a few derogatory comments—but they're the worst thing I discovered about him. Do you think Lucinda will be able to exercise a restraining influence over him?'

Mary stifled a choke of laughter. She felt strangely light-headed, not herself at all. She told herself it was simply the bright sunlight in her face, and the crisp, fresh air in her lungs, but she was afraid it was the feel of Justin's arm beneath her hand. And the new harmony which seemed to exist between them.

Something had changed since yesterday. She was still annoyed that he hadn't believed she'd sold the Blue Boar. But she was overwhelmingly relieved that he finally knew she'd lived a respectable life all the years they'd been apart. And he'd worked it out for himself—she hadn't had to tell him.

She no longer had any secrets from him. He knew her for what she was, and she could once again be herself with him. That freedom was worth a great deal to her. And so, she told herself, was his assurance that he would never again ask her to be his mistress. She could walk beside him, take pleasure in the brief, formalised contact that social convention permitted them, without fearing the consuming passion which threatened her resolve—and her integrity.

'I also made some enquiries about Samuel,' said Justin.

'And?' Mary looked up at him sharply.

'You're right, he is generally well thought of in Bath, but I got Henry——'

'Henry?' Mary interrupted, frowning.

'My tiger,' Justin explained.

'I remember!' she exclaimed after a puzzled moment, as she thought back to that morning on the Bath road when the tiger had introduced her to Barabbas and Mary, the two high-spirited chestnuts who pulled Justin's curricle. 'I'm sorry, go on.'

'It's easier for him to make enquiries among people who wouldn't dream of gossiping about Penrose to me,' Justin said. 'Penrose's servant, Phelps, is not well-liked. He's regarded as a bully who's not afraid to use his fists to get what he wants. Does that tally with what you know of him?'

'It doesn't surprise me,' Mary replied. 'But he didn't try anything at the Lazy Cat. No one picks a fight with Donald unless they have a good reason. Or they want to prove themselves—like cocks on a dunghill,' she aded acidly.

'How *is* Donald these days?' Justin asked. He spoke politely, but Mary heard the undercurrent of hostility in his tone and wasn't deceived.

'He did what he thought was best for me,' she said, meeting Justin's eyes squarely.

'He acted out of jealousy and possessiveness,' Justin contradicted her harshly. 'I'm looking forward to my next meeting with him.'

'No!' Mary suddenly had a dreadful vision of Justin confronting the huge Scotsman.

Justin was fifteen years younger than Donald. Strong, athletic, and quite capable of taking care of himself. But Donald was four inches taller, he carried more weight, and he was a vicious fighter. Mary hated to think what the outcome would be if they came to blows. And, whatever happened, someone she cared about would be hurt.

Donald might have lied to her, but without him it would have been much harder to survive in Church Lane, and she might never have succeeded in selling the Blue Boar to Seb Collins. He had badly damaged her trust in him, but she would never forget how much she owed the Scotsman. And she loved Justin.

'Justin! Let it be!' She clutched convulsively at his arm, turning to face him in the winter sunlight. 'Nothing you say to Donald is going to change anything. Please!'

He looked down into her wide, urgent eyes. For a moment she could see nothing but his face — and the searching, yet quizzical, expression in his eyes.

'Please, Justin!' She shook his arm insistently. 'Don't pursue it.'

He smiled, flecks of gold appearing in his hazel eyes, and her heart turned over at the thought of him being hurt.

'Are you so sure your Scottish Goliath would be a match for me?' he asked, almost chidingly.

'No.' She shook her head, although that was certainly her fear. 'But. . .'

'And what makes you think the situation would come to blows?' he asked quizzically.

'You're angry. . .'

'I'm very angry,' he corrected her. 'But I'm not necessarily going to try to relieve my feelings by trying to pound your over-zealous protector to a pulp.' He smiled crookedly. 'Don't keep looking at me like that, sweetheart, or I may forget where we are.'

Colour flooded Mary's cheeks, and she pulled away from him.

'You *promised*!' she exclaimed.

'I promised not to ask you to be my mistress,' Justin replied calmly. He took her hand and drew it back through his arm. Mary tried to pull away, but his free hand closed over hers.

'Let me go!' she said fiercely.

'No.'

'Justin!'

His fingers encircled her slender wrist, holding her too tightly to allow her to escape, but not tight enough to hurt her. He wasn't wearing gloves, and her hands had been tucked snugly inside her muff before she'd met him. There were no barriers between them. Mary couldn't deny the current of excitement which pulsed between their joined hands, or the fire which leapt within her at his touch. After a moment his grip relaxed, and she felt his fingers softly caress the palm of her hand.

She caught her breath.

'Please don't!' she begged in a whisper. 'It's not fair.'

'Nothing ever is.' He kept his hand over hers, but he began to stroll once more after Lucinda and Peter, compelling her to do likewise. 'Don't keep fighting me, Mary.'

'What are you trying to do?' she demanded in a shaken undertone. 'Get me to plead with you to renew your offer? How could you?'

'No.' He glanced around at their surroundings with an air of barely controlled exasperation. 'Dammit, I'm sick of trying to talk to you in public places. Where's Penrose. . .?'

'I don't——'

'Senior.'

'The Pump Room. No. . .he was going to see his lawyer. . .I think.' Mary struggled to think clearly.

'But he's not at Queen Square?' Justin queried impatiently.

'I don't think so,' she said uncertainly.

'It doesn't matter if he is,' Justin asserted decisively. 'I'm sure he can spare us one room to hold a conversation in.'

'But I don't want. . .'

'You may not want to talk to me, but I have every intention of talking to you,' Justin said grimly. 'I'm sure King will be glad of the opportunity to escort Lucinda back to her mama.'

'But I can't just abandon her,' Mary protested, hurrying to keep up as he lengthened his stride.

'You aren't abandoning her. You're leaving her in the unexceptional care of a very respectable young man,' said Justin. 'No one could blame you for doing so when you've just become the victim of a painful migraine.'

'But. . .' It was too late to protest. They'd already caught up with Lucinda and Peter, and Justin was making their excuses, his manner towards Mary half humorous and half solicitous.

Despite her confusion and agitation, Mary had to grit her teeth at his subtle suggestion that she was fatigued by her recent exertions. For her apparent fragility belied an excellent constitution, and she was rarely ill.

'Dammit, why did you have to make me sound like a wilting violet?' she demanded, as soon as she was free to do so. 'And if I am such a poor thing, why are we striding along as if the hounds of hell are on our heels?'

Justin slowed his pace, a reluctant grin lightening his rather set expression.

'I'm sorry. I didn't mean to overtax your strength,' he said solicitously.

'I've a good mind to kick you in the shins and then cry for help,' said Mary crossly. 'You've got no right to abduct me like this.'

'I'm not abducting you,' Justin retorted. 'I'm escorting you to a place where we can have an uninterrupted—and unobserved—conversation. And don't tell me there isn't anything left to say.'

'I wasn't going to.'

'My God! What an admission!' Justin exclaimed. 'Perhaps all this fresh air is going to your head. We'd better get you within the stuffy security of four walls immediately.'

Mary turned her head away, trying not to give way to the rather hysterical laughter that was bubbling up inside her. She didn't honestly think that Justin was going to renew his offer to be his mistress—nor did she think he'd been callously playing with her feelings in Sydney Gardens.

In fact, she wasn't quite sure what to think. But, strangely enough, she felt closer to him as they walked decorously through Bath—occasionally pausing to exchange greetings with acquaintances—than she had done for seven years.

She was aware of his seething impatience as he replied courteously to Mrs Melville's polite enquiry about his mother. And she had to look down to hide the dancing amusement in her eyes when he was waylaid by a retired captain he had sketched only two days before.

'I showed the picture to my sister, and she said it was a most speaking likeness,' said the grey-haired old soldier. 'You have a rare talent, my lord.'

'Thank you, sir. And please convey my compliments to your sister,' said Justin, controlling his exasperation admirably. 'I'm afraid we cannot delay. Poor Mrs Drayton is feeling unwell, and I promised to escort her home.'

'Of course, of course. I do hope you recover

quickly, ma'am.' The old captain lifted his hat to Mary.

'My father always warned me that I shouldn't treat the whole world as my brother,' said Justin darkly as they continued on their way. 'Now I can see I should have paid more attention to him.'

Mary started to laugh. Justin glanced at her, then his lips quirked in a self-deprecating smile.

'You think I'm being ridiculous?'

'No,' she gasped, catching her breath. 'Justin, how come there are people like the poor captain who treat you as if you were a long-lost friend, yet I've seen you walk across the Pump Room as if you expected the seas to part for you? You cannot behave like that most of the time.'

He slowed his pace, looking down at her, a rueful expression in his eyes.

'I was angry both times I met you in the Pump Room,' he said. 'When I'm angry I have a tendency to become arrogant. And the Lewisham woman didn't help. Here we are. Let's hope Penrose is out—or I may become arrogant again!'

Grigson opened the door. His expression when he saw Justin was a nicely judged mixture of curiosity and disapproval, but Mary ignored it.

'Is Mr Penrose in?' she asked briskly.

'No, ma'am.'

'I see.' She glanced back at Justin. 'I'm afraid you may have had a journey in vain, my lord. But if you would care for some tea, we could wait for my uncle to return.'

'I would be glad to do so—if it won't put you to

too much inconvenience,' Justin replied, smoothly falling in with the mild deception.

'By no means,' said Mary. 'Please have some tea sent up to the drawing-room, Grigson.'

'Yes, ma'am.' The butler bowed and departed in his stateliest manner. Mary caught Justin's eye and a flicker of shared amusement passed between them. Then she turned and led the way upstairs.

Justin glanced around the drawing-room, then went straight over to the window. Mary had a sense that he was impatiently waiting for the tea to be brought before he spoke to her.

Now that she was no longer caught up in his urgency to get to the house in Queen Square, nervousness rose up within her. They'd had many difficult conversations over the past few days, but none quite like this. Her mouth felt dry and it was hard to swallow. She wanted to say something to break the tension, but she couldn't think of anything. And she wasn't sure if she could trust her voice anyway.

He was so close. Just on the other side of the room, looking out across the Square. She could sense the tension in him, and the barely contained energy. She knew it was only rigid self-control that was keeping him silent until they could be reasonably safe from interruption.

What was he going to say? And how would she respond? A wild hope was beating in her heart, nearly choking her with its intensity.

There were footsteps outside the door and Justin moved away from the window.

'You have an excellent view of the Square,' he said as the butler came in with the tea-tray.

'I expect the garden looks particularly charming in summer,' Mary replied, hardly recognising the sound of her own voice. 'But I've never visited Bath before, so I have to use my imagination. Thank you, Grigson.'

The butler went out, closing the door softly behind him. The moment he had done so, Justin came towards her. She stood up instinctively, lifting her eyes to meet his. He caught her hand in his, and she felt the same thrill of excitement which had affected her so powerfully in Sydney Gardens.

'Mary. . .' he began. Then, as she continued to look mutely up at him, she saw his eyes blaze with sudden fire, and he pulled her roughly into his arms.

She gave a soft cry, partly of surprise, partly of protest, and he stifled it with his mouth. She tried to push him away, but her arms felt weak and her efforts were half-hearted at best. He was holding her so tightly, she could feel the urgent warmth of his body through the many layers of cloth that separated them.

Yesterday his lips had been gentle and persuasive on hers; today they were demanding and insistent. An answering flame of passion flared up from deep within her. She had been excited and stimulated by his touch earlier, and now she was almost instantly aroused by his lovemaking. She slipped her arms around his neck, clinging to him eagerly. Her lips were already swollen and throbbing from his fiercely irresistible kisses. But when he drew back slightly, and ran his tongue delicately across her burning lower lip, another, deeper wave of pleasure swept through her.

She trembled responsively in his arms and he pressed her more closely against him. Beneath his urgent, questing hands her dress was creased and rumpled, but she didn't care. And when he lifted his head to look down at her he saw that her eyes were dilated with desire. He groaned softly, and bent to kiss her neck. She felt his lips teasing her tender skin, and she let her head fall back as golden fire coursed through her veins. Her hands clutched convulsively at his shoulders.

Nothing had prepared her for the fierce, uncontrollable passion which filled her. She only knew she wanted more of him—much more. A soft sound of almost desperate longing escaped her, and she twined her fingers in his hair, surrendering herself to him completely, abandoning responsibility for whatever followed to him.

She seemed to dissolve in his arms as the world whirled about her in a dizzying kaleidoscope of lights and colour and fire.

And then the world steadied, and she found herself standing quietly within the circle of his embrace. Her face was pressed against his shoulder. His head was bent over hers, his breath ruffling her hair, but he was no longer trying to rouse her to new heights of passion.

She could hear his heart pounding, and the rasp

of his breathing, but his hand was gentle as he stroked her hair. She felt confused and disorientated, unsatisfied desire still raging through her body. But gradually her trembling lessened and she became more fully aware of her surroundings.

She could hear the clock, its measured mechanical ticking in sharp contrast to the wildly human beating of her heart and Justin's. Then she became aware of the sound of muffled voices from the Square. And the rich yet subdued colour of Justin's coat so close to her eyes.

And then she realised what had happened—and exactly where she was.

Never in her life had she so completely lost control of herself. It was no thanks to her restraint that they were not now lying in a tangle of petticoats and disarranged clothes on the drawing-room floor.

She closed her eyes, shame and embarrassment consuming her. After this she had no one but herself to blame if Justin thought she was a loose woman. How could he fail to see her as a suitable candidate to be his mistress when she had so little propriety?

She wanted to wrench herself out of his arms, but the moment she did that she would have to face him—and see the condemnation in his eyes. She tensed instinctively, and his hand ceased in its gentle stroking.

'Mary?' he said quietly.

She spun out of his arms, turning her back on

him and pressing her hands against her fiery cheeks.

'Don't look at me!' she begged in a strangled voice.

'But I like looking at you,' he replied mildly. 'I cannot imagine an occasion when it will not give me pleasure to look at you.' He touched the back of her neck very softly, but she flinched away from his hand.

'Turn around,' he said, gently insistent.

Mary didn't answer. Her face was buried in her hands, and her shoulders were hunched protectively. She had made a shocking discovery about herself, and she could not bear to meet anyone's eyes—least of all Justin's.

She had known she loved him. And she had known she would find pleasure and comfort in his arms. But she had never before suspected how completely uncontrollable and all-consuming her desire for him was.

He had slept with her once when they'd first met, before he'd asked her to marry him. But she had been much younger then, and still encased in the emotional armour which had protected her from the horrors all around her in St Giles. Now she was older, and paradoxically more vulnerable, and she'd burnt her fingers in the fire he'd ignited. Or had she always had this capacity within her? Was that why she'd struck her disgraceful, unholy bargain with Bill Crawford? The bargain that damned her forever in the eyes of the respectable, pious world. What kind of woman was she?

Her eyes were blank with distress as she remembered every text she'd ever heard or read against the sins of the flesh—and the condemnation reserved for an adulterous woman. And she heard again the pinched voice of Lady Moorcock, Sir Richard's wife, delicately but distastefully alluding to a wife's duties.

In her own mind, Mary had always justified her bargain with Bill on similar grounds. He had, after all, given her the protection she so desperately needed—and which should have been provided by a husband. But she had experienced no pleasure in his bed, and little comfort. It had been easy to imagine she was performing no more than a duty—something which was essential for her survival.

But this was different. In Justin's arms she had been confronted by her true ardent nature. It was impossible to justify what had happened on the grounds of necessity—her own wanton spirit had betrayed her. She had proved she wasn't fit to be anything more than his mistress.

She heard her father's voice, echoing across the years. 'God's dispositions for us cannot be questioned. He must always know what is best for us.'

Was that why He had sent her into the hell of St Giles? Because that was where her unruly, sensual flesh belonged?

CHAPTER NINE

'MARY, turn round,' said Justin. 'Very well,' he added after a moment. 'As long as you don't decide to imitate a spinning top, I should be able to resolve this impasse.'

She heard the undercurrent of amusement in his voice and burned with fresh embarrassment.

In a moment she knew he was standing in front of her. She was staring at his feet, but she couldn't bring herself to lift her head and meet his eyes.

He sighed. 'And which ghostly voice are you listening to now?' he asked, almost conversationally. 'There are so many to choose from, aren't there? Your father, Alf, Sir Richard—I've never understood how he could let Alf walk off with you without making any enquiries about his suitability to take care of you.'

She did look up then, staring into his face with huge, desolate grey eyes, because he had so accurately divined the direction of her thoughts. His mouth twisted as if he was in pain, and he reached out to touch her cheek.

'My love, if I could line them all up in front of a firing squad I would do so,' he said, his voice not quite steady. 'But if you don't *tell* me I can't help.'

'I *can't*!' She pulled away from him.

Perhaps he hadn't noticed how wildly she'd

responded to his caresses. How she hoped that was the case. And if he hadn't noticed she could never admit to him the vision she'd just had of herself. She could never admit that to anyone, as long as she lived.

Then she caught sight of herself in the mirror, and a moan of distress escaped her lips as she saw the marks of passion still vivid on her face. She made a sudden movement as if she was about to run from the room, and Justin caught her arm.

'Don't touch. . .' The words stuck in her throat. After what she had just discovered about herself, it seemed almost hypocritical to order him to leave her alone.

'Let's have a cup of tea,' he said, guiding her back to a chair. 'It should be nicely stewed by now. We must hope no one in Bath ever discovers I've drunk any. My reputation would be completely destroyed.'

Mary stared at him numbly, unable to make any sense of what he'd just said.

'If you remember, I assured Miss Lewisham I couldn't drink anything with water in it,' he reminded her, pouring out a cup of tea. 'Perhaps we ought to get the butler to send up some vinegar later, just to add verisimilitude to my claim.'

Mary's lips curved into a faint smile, and she took a sip of tea. Justin watched her for a moment, then stood up and went to lean against the mantelpiece, staring down at the fire burning low in the hearth.

'Have you had any news about Samuel's whereabouts?' he asked abruptly, over his shoulder.

'No.' Some dim sense of normality was returning to Mary. She was no longer blind to everything around her, and she saw Justin's hand close into a fist at her reply. But his voice was quite calm when he next spoke.

'Has Penrose changed his will?'

'So he tells me.'

'Good. I can't see any reason for you to stay in Bath. Lucinda's well on the way to falling in love with Peter King, and Penrose can take care of his own affairs. I'll take you home.'

'Home?' Mary repeated. She seemed to have grown unbelievably dull-witted over the past hour. She had no idea what he was talking about.

'To your inn,' Justin said impatiently. 'That's where you want to go, isn't it?' He came back to her side, and once again she was aware of the barely contained energy seething within him. 'Perhaps when you are in familiar surroundings you will feel more comfortable and we'll do better,' he continued.

Mary stared at him blankly, and he suddenly dropped on his knees beside her, taking one of her hands in his.

'I didn't mean to frighten you,' he said roughly. 'My God, Mary! I know how many people have used you and hurt you in the past. It was just. . . it's been such a long time—I couldn't help myself. You have so much courage I forget. . . I'm sorry.'

The saucer tilted unnoticed in Mary's other

hand. It seemed so unbelievable that he should be apologising to her—and yet he was. She smiled tremulously and saw the golden flecks appear in his eyes as he brushed a tendril of her hair back from her face.

Suddenly things didn't seem so bad. It was hard to believe that where there was so much care and tenderness there could also be sin. Justin saw her eyes lose focus as she tried to make sense of her feelings.

Then half a cup of tea landed in her lap and she was jerked back to reality.

Justin helped her mop it up. Neither of them had any inclination to ring for help.

'I hope you aren't particularly fond of this gown,' he remarked after a while. 'I don't think it's ever going to be the same again.'

'It doesn't matter,' said Mary. 'Oh, dear, I'd better go and change it.' She stood up, and then looked at him doubtfully.

'I'm not going anywhere,' he said, a half-smile on his lips. 'Not until we've settled a few things. Do you want to go home, Mary?'

He meant to the Lazy Cat. But Mary suddenly realised that the Lazy Cat was no more her home than the Blue Boar had been. Her business provided her with security and independence—but it wasn't her home. She had left the inn soon enough when the opportunity arose. And going back there after everything that had happened would be very difficult.

'I cannot desert Mr Penrose now,' she said, evading the question.

'In that case, when you've changed your dress we must decide what can be done to expedite this business,' said Justin grimly.

Mary poured water from the jug into the basin and washed her face. The cold water was both refreshing and soothing. Then she looked at herself in the mirror.

Her hair was dishevelled, her gown was stained, and her eyes were haunted by her secret fears. No sly serpent had ever tempted her with the apple of knowledge. When she was fourteen she'd had it shoved in her mouth so forcefully that she'd nearly choked. She'd been choking on it ever since.

She had always been too angry and too obstinate to give up the fight for survival, but she'd sacrificed so much in the process. And for twelve years she'd been torn between defiance and shame.

On a day-by-day level she had become a pragmatist, responding to the demands of each situation as it arose, without questioning the impact of such accommodations on her fundamental beliefs. Of course, she had been forced to modify many of her childhood assumptions, but she had done so piecemeal, without creating any new, coherent code of values. There had never been time—and perhaps she had lacked the inclination.

Now she felt like a rudderless, anchorless boat,

tossed helplessly before the storms of half a life-time of fierce, painful, bewildering emotions.

She had told Justin only three days ago that she had never broken the laws of men—leaving it open as to whether she had transgressed against heaven's commandments. But the second greatest commandment, the one which transcended all others except the commandment to love God, was to love one another—one's neighbour as oneself.

Despite everything that had happened to her, she had always dealt as fairly as she could with other people. And surely the overwhelming pleasure she had experienced in Justin's arms had been born of love—not simply of lust? So how could it be evil?

She gazed at herself in the mirror, hope dawning in her eyes. Justin must have known how passion-ately she'd clung to him, but he had not con-demned her. He had been afraid that he'd frightened her. She frowned, trying to discover the significance of this new idea. She valued his opinion, and his insight.

But he came from a different social station. As Miss Lewisham had pointed out, a certain laxity of morals was forgiven the aristocracy. Could she really rely on his judgement on this matter?

Then she remembered that he'd dragged her back to Queen Square to talk to her—but he hadn't said anything. He'd simply kissed her. Had that been his intention all along? Or had he really meant to say something? And, if so, what?

For a few glorious moments while they'd been

waiting for Grigson to bring the tea she'd wondered if he was going to ask her to marry him. But
that was before he'd kissed her. Now she found
the possibility that he might do so almost alarming. Her heart and soul were too confused. She
had been ruthlessly confronted with the realisation
that she no longer knew what she believed. And,
until she found out, she could not deal honestly
with Justin.

She suddenly noticed that nearly twenty minutes
had elapsed since she'd left the drawing-room.
She stood up hurriedly and began to change her
dress. There was no time now to think. For the
moment she would have to do what she'd always
done—face each problem as it arose, and hope
there would be time for reflection later.

When Mary went downstairs, she found Mrs
Knightley in the drawing-room with Justin. He
was sketching her. The sight was so unexpected
that Mary stopped short in the doorway. Then she
noticed the innocent self-importance with which
Mrs Knightley was posing, and a flicker of a smile
illuminated her eyes.

'Mrs Drayton!' Mrs Knightley exclaimed.
'Oh. . .'

'Please don't get up,' Mary said hastily. 'I'm
sorry, I hadn't realised you were here.'

'I came to call upon you,' said Mrs Knightley,
careful not to open her mouth too much. 'Lord
Hawkridge said you'd spilt some tea on your skirt
and had to change your gown. But he said he was

waiting for Mr Penrose, and we might as well wait together. And then he asked if he could draw me!'

'So I see,' said Mary, smiling, wondering why Grigson hadn't sent a maid to tell her of Mrs Knightley's arrival. Perhaps he'd hoped she'd be disconcerted to find Mrs Knightley ensconced with Lord Hawkridge. By now Bath gossip would have informed him that Justin was far more interested in her than he was in Mr Penrose. There was nothing she could do about it, and she didn't intend to worry about it.

She went to stand at Justin's shoulder. It was a good sketch, executed swiftly and cleanly in the small sketchbook that he carried everywhere in the large pockets which he always insisted his coats possessed. Mary wondered briefly and irrelevantly what his tailor had to say about that. Had he even carried a sketchbook when he'd gone to Lucinda's party?

But, despite the skill with which Justin had captured Mrs Knightley, Mary suspected that his suggestion had been motivated more by a wish to distract the lady than to flatter her. He could hardly have been in the mood for trivial conversation with a woman he barely knew.

'It's very good,' said Mary appreciatively. 'You are fortunate to possess such a talent, my lord.'

He glanced up briefly, a smile warming his hazel eyes.

'Thank you, ma'am,' he replied. 'I've never regretted it, although it has led me into some uncomfortable situations.'

'My lord?' Mrs Knightley exclaimed, fascinated.

Mary sat down and listened quietly while Justin related a couple of humorous incidents provoked by his habit of sketching anything that interested him. It seemed unlikely that they would have any further opportunities for private conversation in the immediate future and, on the whole, she was relieved. She had too much to think about.

When Justin had finished, and presented Mrs Knightley with her picture, Mary suggested that she might like another cup of tea to recover from the strain of posing.

'I'm afraid it doesn't look as if my uncle is going to return, my lord,' she said pleasantly to Justin. 'If you wish, I would be happy to give him a message for you.'

'Thank you, ma'am.' He stood up, accepting his dismissal, but she knew from the expression in his eyes that he would not leave quite so easily. 'He visits the Pump Room most mornings, does he not?' he said. 'Perhaps I may see him there tomorrow.'

'I will certainly tell him that you hope to do so,' Mary replied, ringing the bell as she tacitly agreed to Justin's suggestion. It would mean another public meeting but, in the circumstances, that might be a good thing. And by tomorrow she might have had a chance to bring some kind of order to her confused emotions.

'Please show Lord Hawkridge out,' she said when Grigson appeared. 'And then please bring us some more tea.'

*   *   *

'I've seen Samuel!' Mr Penrose burst into the drawing-room with far more haste than usual. He stood in front of Mary, almost wringing his hands in his agitation.

'Have you spoken to him?' she asked sharply. She had been sitting alone, her thoughts very far from the problem of Mr Penrose's nephew, but she responded immediately to his announcement.

'Only to ask him to call upon me here,' Mr Penrose replied. 'Oh, dear, oh, dear. . .'

'Is he coming?' Mary interrupted Mr Penrose's exclamations of distress without hesitation. 'When may we expect him?'

'Later this evening. He was most offhand with me. He said he had other appointments he could not break this afternoon. I didn't invite him to dinner. I couldn't tolerate the thought of sitting down to eat with him!'

'Of course not,' said Mary calmly. 'Well, it seems we have some time to prepare for him. Please don't feel so anxious, sir.'

He stared at her. His thin face seemed more lined than ever, and a nervous tick kept twitching at his right eyelid. He rubbed his eye distractedly. Mary stood up.

'Please, sir. Don't be so distressed.' She took his arm and urged him to sit down beside her on the sofa. 'I'm sure we're going to have an unpleasant interview with Samuel—but no more than that. You've changed your will, and done everything necessary to put him in control of his own affairs. As soon as we have informed him of both those facts you can safely wash your hands of him.'

'It's so hard to credit such villainy,' said Mr Penrose fretfully. 'I wish none of this had ever happened!'

'I'm sure you do,' Mary agreed. 'But, however unpleasant it makes life, surely it's better to know what he was planning than to continue in ignorance?'

'I suppose so,' said Mr Penrose miserably. 'Oh, why couldn't he be a gentlemanly, well-regulated youth? What a scandal there's going to be.'

'Don't think like that,' said Mary firmly. 'You have always done what is right and proper, and you have nothing to reproach yourself with. What Samuel does in the future is no concern of yours. You are not accountable for him.'

Mr Penrose looked at her, then his expression cleared slightly and he almost smiled.

'You are not at all daunted by the prospect of confronting him with our suspicions, are you?' he said wonderingly.

'I'm not looking forward to it,' said Mary frankly. 'But he is not my nephew, so I can consider the problem more objectively.' She laid her hand reassuringly on his arm. 'Soon it will all be over and you can go home, sir, I assure you.'

'You have been so kind to me,' said Mr Penrose distressfully. 'I don't know why you should put yourself to so much trouble for me. I cannot begin to——'

'I have only done what anyone would have done

in the same situation,' Mary interrupted briskly. She could see a certain warmth developing in Mr Penrose's eyes which she didn't want to encourage.

'I don't think so,' he replied sadly. 'I cannot be sure that I would have acted in the same way if our positions were reversed.' He sighed, and then took a deep breath, meeting her eyes almost reluctantly. 'I have not always been entirely courteous to you since we came to Bath,' he said with difficulty. 'I am sorry if I have ever seemed to criticise your behaviour.'

'You've been under great strain,' Mary replied. 'You've never been less than a generous host. And our visit here was hardly of your choosing.'

'Nevertheless. . .' He stood up abruptly, taking a turn around the room. 'Well, we must wait until we have spoken to Samuel,' he said at last.

'Yes, sir.'

Mary briefly wondered whether she should let Justin know what had happened. He would certainly be interested to know that Samuel had returned to Bath. But, on the other hand, there was little he could do to help. He could hardly be present at their interview with Samuel without giving rise to all kinds of questions which Mary was reluctant to answer.

Besides, it still rankled that he'd chosen to believe that she'd needed the protection of a rich man, rather than being able to fend for herself, when she'd left St Giles. She would not go running to him with this problem as if she were an empty-headed, panicky fool.

'Mr Samuel Penrose,' the butler announced.

'Thank you, Grigson, that will be all,' said Mary, when she realised that Mr Penrose was too perturbed to speak.

Samuel glanced sharply in her direction as the butler closed the door. A frown appeared in his eyes. Mary guessed that, although she seemed familiar to him, he couldn't quite place where he'd met her.

He was of average height, with a good figure and a handsome face. He dressed with elegance and propriety, and when it suited him he had a conciliatory manner. But Mary had seen him at his worst, his face flushed with brandy, his demeanour crude and disgusting.

There had been occasions, before seeing him again, when even she had doubted the seriousness of his threats. But when she looked at him now she knew she'd been right to worry. His eyes were hard and suspicious as they rested on her, and she could sense the potential for violence in him.

'Uncle,' he said, turning on Mr Penrose, 'I was not expecting you to have company.'

Mary found that hard to believe. Bath gossip would surely have informed him already that she had accompanied Mr Penrose. And Samuel of all people would know that he didn't have a cousin called Mary Drayton.

'Good evening, sir,' she said, when once again

it seemed that Mr Penrose wasn't going to speak. 'We've met before, althought I dare say you don't remember me. My name is Mary Drayton.'

Her hands were concealed in the shawl she was wearing to protect her from the winter draughts, and she didn't offer to shake his hand.

'My cousin Mary?' he asked, a hard, ugly note in his voice.

'No, sir.' Mary didn't offer an explanation for the deception. She didn't feel she owed Samuel anything. 'I'm the landlady of the Lazy Cat.'

She saw a hint of recognition in his hot eyes as that piece of information allowed him to place where he'd seen her before.

'Then you're a long way from home, wench,' he said jeeringly. 'What wiles have you played off on the old fool to persuade him to come jaunting so far from Hertfordshire—and with such a questionable companion?'

'How dare you speak so?' Mr Penrose burst out. He spoke with a kind of nervous indignation, as if his feelings of outrage had overcome his anxiety. 'Mrs Drayton is a respectable woman who has been put to great inconvenience by you! You and your dreadful, *dreadful* threats!'

Samuel threw his uncle a hard, contemptuous glance, but it was on Mary that his eyes came to rest. She could see him making a rapid assessment of her character and intentions, but when he spoke his tone was scornful.

'Hardly respectable, sir, if she is prepared to masquerade as your niece. What lies did she tell you about me to insinuate herself in your favour? She must know very well you're a rich man.'

'Are you denying you threatened to kill me to obtain control of your father's fortune?' Mr Penrose demanded excitedly.

'For God's sake!' Samuel's lip curled contemptuously. 'I may not appreciate your interference but in two years' time I'll be free to tell you to go to hell. Why should I risk the gallows to kill you now?'

'Because Smash Burke threatened to consign your corpse to the Thames if you didn't pay your debt to him,' said Mary coldly before Mr Penrose could speak. 'I don't suppose either your fine friends in London or even the brutish Phelps will be enough to protect you from Burke indefinitely.'

Samuel's eyes narrowed dangerously, then he swung round to confront Mr Penrose.

'You stupid old fool!' he snarled. 'Don't you see what she's trying to do? She knows you're too prudish and respectable to give her house-room in normal circumstances so she's invented the most outrageous lies she can think of to get close to you. Look at her!' He flung out a hand towards Mary. 'Standing there so demure and modest. She knows exactly how to twist you round her finger!'

Mr Penrose stared at his nephew.

'Are you denying that you threatened either to marry Miss Burleigh or to kill me to recoup your fortune?' he said. Two hectic spots of colour were burning on his parchment cheeks, and his hands were clenched convulsively by his sides, but his voice was steady.

'Of course I am,' Samuel declared impatiently. 'Dammit, I've never pretended to like you, but I'm not that base!'

Mr Penrose took a deep breath. Now that battle was well and truly joined, he seemed to have his nervousness under control.

'I don't believe you,' he said.

Samuel stared at his uncle, an ugly expression on his face.

'Don't you?' he said insultingly. 'And what do you intend to do about it, you stupid old buzzard? Do you think anyone would believe such an accusation—supported only by the word of an alehouse doxy?'

Mr Penrose's features were rigid with uncharacteristic anger. For a moment it was almost possible to see a likeness between uncle and nephew.

'You will speak courteously of Mrs Drayton,' he said bitingly. 'As to what I intend to do, I have already done it. It wants only two more signatures and you may have control of your fortune. Though you would have done better to wait another two years. Your father was nearly as big a wastrel as you, but I've done my best to recoup his losses these past five years.'

Mary glanced sharply at Mr Penrose, suddenly realising that there might be undercurrents here that she had not suspected.

'If that is the consequence of having false allegations laid against me, I can only be grateful for them,' said Samuel sarcastically. 'If you have nothing more to say, I will take my leave of you. But may I suggest you take a closer look at the credentials of your fair informant, uncle? I would hate to see her turn you into an even bigger fool than you already are.'

'There is one more thing to say,' said Mary as Samuel reached for the door-handle. 'In view of the circumstances, I advised your uncle to change his will to exclude you. He has done so. A copy rests with lawyers in Bath, and information to that effect has been transmitted to his lawyers in Hertfordshire. His death is no longer of any benefit to you at all.'

'You *bitch*!' Uncontrollable fury suddenly distorted Samuel's handsome features, and he lunged towards Mary. He had been angry before, but this was different. His temper had exploded beyond all reasonable levels. His lips were curled back in a terrifying snarl and his fist was raised to strike.

Mary heard Mr Penrose give an exclamation of pure horror, but she didn't pay any attention to him.

'Stand still!' The icy command in her voice cut through even Samuel's fury—but even more important was the small pistol she was pointing steadily at his heart.

He slammed to a halt.

'Harpy! You wouldn't *dare*!'

'If you make another move against me I will shoot you,' she said. Her voice was ruthless and inflexible, and her eyes as cold and penetrating as steel. There was no wavering in either her gaze or the hand which held the pistol. The concealing shawl had fallen, unheeded, to the floor. She stood straight and slender in the unexceptional surroundings of the drawing-room. But there was nothing commonplace or fragile about the way she confronted Samuel, and neither of her companions had any doubt that she would do exactly as she said.

Mr Penrose stared at her in shocked amazement. Though he didn't know it, she looked very much as she had done the day she forced Seb Collins to hand over a fair price for her uncle's alehouse. She had held the pistol in her hand that day also—but then she had had the added reassurance of Donald's presence. Today she knew she must deal with Samuel alone.

She held Samuel's savage glare with her own, diamond-hard gaze.

'You little bitch! Do you really think you can get away with threatening *me*?' he demanded harshly. The blind fury had been kicked out of him by the sight of the pistol, but his sullen rage was almost more frightening.

'Why not?' said Mary. 'If your response to Smash Burke is anything to go by, threats seem to work.' She lifted her hand slightly as he made a hasty movement, and he snarled in frustration.

'There are two points I'd like to draw to your attention,' she said coldly. 'Then you can go. As I've already mentioned, you no longer stand to gain any financial or other practical benefits from

Mr Penrose's death. Nor do I, incidentally—in case you were planning to overturn the will on the grounds that I've manipulated his affections. But it occurs to me that you might wish to take revenge, either upon your uncle or me—and that would be a very bad idea.'

'Why?' He stared at her offensively. 'Do you intend to stand guard over him with that insignificant little gun for the rest of his life?'

'No,' she replied. 'But a statement of what I overheard at the Lazy Cat is already lodged with the lawyers. And first thing tomorrow morning an account of this interview will join it. If anything untoward happens to either of us, you will immediately fall under suspicion. Just as important, from your point of view, is the fact that I have several powerful friends who won't wait for legal sanction to avenge me if any harm befalls me.'

'Really? Then why aren't they here now?' Samuel sneered.

Mary's smile was coldly unamused.

'Do we look as if we need them?' she asked. 'But I am handy with a pen, sir. And when I wrote my statement I also wrote to several friends—not least to Donald Campbell. What do you think Donald would do to you if you hurt me?'

She saw Samuel's expression change.

'The ugly Scotsman at the Lazy Cat?' he demanded.

Mary didn't answer, but she saw that her threat had gone home. She wasn't comfortable using Donald in such a way, but she didn't think she was putting him at any great risk. All she wanted to do was impress upon Samuel that the possible satisfaction of taking revenge upon either Mr Penrose or herself was far outweighed by the potential consequences to himself. To some extent she thought she'd done that, but it was hard to tell. Samuel was too sullen and angry for her to be sure that he would see things rationally.

'I don't think there's anything left to say,' she said. 'You have got what you most urgently wanted—control of your own fortune. And, as far as Mr Penrose and I am concerned, there should be no reason for us to discuss this meeting with anyone else in future. Nor for anyone to read the statement I've left with the lawyer—unless you give them cause to.'

'I could ruin you,' said Samuel viciously. 'Think of the scandal if it ever came out that you're not his niece! And after you've been living with him these many days! You'd never be able to show your face in respectable society again!'

Mary laughed, although the pistol remained steady in her hand. 'After tonight I have no further need to stay in Bath,' she pointed out. 'And if you raise a scandal about us we might just choose to be less discreet about your affairs. Besides, I'm sure it won't do any harm for my business to be known as the landlady in the notorious Penrose scandal! The curious will come from miles around to stay at the Lazy Cat!'

Samuel snarled impotently. Then he turned and slammed out of the room. Mary heard his feet on the stairs and the banging of the front door. She went to the window, too cautious to assume that Samuel had really left the house until she'd seen with her own eyes that he'd done so.

Looking down, she saw his shadowy figure striding away. Then she saw another, even more familiar figure loitering in the Square.

She leant her head briefly against the cold window-pane. How on earth had Justin known Samuel was there? She wondered what he would have done if she'd fired a shot.

He'd seen the movement of the curtains and came over to stand beneath the window, looking up at her. She was still holding the pistol, but her hand was by her side, half hidden by her skirts, and she kept it there. She waved with her other hand, in a gesture indicative that everything was all right. He hesitated, and she thought that maybe he intended to come in, but then he lifted his hat and swept her a magnificent bow. He would see her in the Pump Room tomorrow morning, and he was undoubtedly aware that Mr Penrose was with her.

He strolled away, in the same direction Samuel had taken, and Mary experienced a sudden, over-whelming desire to run down and call him back. Samuel had frightened her more than she'd antici-pated and she wanted the reassurance of Justin's company. She wanted to tell him what had hap-pened, hear his opinion and take comfort from his calm judgement.

But Mr Penrose was standing behind her, and

he was undoubtedly even more disturbed by
Samuel than she was. And she had undertaken to
deal with this business. She could not throw her
hands up in dismay now.

CHAPTER TEN

MARY closed the curtains carefully, and turned back to look at Mr Penrose. His face was drained of colour, the bones beneath his face very prominent. He was clearly terribly disturbed and Mary couldn't blame him. She was feeling sick and shaken herself.

'I'm just going to check that the front door is secure, then I think we should both have some brandy,' she said quietly.

'I. . .' The word came out as little more than a croak. He swallowed convulsively and tried again. 'Mrs Drayton. . .'

'Why don't you pour out the brandy while I run downstairs?' she suggested.

If there was one thing she'd learnt in St Giles, it was never to take anything for granted. She wouldn't be able to rest completely easily until she'd seen the front door firmly bolted.

She ran lightly downstairs, shot the bolts, and went back up to Mr Penrose. He'd poured the brandy and taken a large gulp, but he didn't look much better for it. Mary laid the pistol down on the sideboard and picked up her own glass. Now that the crisis was over she could allow herself to feel the horror and disgust that Samuel had aroused in her, and her hand wasn't quite steady.

It had been an ugly interview, and she hadn't liked Samuel's response. Seb Collins had been a dangerous villain, but he had also been a practical businessman. Mary knew she'd gained a certain measure of respect, if not liking, from him. She'd never been afraid that he'd pursue her beyond St Giles.

Samuel was different, and neither she nor Mr Penrose could hide from him, even if they'd wanted to. She could only hope that she'd made the reasons for leaving them alone sufficiently compelling—but she wasn't convinced.

'My dear. . . Mrs Drayton. . . My God, ma'am!' Mr Penrose croaked helplessly.

Mary forced her bloodless lips into a smile.

'I hope I haven't shocked you too much, sir,' she said, trying to speak lightly. 'It was hardly ladylike of me to behave so forcefully.'

'You were. . .tremendous,' said Mr Penrose, finally managing to form a coherent sentence. 'I never guessed. . .' He coughed and cleared his throat, dabbing his lips with his handkerchief.

'That I was such a harridan?'

'That Samuel was so unspeakable.' He closed his eyes for a moment as if he couldn't bear to remember the horror that had just passed. 'My dear, I have been at fault throughout,' he said painfully. 'I have put you at risk, and I have given no proper thought to your safety. Tonight. . .if you hadn't been so capable of defending yourself. . .'

'But *I* knew what kind of man Samuel is,' said

Mary gently. 'I came to Bath with my eyes open—and prepared to deal with whatever arose.'

Mr Penrose stared at her. He was slowly recovering from his first shock, but he was far from being his normal self.

'I think you omitted a few important details when you were telling me your family circumstances, sir,' Mary said ruefully. 'I hadn't realised that Samuel's anger at being cut out of your will would outweigh his relief at getting control of his own fortune.'

Mr Penrose shook his head, as if trying to clear it.

'My brother was not provident,' he said distractedly. 'It was one of the ironies of the situation that he disposed of his property as he did. And one of the reasons why Samuel was so angry about the limitations on his inheritance. But there was still a substantial sum left when I took control of it, and I have done my best to build it up.'

'But your own fortune is considerably greater,' said Mary, stating a fact rather than asking a question.

Mr Penrose glanced at her, something almost approaching an apologetic smile in his eyes. 'I am much better at dealing with business matters than I am at dealing with people,' he said simply. 'Within certain limits I am prepared to take quite large risks on the movement of pieces of paper—and my judgement is usually sound. I have trebled the fortune my father left me.'

Mary took a deep breath.

'That might account for Samuel's irrational fury when he discovered you'd changed your will,' she said drily.

'I'm sorry. I should have told you,' said Mr Penrose contritely.

'I don't suppose it would have made any difference,' Mary replied. She took a sip of her brandy and then put the glass down. 'Except that I'm even more glad you changed your will. You don't live like a nabob,' she added, trying to lighten their mood.

'I'm not comfortable with ostentation,' Mr Penrose said. 'It's the challenge of the game I enjoy — not the fruits of my success.'

'Nevertheless,' said Mary, 'you must have considerable resources at your disposal. I think it's time you employed them against Samuel.'

'You don't think it's over?' Mr Penrose asked sharply.

'Do you?' Mary challenged him.

Mr Penrose stood up and took an agitated turn around the room. 'No.' He chewed his lip nervously. 'I didn't like the wild way he left here.'

'Nor did I.'

'What do you suggest I do?' Mr Penrose looked at her as if he was fully confident of her ability to advise him.

'In the first instance I think you should employ someone to make close enquiries about Samuel's activities,' said Mary. 'I'm not happy about relying on Donald's reputation to act as a brake on Samuel's worst instincts. You need another, more compelling method of bringing him to heel.' She tapped her fingers thoughtfully on the edge of the table.

'And then?' Mr Penrose prompted her, watching her with fascination tinged with admiration.

'If you can find a way to break him, do it,' said Mary bluntly.

'He's still my nephew!' Mr Penrose exclaimed. 'And you told him that as long as he behaved himself we wouldn't take any action against him.'

'I know, but he's dangerous,' said Mary. 'I had not realised until tonight how dangerous. And from what you've said it may be that his own fortune isn't going to be enough to pull him out of the hole he's in. We are not the only people who could suffer from his frustration.'

'Miss Burleigh!' Mr Penrose gasped.

'I think she's safe enough,' said Mary reassuringly. 'She was showing signs of being infatuated with him when we arrived in Bath, but I think her affections have taken a different turn since then. All the same, I think I may visit Mrs Burleigh tomorrow morning.'

'I'll come with you,' said Mr Penrose immediately.

'You won't find it an easy interview,' Mary warned him. 'But if you'd engage to distract Miss Lewisham's attention, that would be a great help.'

She looked up and found that Mr Penrose was steadily watching her, an odd expression on his face.

'Mrs Drayton. . .Mary, aren't you ever at a loss?' he asked her.

'Very often,' she said ruefully, as an image of her complete disintegration after Justin had kissed her flashed across her mind. 'But this is a practical problem, and I've always been able to deal with them.' She glanced at the pistol still lying on the table. 'Aren't you going to ask where I acquired such unladylike tendencies?' she asked curiously.

'I don't care,' said Mr Penrose surprisingly. 'It's enough to know that you are making such enormous efforts on my behalf—without asking anything in return.'

Mary flushed, disconcerted. 'I have only done. . .what seemed right,' she said uncomfortably. 'If we can bring this business to a satisfactory conclusion I will be happy.'

'Will you?' Mr Penrose's words seemed to fall like stones into the sudden silence. 'Forgive me, ma'am,' he continued hastily. 'I am not wise, and I often make mistakes in my dealings with other people, but I have known you for several days now, and I cannot believe that you are completely happy as the landlady of a coaching inn.'

'I assure you. . .' Mary began, startled by his uncharacteristic eloquence. She suspected that he was still being carried along on the tide of over-excitement that Samuel's visit had induced in him.

'You have done an excellent job,' he continued, unheeding of her interruption as the words seemed to flood out of him. 'And I am sure you are justly proud of the reputation the Lazy Cat has built up since you became its proprietor—but that's not the same thing, is it?'

'No.' Mary looked away. Too much had happened that day for her to be able to maintain any pretence about her contentment with her life.

'I'm a relatively old man,' Mr Penrose rushed on. 'There are many things which perhaps I cannot give you that you deserve to have. But I would be honoured. . . You would have security and comfort. . .and maybe even a chance to marry again— since I am so much older than you.' In the end his eloquence failed him, and he stared at her with painful hopefulness.

Mary looked at him. Her first response was astonishment, coupled with an instinctive rejection of his proposal. But that was quickly followed by an overwhelming sense of gratitude for his generosity.

'But you don't know anything about me!' she exclaimed.

'I don't need to know,' he replied. 'I know. . .I know I am only offering you a very poor bargain compared to what you deserve. But my dear. . . Mary, you know there can never be any future in your friendship with Lord Hawkridge. A man like that—he takes his amusement where he can find it, but he marries within his own station. I'm sorry,' he added as Mary stood up.

She moved away from him to stand looking down at the fire.

'I know that,' she said at last in a low voice, without looking round. 'I have no such expectations.' Then she lifted her head and met Mr Penrose's troubled, anxious gaze. 'Thank you, sir,' she said softly. 'I cannot tell you how much your offer means to me, but I can't accept it.'

'I know I'm a poor bargain, but please consider it—I beg you,' he urged her. 'It would mean. . .so much to me.'

Mary smiled tremulously.

'I think it is you who would have the poor bargain if I agreed,' she said. 'Come, sir, let us be friends.' She held out her hand to him. 'I would so much rather be a good friend to you than an unsatisfactory wife. And now,' she added as he took her hand, 'let us write an account of what happened here tonight to lodge with the lawyer tomorrow. I will feel much more comfortable if I know we've taken every possible precaution.'

When Mary and Mr Penrose arrived in Lansdown Crescent they'd already visited his lawyer, and they were making their morning call on Mrs Burleigh as early as they reasonably could.

'Wait a minute,' Mary said suddenly, just as they were approaching the Burleighs' front door. 'I've seen that fellow before somewhere.'

'Who?' Mr Penrose looked round anxiously. 'Where?'

'That thin, round-shouldered lad with a face like an underfed rat,' Mary said, indicating a nondescript personage hovering unobtrusively on the other side of the street.

'Do you think he's anything to do with Samuel?' Mr Penrose asked nervously.

'Well, it's not Phelps,' Mary replied. 'And why. . .? Dammit! I know who that is!'

She spun on her heel and strode straight over to the man, leaving Mr Penrose to tag anxiously behind.

At her approach, the thin man tried to look even more inconspicuous and started to sidle away down the street.

'Henry!' said Mary imperatively.

He turned towards her instinctively at the sound of his name, and then she saw the suspicion of a reluctant grin flit across his face.

'Who? Me, ma'am?' he asked innocently.

'What are you doing here?' she demanded. Her first thought was that Justin had sent his tiger to keep watch over her, but she dismissed that possibility immediately because Henry had been in Lansdown Crescent before they'd arrived. 'Is Samuel Penrose inside?' she asked sharply.

An admiring grin spread across Henry's face. ''Is Lordship said you were as sharp as a tack,' he said approvingly. 'No, ma'am.'

'Then why are you here?' Mary asked, ignoring Mr Penrose's exclamation of surprise.

''Is Lordship didn't trust the look of Master Samuel when 'e left Queen Square last night,' Henry explained. 'So 'e set me to keep watch over 'im. Which same I've bin doing——'

'Then where is he now?' Mary interrupted impatiently.

'I'm *telling* you, ma'am,' the tiger replied reprovingly. ''E went for a carriage ride this morning and picked up Miss Burleigh and the old biddy when they were out walking. I tried to follow, but I was on foot and I lost 'em, so I went back to tell 'is lordship. 'E said to come back 'ere and let 'im know as soon as they returned.'

'I see.' Inside her muff, Mary's hands closed into fists.

'Surely not a significant event,' Mr Penrose said anxiously. 'And Miss Lewisham——'

'Is coming down the street towards us,' said Mary tautly.

'I'll get 'is lordship.' Henry prepared to dash off.

'Wait!' Mary said sharply. 'The more information you can give him the better. Miss Lewisham! What has happened?' She went forward to take Mrs Burleigh's elderly companion by the arm.

'Mrs Drayton!' Miss Lewisham was too distressed to feel any surprise at meeting Mary. She was out of breath and flushed, and her skirts were muddy. 'He's taken her!' she cried, horror in her eyes.

'How?' Mary demanded.

'There was a coach!' Miss Lewisham's lip began to tremble and tears started in her eyes. At any moment she was going to give way to a fit of weeping.

'Where?' Mary's voice cracked like a whip, and

she seized Miss Lewisham by the shoulders, start-
ling her out of her incipient hysteria.

'On the London Road.' Miss Lewisham stared
at Mary in blank surprise. 'He threw me out on to
the side of the road and forced Lucinda into the
coa-coa-coa——'

Mary thrust the weeping woman into Mr
Penrose's appalled arms.

'Take her inside,' she commanded. 'Henry, go
and tell Lord Hawkridge what has happened, and
ask him to meet me at the house in Queen
Square.'

'Yes, ma'am!'

'And Henry. Make sure he does call for me.
Lucinda will need me.'

'Yes, ma'am.' The tiger sprinted away, leaving
Mr Penrose to stare at Mary over Miss Lewisham's
wilting body.

'I'm sorry, sir,' said Mary, a cold, grim
expression in her eyes. 'I don't have time to come
in and talk to Mrs Burleigh. But please assure her
that we will find Lucinda and bring her back. No
harm will come to her—and no scandal will touch
her. Be sure to tell her that. She will be in an
agony of worry and she is not strong. Don't let
her become too distressed.'

'But Lord Hawkridge. . .' Mr Penrose began.

'Has an aversion to innocent girls being hurt by
scoundrels.'

Mary picked up her skirts and began to walk as
fast as she could back to Queen Square. Once she
was well away from Lansdown Crescent and the

only reputation she had to worry about was her own, she ran.

She arrived in Queen Square just as the curricle with the glossy chestnuts drew up outside the house. 'Wait! I will be with you in two seconds,' she said breathlessly, giving Justin no time to speak.

She brushed past Grigson and ran up the stairs to her bedchamber. She paused only to collect her pistol and hide it in her muff and to take several coins out of her purse.

'Is there anything wrong, ma'am?' Grigson asked when she came back downstairs.

'No,' said Mary. 'My uncle has been called away, but I dare say he will be back by this evening. I am not sure when I will be returning. But if not today then I'm sure it will be tomorrow. In the meantime, please tell callers that we are not at home.' She put the coins into his hand, and went to climb swiftly into the curricle.

'Where's Henry?' she asked.

'He took a horse and went ahead to see if he could discover anything more,' said Justin, immediately setting the chestnuts in motion. 'What the devil happened last night?' His voice was harsh and his expression grim.

Mary leant back against the leather upholstery and tried to catch her breath. Now that, for the time being, she had done everything she could, she found that her hands were trembling. She gripped them together and took deep breaths, waiting for her heart to stop pounding so furiously.

Justin didn't repeat the question. He took one glance at her flushed, panting face and then concentrated on getting out of Bath as quickly as possible.

As soon as Mary had enough breath to speak coherently, she told him all about the meeting with Samuel Penrose.

'Dammit!' he swore when she'd finished. 'I knew I shouldn't have let you become involved in this business.'

'You didn't let me!' Mary snapped back. 'I was the one who initiated this. And even I didn't guess how unstable and vengeful Samuel is.'

'I should have come in last night,' Justin declared tensely.

'It wouldn't have prevented this. How could we have known what he intended to do?' Mary demanded. 'But I wish to God I'd warned the Burleighs against him when I first wanted to. If anything happens to Lucinda it will be my fault.'

'Don't be ridiculous! Besides, nothing's going to happen to her. We'll catch up with them first.'

'I hope so.' Mary let out her breath in a long, unsteady sigh, trying to ease the tension in her slight body. 'I was so determined to discourage him from taking his revenge on Mr Penrose or me that he is taking out his spite on Lucinda instead,' she said wretchedly.

'Or he may simply be trying to obtain a rich wife,' Justin pointed out. 'Judging by the route we're taking, Scotland is their destination. Lucinda's still a minor, isn't she? He may even be intending to hold her hostage in the expectation that Penrose will pay up to avoid a scandal. In which case he certainly won't hurt her.'

Mary didn't reply. She was remembering the expression in Samuel's eyes when he'd lunged towards her the previous night. A practical, cool-headed man might try to make good his losses by a scheme to blackmail Mr Penrose or the Burleighs, but she doubted if Samuel was capable of thinking so rationally.

She didn't voice her fears; there was no point. Nothing she said or thought would make any difference. All that counted was catching up with Samuel and rescuing Lucinda.

They travelled quickly, and Henry continued to range ahead of them, occasionally leaving small, badly scrawled messages for Justin at staging posts. It was lucky that he did so. For with his greater turn of speed he was twice able to back-track when Samuel's route became unclear, and leave messages which prevented Justin from taking a wrong turning. That he was riding his horses into the ground to do so was apparent from a comment made by one of the ostlers when Justin stopped to change horses.

'We're gaining on them,' said Justin as he set the curricle in motion again.

'Yes.' Mary flicked a stray lock of hair out of her face, and put her hand back inside the comfort of her muff. 'But Samuel's not wasting any time. He's changing his team at nearly every stage.'

'Better for Lucinda, perhaps,' Justin replied,

negotiating a tricky corner with consummate ease. 'The more his mind is concentrated on the need for speed, the less attention he may give to her.'

'Phelps is in the carriage with them,' said Mary. 'I dare say Lucinda's too frightened to cry for help even when they halt.'

'We will catch them,' said Justin grimly. 'Are you cold?' he added, glancing at her briefly as she shivered.

'No.' It was a damp, grey, miserable November day. The sun had barely appeared from behind the clouds, and even Mary's new pelisse and muff were no protection from the cutting wind. But she was hardly aware of her own discomfort. All her thoughts were with Lucinda.

'We will catch them,' said Justin again, this time more gently.

'I know we will.' It was true; Mary had no doubts on that score. She was with Justin, and Justin would catch Samuel. It was only what happened to Lucinda in the meantime that worried her.

She lapsed into silence, watching the horses as they ate up the miles. Justin was hiring the best, and Mary was dimly aware that both he and Henry were laying out money very freely on this venture.

It didn't surprise her. Whatever his relationship with her, Justin would have done his best for Lucinda Burleigh. He had a deep-rooted objection to cruelty and unkindness.

'How did you know Samuel was coming to Queen Square last night?' she asked suddenly.

'Henry was watching for his return to Bath,' Justin explained briefly.

'Of course he was,' said Mary, wondering how she had failed to realise that Justin would take such a precaution.

'It isn't you who should be rebuking yourself for not taking this matter seriously enough,' he said harshly, as if he was aware of what she was thinking. 'I had not fully grasped the nature of the man. When Henry came back and told me he'd taken up Lucinda in his carriage. . .'

Justin pressed his lips together grimly; his jaw was rigid.

'I think, my love, that we'd better make haste to resolve our differences,' he continued after a moment. 'We will then be in a position to give our combined attention to any problems which arise in future—and we might do better.'

Mary turned her head to look at him. His profile was stern and unyielding, his concentration fixed on the horses and the road. He was hardly in the mood for pretty speeches, but he seemed to take it for granted that they would have a future together. Her thoughts slipped back to their meeting yesterday. She had never yet had any opportunity to come to terms with the confusion she had experienced then.

She didn't question that she loved him. She had always loved him for his insight, his kindness and his humour. When she had met him in St Giles she had felt for the first time in her life that here was someone who could understand her, someone in whom she could place her trust.

She still felt that. But the lost years, his hurtful assumptions about her, and her own unruly emotions, had tarnished the first purity of their love.

And, even now, when her thoughts should have been entirely given over to Lucinda's plight, she was profoundly conscious of his powerful body so close beside her. She was aware of the tension in his arms as he held the reins and the forceful thrust of his legs as he braced himself to obtain every reasonable ounce of speed he could from his team. He was not a cruel or violent driver. The horses responded to his hands and his voice, not to the lash of his whip.

Mary was shamefully conscious of how much she longed to have him make love to her. To lie in his arms and surrender to the urgent desire he aroused in her. It was not a maidenly or a modest emotion—but then, ultimately, she wasn't a maidenly or modest woman. She could deny what she was, or she could accept it. But if she accepted it, did she scourge herself for her unruly passions—or did she embrace them willingly?

She did not know. But she was beginning to recognise that there might be other reasons for her uncertainty besides the strictures of her childhood.

When she had lost herself in Justin's arms, she had also lost all control of herself and the situation. And she had spent all her adult life struggling to achieve control and independence. She had been more self-assured when she'd been facing Samuel with a pistol than she had been when she'd tried to handle the emotions which Justin aroused in her. Was she simply afraid of what might become of her if she truly surrendered to him?

A few spots of rain fell, but she ignored them. She was thinking about the consequences of giving in to Justin—and how little she really knew about him. These past few days had been the only time she had ever come remotely close to inhabiting his world.

The aristocracy were different.

She remembered Miss Lewisham's scandalous story that Justin kept mistresses along the main post roads in the way that some men kept horses. He'd denied that—but there must have been some reason why the story had gained currency.

She glanced at him surreptitiously. The virile energy which created so much disturbing excitement in her must have found an outlet over the past seven years.

'What are you thinking?' he demanded suddenly.

'Have you had many mistresses?' she asked, her voice sounding harsh in her ears.

He didn't answer immediately.

'There have been several, over the years,' he replied at last in an unemotional voice.

'Do you have one now?'

'Yes.'

Mary's hand closed into a fist so tightly that her nails dug into the palm of her hand. She had known it must be so, but hearing it didn't make it any easier. Dear God! What was to become of her? She was in love with a man who could calmly tell her that he had another mistress. She was suddenly unbearably jealous of the woman—and furious with Justin.

'What's her name?' she grated.

'Bernadette. She claims her father was a French nobleman,' he said drily. 'I don't think she'll be disappointed to terminate our liaison. I don't spend enough time in London for her—and I don't pander sufficiently to her whims.'

'Terminate. . .?'

Justin checked the horses, and they dropped back to a walk. He turned to look at her.

'I would have done it the moment I first laid eyes on you,' he said quietly. 'But, as I said, she lives in London and I've been in Bath. Mary, I'm not going to lie to you about my virtue—or lack of it. But it doesn't make any difference to the way I feel about you. I was hurt and angry when I thought you'd deserted me. I wasn't looking for love from a woman.' He sighed, seeing the doubting, disturbed look in her eyes. 'Would you be more willing to marry me if I'd lived as a monk these past seven years?' he asked, half jokingly, half seriously.

'*Marry* you?'

'What did you think I meant to ask you yesterday?' he asked, whipping up the horses again.

Mary closed her eyes, a maelstrom of conflicting, overwhelming emotions flooding through her. Relief. Happiness. Doubt. Fear.

In the same moment Justin had admitted to having a mistress in keeping he had asked her to marry him. She had heard many times about the capacity of men to separate lust from love, but that didn't make it any easier to come to terms with the phenomenon in the man *she* loved.

Besides, just as she'd been coming to believe that her own fierce desire for him was acceptable, he had inadvertently raised the possibility that perhaps it was comparable to the feelings he'd had towards his mistresses.

CHAPTER ELEVEN

BEFORE Mary had time to respond to Justin's question she saw Henry coming towards them. His horse was lathered, but his face was flushed and bright with excitement.

'I've seen 'em, guv'nor!' he announced immediately. 'They're changing horses at the Red Lion. I went right past the coach and it's them all right. Only one way they can go now for the next ten miles!'

'Good!' said Justin with satisfaction. 'We can't be more than three or four miles behind them.'

'I'll have a fresh team ready for you at the Lion, guv'nor,' said Henry. 'This pair's blown. Leave the lady there?'

'You'll do no such thing!' Mary said fiercely.

Justin glanced at her, doubt in her eyes. She was sure he would have preferred to leave her in the safety of the inn, but she met his gaze with unswerving determination. After a moment a brief smile of reluctant acceptance curved his lips and he nodded imperceptibly.

'Mrs Drayton stays with me,' he said. 'Miss Burleigh may need her. Have the horses ready.'

Henry needed no second telling.

'He could have been a jockey,' said Mary, looking after the tiger's disappearing figure. Her mouth was suddenly dry, and her heart was thudding, but she still managed to sound calm.

'He finds it more interesting working for me,' said Justin. 'But I think we've exceeded all his expectations of excitement today.'

'I hope we don't exceed them any further!' Mary replied, her hand closing around the comforting handle of her pistol within her muff.

'So do I.'

Justin's profile was ruthlessly determined, and she was conscious of the coiled, fiercely contained energy within him.

'Do you know this part of the country?' she asked, suddenly remembering the familiarity with which the tiger had referred to the inn ahead.

'I've a house not far from here,' said Justin briefly.

After that, no further conversation passed between them. The curricle dashed into the inn yard and, at Henry's fiercely worded behest, the ostlers flew to their task.

With a fresh team, and the end of their quest in sight, Justin pushed the horses hard. Mary had to cling to the edge of the curricle to avoid being thrown out, but she made no complaint.

They rounded a bend and saw the coach. It was rumbling along on a straight, relatively good stretch of road. Justin gave a grunt of satisfaction, completely intent on his task. The horses sprang forward with even greater eagerness, and the gap between the two vehicles slowly closed. The curricle went past the coach at a clipping pace, barely inches between the wheels, and Mary saw the startled glance that the postilion threw at them.

In another few moments, Justin had turned the curricle and brought his horses to a quivering standstill. It was a display of driving skill which would have left a disinterested bystander open-mouthed with admiration, but Mary simply took it for granted.

Justin leapt from the curricle and ran towards the coach as the swearing postilion tried to control his plunging, snorting team. Henry grabbed Justin's whip and followed his master, still mounted. Mary wasn't far behind, her pistol in her hand.

'What the devil. . .?' Samuel's head appeared at the window of the coach.

Justin hauled open the door, seized him by the front of his coat and dragged him out of the carriage. Samuel struggled furiously, raising his fists, but he was taken by surprise and caught off balance. A crashing blow from Justin's right hand sent him sprawling on the muddy road, and Justin spun round in time to intercept a more calculated assault from Phelps. Mary heard Lucinda cry out in horror, but she paid no heed. Her attention was locked on Justin and the manservant.

As she had once said, Phelps was a swaggering bully, but he wasn't a coward. She knew immediately that he was a far more dangerous opponent than Samuel, and her pounding heart threatened to choke her when she saw how narrowly Justin evaded his first rushed attack. But Justin was aware of the danger too, and Henry was standing over Samuel's prone body with his master's whip. Mary took the time to look up at the postilion who was still struggling to calm his horses.

'For God's sake! What's going on?' he demanded frantically.

'Attend to your horses and don't interfere,' said Mary coldly. 'Did you know the lady wasn't a willing passenger?'

'It wasn't my place to know,' he said desperately. 'The servant hired the coach this morning. I didn't know what he had in mind.'

Mary's eyes flashed contemptuously, and she turned her attention back to Justin.

Phelps was down on one knee, half turned away from Justin as he struggled to get to his feet. Then he swung back towards Justin and she gasped as she saw the dull gleam of a knife in his hand.

She lifted her pistol, but she didn't fire. Justin was between her and the manservant, and he was moving too fast to give her a clear shot.

Henry's eyes were fixed on his master, but he didn't use the whip. If Mary had had any time to spare him a glance, she would have seen him watching the fight with grim satisfaction tinged with expectation.

Phelps lunged towards Justin. Justin sidestepped swiftly and seized the wrist of the manservant's knife-hand in a bone-crushing grip. In one continuous movement he yanked Phelps off balance and forward to receive a thundering blow in his stomach. Phelps doubled up and landed groaning beside Samuel.

Justin picked up the knife and tossed it into the field beside the road. Then he looked down at his victims, absent-mindedly rubbing his bruised knuckles as he did so. Both men were dazed, and Samuel was barely conscious. It wasn't in Justin to continue pounding them. He looked up at Henry, still mounted on his horse.

'Watch them,' he said curtly.

'Yes, guv'nor.' The tiger stared down at the two men with hot, angry eyes. He didn't hold with anyone attacking his master with a knife, and the whip was ready in his hand.

Justin glanced back at Mary, and smiled faintly as he saw the pistol she was holding. 'I should have guessed you would not be standing idle,' he said, a note of proud affection in his voice. 'If you will cover them for a few minutes, I'll reassure Lucinda and then find some cords to restrain them.'

'As long as it takes,' Mary told him grimly.

'Not long, I hope,' he said, and turned to the coach. 'Miss Burleigh?' he said gently, reaching out his hand to her.

She was shaking with shock and fear, hardly able to realise that she'd been rescued. Her muscles were too knotted with tension to allow her to move. She simply stared at Justin with huge, terrified eyes.

'Miss Burleigh. . .Lucinda, you're safe now,' Justin said quietly. 'Mary—Mrs Drayton—is with me. She'll look after you. But first I must tie up the two villains who abducted you.'

Phelps groaned and tried to push himself upright.

'Stay where you are!' Henry growled, and the whip cracked inches before the manservant's face.

Phelps subsided in the mud, the spirit knocked out of him.

Samuel stirred, his gaze still dazed and unfocused. He had no more fight left in him than his henchman.

Then he caught sight of Mary. His eyes focused and his expression changed. His face distorted in an ugly grimace of hate and he surged to his feet, taking Henry by surprise. The tiger's horse shied away and Justin spun round.

Henry had the horse under control in an instant, and Justin was already lunging after Samuel, but Samuel was in the grip of ungovernable rage. His lips were curled back in a hideous snarl and his eyes blazed with mad fury. He ignored both the lash of the whip across his face and the pistol levelled at him as he charged down on Mary.

She didn't waver. Her bullet hit him in the right shoulder at the very same instant that Justin seized him from behind and sent him crashing, unconscious, to the ground.

In the sudden silence, disturbed only by the sounds of uneasy, restless horses and the jingle of harness, Mary let out an unsteady breath.

'I do hate having to do that,' she said vaguely.

'Mary!' Justin reached her side and took the

pistol out of her numb hand. He slipped his arm around her waist and supported her against him. 'My God!'

For a moment she leant against his broad chest. She would have liked nothing better than to give way to her overwrought nerves within the protection of his arms. But she knew she couldn't allow herself the luxury of such self-indulgence. There was still Lucinda to think of—and Mary was desperately worried about what Samuel might have done to her.

'I'm all right,' she said, pushing herself away from Justin.

'Dear God! I'm sorry,' he said, and she knew he was as shaken as she was. 'I should have——'

'I'm all right,' she repeated. 'No one could have anticipated such blind craziness, and I know you would have stopped him even if I hadn't shot him.' She lifted her head and managed to smile at him, and felt his arm tighten around her. 'I must take care of Lucinda,' she said. 'And God knows what we're going to do about. . .them.'

She slipped out of his embrace and went over to the couch, careful to leave a wide berth between herself and both Samuel and Phelps.

Behind her Justin looked up and met his tiger's shocked, admiring gaze. 'You won't find another lady like her in a million years, guv'nor,' Henry croaked.

'I know.'

Then Justin looked down at Samuel's unconscious body, black fury in his eyes.

'Today you made your last mistake,' he said, his voice quiet, cold and implacable. 'You'll never have an opportunity to make another one.'

Mary got into the coach and sat down beside its frightened occupant.

'Lucinda,' she said gently. 'It's all right. You're safe now.'

Lucinda gave a little choking gasp and started to cry, heart-wrenching sobs racking her whole body. Mary took the girl in her arms and stroked her hair, murmuring reassurances.

It took a long time for any vestige of self-control to return to Lucinda. But, despite her own agony of anxiety to know what had happened to the girl, Mary didn't hurry her. Outside she heard voices and the sounds of movement, but she ignored them. She had no idea what Justin intended to do next, but she was content to leave the decisions in his hands.

'Did he hurt you?' she asked at last, when Lucinda's storm of tears finally subsided.

'He di—didn't touch me,' Lucinda choked out. She scrubbed at her pale, tear-stained cheek with her sleeve. 'He ju—just talked to me. He s-said *such* things! About. . .about *you*, ma'am. He *hates* you.'

'I know.' Mary pushed Lucinda's damp, straggling hair out of her face. 'But he didn't hurt you?' She looked deeply into Lucinda's eyes.

Lucinda gulped back a sob and mutely shook her head.

'Thank God for that!' Mary said, heartfelt relief in her voice.

She looked up as Justin appeared beside the carriage. He had a hard, anxious question in his eyes, and she smiled reassuringly.

'She's just shaken,' she said softly. 'He didn't touch her.'

Justin's expression relaxed slightly.

'Miss Burleigh,' he said quietly, 'if you can bear to travel a short distance in my curricle, Henry will take you and Mary to a house of mine not far from here. It's about eight miles away, I'm afraid, but you'll be able to rest there—and Henry can ride post-haste to Bath to reassure your mother that you're safe.'

Lucinda nodded, still clinging to Mary, but she didn't say anything.

'What are *you* going to do?' Mary asked, keeping her voice subdued, but there was a sharp question in her eyes.

'I'm going to take this coach and the unholy pair outside to a friend of mine who's also a magistrate,' Justin replied evenly, but there was a cold, ruthless expression in his eyes. 'Between us we should be able to make sure that they never hurt anyone again—and without causing a scandal.'

Mary held his gaze for a moment, then she nodded, accepting his decision.

'Come on, Lucinda,' she said, helping the girl out of the coach.

The curricle had been turned to face the direction from which they'd come, and Henry was already holding the reins. He was looking mulish, and Mary suspected that he was reluctant to leave his master's side. She sympathised, but didn't say anything.

Justin's greatcoat was lying on the seat. He had taken it off when they'd stopped at the Red Lion, and now he put it around Lucinda's shoulders. He helped Mary up into the curricle, so that she was sitting beside Henry, and then gave Lucinda his hand.

Mary was sure he'd arranged the order of their seating deliberately, so that Lucinda did not have to sit next to a stranger.

'I will come as soon as I can,' he said. 'And Henry will take a message back to Bath.'

'Thank you, my lord,' said Mary.

'You watch that bas——' Henry snapped off what he'd been about to say and urged the horses into motion before Justin could reprimand him.

Mary looked back as they drove away, but she couldn't see either Samuel or Phelps. They were hidden from her by the coach. She wondered what Justin intended, but she wasted no time in speculation. She only wished she didn't have to ride away and leave him. Like Henry she would have been much happier to see the business through to its end—but they also had to think of Lucinda.

Even huddled in the greatcoat, the girl still shivered with cold and shock. Mary wondered if it would be better to take her the lesser distance to the Red Lion rather than to Justin's house—but then they would have to provide an explanation for their presence. There was no point in causing unnecessary gossip about what had happened.

'I've got some gin in me pocket,' said Henry suddenly. 'I know it ain't what she's used ter but it might 'elp.'

'Thank you.' Mary took the small flask from him and held it for Lucinda to take a sip.

Lucinda choked on the raw spirit, her eyes watering. 'That's horrible!' she gasped.

'I know.' Mary sniffed the cheap gin with reminiscent distaste, then screwed the lid back on. 'I've never acquired a liking for it either. But some people swear by it, don't they, Henry?'

'Me uncle, for one,' he agreed, picking up her light tone. 'Swore all the way down three flights of stairs one night when 'e'd taken a glass too much.'

'Oh, dear,' said Mary. 'I hope he didn't break anything.'

'Only 'is leg,' Henry replied. 'And 'e'd been meanin' to get a new one anyway, so it wasn't a problem.'

'A new leg?' Mary repeated encouragingly.

'Well, you see, ma'am, it was wooden,' Henry confided. 'And the woodworm had got into it. Riddled with holes, it was. Every time 'e stumped across the floor 'e left a trail of dust be'ind 'im. Made the devil of a lot of work for his old woman. She'd been on at 'im to change it for months. So getting drunk and fallin' downstairs was a blessing in disguise, really.'

'I can see how it must have been,' Mary agreed,

putting her arm comfortingly around Lucinda. 'I had an uncle once who. . .'

She went on to make up a completely spurious story about a non-existent uncle which Henry topped with an even more outrageous anecdote about an old aunt. She was grateful for the tiger's help. She knew that nothing they said was of any comfort to Lucinda, but it might provide her with a distraction to hasten the journey—as long as the stories didn't become too frivolous.

At last Lucinda stirred restlessly, and Mary silenced Henry with a swift glance.

'I didn't want to get in the carriage with him,' Lucinda said abruptly. 'When he stopped and asked us to go for a drive with him, I didn't want to go—but Cousin Emma made it so hard to refuse. I really didn't want to go.'

'I know you didn't.' Mary hugged her reassuringly.

'What's going to become of me?' Lucinda asked helplessly. 'The scandal. . .'

'There won't be any scandal,' said Mary firmly. 'You're safe now. We'll take care of you.'

'I wanted someone to come. I wanted someone to come. . .but since Papa died. . .' Lucinda buried her face in her hands. 'I was so frightened,' she whispered, her voice muffled. 'I was so fr— fr—frightened.' She turned in Mary's arms, sobbing against her friend's shoulder.

'I know,' said Mary. Her eyes were bleak. She was remembering the days when she had been as afraid as Lucinda and there had been no one for her to turn to. 'But you'll never be frightened like that again,' she continued gently. 'Because next time someone tries to persuade you to do something against your better judgement you'll refuse—won't you?'

Lucinda lifted her tear-stained face and looked at Mary.

'The only mistake you've ever made is to be too deferential to those who don't deserve your respect,' said Mary, smiling reassuringly. 'You had some doubts about Samuel from the first, didn't you? You should be proud of your insight. You have nothing to reproach yourself for.'

'I don't know,' said Lucinda uncertainly.

'And in future you will have more confidence in your opinions,' Mary continued. 'That's all you need, Lucinda. That's all you've ever needed.'

A very tremulous smile wavered on Lucinda's lips. Among all the other horrors that had assailed her that day was the fear that, somehow, she had been responsible for encouraging Samuel's behaviour. But Mary seemed to have no such concern, and she was doing her best to reinforce Lucinda's faith in herself.

'Did you really threaten to shoot him last night?' Lucinda asked wonderingly.

'She *did* shoot him today!' Henry exclaimed before Mary could reply.

'Ma'am?' The girl looked startled.

'I wounded him in the shoulder,' said Mary, glancing at Henry reprovingly. 'I'm afraid I made him angry yesterday. I told him Mr Penrose had cut him out of his will—and then I wouldn't let him throttle me to relieve his feelings.'

Lucinda shuddered.

'He hates you,' she said in a low voice. 'All he talked about was what he was going to do to you when he had the chance. But he was also afraid of someone called Burke—that's why he was taking me to Scotland. He said if Burke knew he was married to an heiress he'd hold off for a few more months. Then he was coming back for you. He said he knew where you lived. And something about a man called Donald. He said he was going to shoot Donald first. And then. . .' Her voice faltered. 'Oh, ma'am. I can't tell you what he said he was going to do to you.'

'It's all right, Lucinda, I can guess,' said Mary quietly. 'Don't think about it any more. He's not going to hurt you or me—or anyone else—ever again. We're quite safe now.'

'What's Lord Hawkridge going to do?' Lucinda asked anxiously.

'I don't know. But I know neither of us has any reason to worry about Samuel any more,' said Mary with absolute certainty. 'When Justin makes up his mind to do something, he does it. And I think he hates Samuel even more than we do.'

'Justin?' said Lucinda questioningly. 'Mrs Drayton, how did it come about that it was Lord Hawkridge who came with you to rescue me? How did either of you even know I needed rescuing?'

'It's a long story,' said Mary wryly, 'and Henry probably knows as much of it as I do by now. If

Samuel was ranting on about me in the coach you must have realised I'm not Mr Penrose's niece. . .'

'He said you were a dox—an innkeeper.' Lucinda hastily amended what she'd been about to say.

'I'm the landlady of a coaching inn called the Lazy Cat,' said Mary calmly. She was aware that Henry was also listening with interest but if he hadn't already known that fact he probably soon would have anyway.

'Several days ago I heard Samuel talking to Phelps at the inn,' she continued. 'He was making threats against his uncle, and he also mentioned the possibility of coaxing you to marry him. So I went to tell Mr Penrose what I'd overheard, and we came to Bath to confront Samuel. I'm sorry, Lucinda,' she added regretfully. 'If I'd taken you and your mother more fully into my confidence, today would never have happened. I feel very responsible.'

'It's not your fault, ma'am,' said Lucinda softly. 'I don't suppose Mr Penrose wanted you to tell me, did he? He seems a very anxious man. And you did warn me against Samuel. I knew that was what you were trying to do, and I understood. I should have been firmer with Cousin Emma.'

'That's the ticket,' said Henry admiringly. 'You're a lady after me own 'eart, miss. I'm proud to 'ave assisted in your rescue.'

'Thank you,' said Lucinda, looking both surprised and pleased.

* * *

''Ere we are, ladies,' Henry announced, bringing the curricle to a halt before a large, elegant house built in the classically grand style of the previous century. 'Allow me to welcome you to 'is lordship's Worcestershire residence. Famous for its helegant architecture and pictureskew surroundings. Mind you, it doesn't look its best at this time of year. You ought to come back in the summer.'

He jumped down from the curricle and went to knock on the front door, before coming back to help Mary and Lucinda down.

'Mr Dibley,' he said, when an elderly butler appeared at the door, 'we've got guests. This is Mrs Drayton and Miss Lucinda. They was involved in a carriage accident and 'is lordship said to bring them 'ere while 'e sorted everything out on the road.'

'Thank you, Henry,' said Mary with quiet dignity. She wondered whether Justin had told his tiger to provide them with an unexceptional reason for their presence or whether he'd made up the excuse on his own initiative. She smiled at the butler. Her manner was friendly, but neither over-familiar nor ingratiating. 'I hope we won't put you to too much inconvenience,' she told him, 'but we would be grateful to sit by the fire and perhaps have a cup of tea. Lord Hawkridge said he would come as soon as he had everything arranged, but I don't know how long that may take.'

'Of course, Mrs Drayton, please come in,' said Dibley. He spoke courteously, but she thought she detected a hint of disapproval in his bearing. 'I hope you are not hurt,' he added, stepping back to allow them into the house.

'Only a little shaken, thank goodness,' Mary replied. 'Oh, Lord Hawkridge did say we could send a message to our family to let them know we're safe.' She glanced towards Henry.

'I'll be back to take the message from you as soon as I've taken the curricle round to the stables,' he said instantly.

'This way, please, ladies,' said Dibley. He led them into a small sitting-room. 'I'll have the fire made up directly, and bring you some tea.'

'And some writing materials, also, if you please,' said Mary.

'Certainly.' He bowed and went out, and a few minutes later a maid came to make up the fire. Shortly after that a footman appeared with paper, pen and ink, and then the butler himself returned with a tea-tray loaded not only with tea but with a substantial cherry cake and several smaller savoury items too.

'Mrs Marlowe, the housekeeper, thought you might be hungry,' he explained. 'Please ring if you need anything else.'

'Thank you very much.' Mary's smile illuminated her eyes. 'And please thank Mrs Marlowe for her thoughtfulness. I think we will both be glad of something to eat.' She glanced at Lucinda who nodded.

'We will be serving dinner later,' said Dibley

rather austerely. 'Do you have any idea when his lordship will be returning, ma'am?'

'I'm afraid I don't,' Mary admitted.

'Henry says his lordship wishes you to have every comfort during your stay,' said the butler. 'I'm sure he would not want you to wait unduly for him. We will serve it at the normal hour.'

'Thank you.' Mary watched the butler leave the room, an odd smile on her lips. She was in Justin's house, talking to his servants. If Justin had meant what he'd said about marrying her, they might one day be her servants. It was a very strange notion.

She wondered what the stately Dibley would say if he knew about her relationship with his master. Would he approve? Or would he think she was completely unsuitable to be Lady Hawkridge?

She glanced around at her surroundings. Even this small sitting-room was imposing, and the glimpses she'd caught of the rest of the house had been similarly grand. *One* of Justin's houses, Henry had said.

Of course she'd know that Justin inhabited a world that was different from anything she'd ever known, but her vision of it had been vague and cloudy. The reality was rather daunting. Even Sir Richard had not lived in such a magnificent house. And, until now, the squire's house had been the most imposing country residence she had ever visited.

The houses she'd visited in Bath had somehow been different. Perhaps because she'd been aware that the Mr Penroses and Mrs Knightleys of the world were not so very much grander than she was. If they'd met her at the Lazy Cat they would undoubtedly have responded to her differently than they had when she was a guest at Mrs Burleigh's party. But her memories of her childhood had given her the confidence to treat them as equals.

She had no such memories to fall back on to tell her how to behave in a nobleman's house. She glanced at Lucinda and saw from her wide-eyed stare that she was feeling similarly overawed.

'Oh, ma'am,' Lucinda breathed. 'I had no idea Lord Hawkridge would live in a house like this. I hope he comes back before it's time for dinner. I shall be so nervous if we have to sit down to eat with all his servants watching us.'

'So shall I,' Mary admitted. 'But I'm sure we'll both rise to the occasion if we have to. In the meantime, we'd better write some messages for Henry to take back to Bath.'

CHAPTER TWELVE

JUSTIN didn't return in time for dinner, and they ate alone at one end of an imposing dining-table in an even more imposing dining-room.

There were several large oil-paintings on the wall, but none by Justin. Mary wasn't surprised. He wasn't the kind of man to make a vulgar, ostentatious show of his work in his own house.

It was an uncomfortable meal for the visitors. Both of them were preoccupied by the events of the day, but neither of them felt able to speak naturally in the presence of others. And their discomfort was increased by the fact that they were waited upon by expressionless servants in magnificent livery.

Mary felt particularly uneasy. Not only did she feel out of her depth in such surroundings, but she was desperately afraid that someone in the household might have recognised her. Justin had sketched her several times at the Blue Boar. There would inevitably be pictures of her in his old sketchbooks. All it needed was for someone to remember and put two and two together. . .

What made it worse was that if anyone did know anything about her they would also inevitably believe that she had run away to be the mistress of a richer man. That was what Justin had believed until a few days ago, and there was no possible way that anyone in this household could know differently.

She glanced at the servants surreptitiously, but their faces were so expressionless that it was impossible to guess what they were thinking. She thought she detected a certain air of disapproval in Dibley's bearing, but that might simply be because he didn't like the unconventional way the guests had been foisted on the household.

There was nothing she could do to reassure herself; she just had to brazen it out. But she was becoming increasingly anxious not to stay in the house any longer than she had to. Justin had implied that he still wanted to marry her, but sitting in such stately splendour, painfully conscious of how out of place she was in such surroundings, Mary could hardly believe that he meant it.

She was glad when the meal was over, and they went back to wait in the small sitting-room. Lucinda had recovered her composure very well, but she was still extremely nervous, and both women jumped and looked startled when a servant came to build up the fire.

When they were alone again, Mary smiled ruefully at Lucinda.

'This will never do,' she said. 'We'll be as skittish as a pair of kittens on a windy day by the time Lord Hawkridge gets here if we're not careful.'

'What do you think he's doing?' Lucinda asked nervously.

'I don't know. He was taking them to a friend of his. But we don't even know how far he had to go.'

'Is he going. . .do you think he means it to come to court?' Lucinda asked, pleating the folds of her skirt convulsively.

'I don't think so.' Mary remembered the expression in his eyes as he'd looked at Samuel. Justin was a tolerant man, but he had an overwhelming hatred of the kind of vindictive cruelty which characterised young Penrose. He would not allow him to escape unpunished for his actions, but nor was he likely to do anything which would expose the innocent Lucinda to malicious, damaging gossip. 'Anyway, I dare say we will find out soon enough. In the meantime, perhaps we should find some way of distracting our thoughts from what's happened.' She glanced at a piano on one side of the room. 'Can you play?' she asked.

'Oh, yes,' said Lucinda eagerly, as if she was glad of the suggestion. 'Oh, ma'am, do you think anyone will mind?' she added doubtfully.

'Lord Hawkridge certainly won't mind,' said Mary firmly. 'And I would be grateful. I've always enjoyed music.'

'Do you not play yourself?' Lucinda asked, going to the instrument and opening the highly polished lid.

'I'm afraid not,' Mary replied. She had played once, but that had been over twelve years ago, and she had no confidence in her ability to do so now.

Lucinda touched the keys tentatively, drawing soft random notes from them. Then she sat down and played a simple melody. Her playing was very characteristic of her—hesitant at first, yet growing in confidence.

Mary leant her head against the high back of her chair and listened, relieved that she no longer had to try to make conversation with Lucinda. Too many confusing emotions were churning within her, and she knew she was as concerned about her own problems as she was about her friend's.

When this ugly business was over she would finally have to confront her feelings for Justin. None of her doubts or uncertainties had resolved themselves. Now that she had seen the house he lived in she believed more firmly than ever that their union would be a mismatch—unless she accepted the role of his mistress.

That thought reminded her of the unknown Bernadette and her hands tightened instinctively into fists. It was unreasonable to feel such violent antipathy towards the woman, but she did. Bernadette had had what Mary wanted yet was afraid to take.

And why did Justin wish to marry her? Was it simply because he'd been frustrated in his attempt to do so seven years ago? Did he love her? Or did he think he owed it to her? He must know how unsuitable and outrageous their marriage would be.

Because even if she discounted her life in St Giles there was still the unalterable fact that she was no more than the landlady of a coaching inn. And everyone who met her would know that—and whisper about her behind her back. Justin might think he loved her now, but would his love withstand years of knowing that his friends and family disapproved of her?

She suddenly realised that instead of becoming calmer she was growing more agitated, and she tried to force herself to listen more attentively to the piano. But there was a certain passionate energy in the way in which Lucinda was playing which echoed Mary's heightened emotions. Mary suspected that the girl was using the music to exorcise some of her own feelings about the day's events. She was pleased for Lucinda's sake, but the torrent of music did nothing to soothe her own restlessness.

She got up and went to admire a fine porcelain clock above the fireplace. It was all she could do not to pace up and down the room. But then the chords modulated, and Lucinda moved into a quieter, more melodic piece. It was familiar, but at first Mary couldn't place it.

Then she remembered. With unexpected, heart-wrenching force she was drawn back to her childhood. She stood frozen, one hand still reaching up to the mantelpiece, as she recalled the last time she had heard that tune.

She had been sitting in the garden with her father, listening to him working on his sermon. They had been surrounded by sweet-smelling honeysuckle and lavender. And through the open window of the house she could hear her mother playing the piano. It was a scene which, with slight variations, had been repeated hundreds of times in her childhood.

She had been happy then, with no awareness of how precarious her happiness really was. She had listened to her father preach about the importance of building one's spiritual house upon the rock—not the sand—and she had never questioned the security of her physical surroundings. After all, God dressed the lilies of the field, and watched over the smallest sparrow. Naturally He was watching over her.

But then her mother had died. And two years later her father had died—and her uncle had taken her to Church Lane.

She very rarely allowed herself to think about her first uncomprehending horror at being confronted with the rookeries of St Giles. It was still too unbelievably painful for her. But the combined stimuli of Lucinda's earlier terror in response to a similar shock and the sound of the achingly familiar melody stripped away her defences.

'*Mary*?'

Justin closed the door behind him and strode across the room, taking her into his arms without any hesitation.

Her face was bleached and her eyes were blank
with distress. She was shaking with remembered
fear and dread, but she made no sound. Justin
wasn't even sure if she knew he was there,
although he was holding her and speaking softly
to her, and she was clinging to him in white-
knuckled desperation.

The music stopped with a jarring chord and
Lucinda started up. Justin met her eyes across
Mary's head. 'It's all right,' he said quietly, and
he was speaking to both women.

He held Mary close to him, his hand moving
gently against her hair as he waited for the uncontrollable shaking of her body to ease. Lucinda
watched, her lower lip caught between her teeth
in painful concern. It was clear that she wanted to
help yet she didn't know what to do. Justin smiled
at her reassuringly, although his eyes were
sombre, and glanced at a nearby chair. Lucinda
perched on the edge of it, her hands gripped
together in her lap, and waited.

Mary slowly became aware that she was in
Justin's arms. She didn't yet know where she was,
or how he came to be with her, but she didn't
care. She could hear his voice, and the remembered voices of all her tormenters from the past
began to recede. In the worst of her horror she
had not wept, but now tears of relief sprang to her
eyes and she gave a sobbing gasp.

'Mary, it's over,' said Justin softly. 'You're here
now. You'll never have to go back. My love, I'm

not letting you go again,' he added unevenly, a crooked half-smile on his lips.

Mary pushed herself away from him, her hand laid flat against his chest. She looked up at him, still confused and shaken—and then, in one flashing instant, she remembered where she was and realised what had just happened.

She glanced round wildly and saw Lucinda watching her anxiously.

'Mrs Drayton. . .' the girl said very tentatively.

At that moment Mary reached breaking point. She no longer had any resources left to deal with anyone or anythng. She just wanted to escape.

She wrenched herself out of Justin's arms and ran. She fumbled desperately with the door-handle for a few seconds, then she fled up the stairs to the bedchamber that the housekeeper had earlier assigned to her.

Lucinda jumped up.

'I must go. . .'

'No.' Justin caught her arm and drew her back.

'But. . .'

'She's too upset just now,' he said. He sighed. 'Come and sit down again, Miss Burleigh. I hope you've been well looked after in my absence.'

'Oh, yes,' she said, but her expression was distracted. 'It was like the time at my party,' she said slowly. 'Only this time was much worse. I'm so glad you were here. But what distressed her so much? I'm sorry,' she added, flushing, as she realised how inquisitive she was being. 'I didn't mean. . .'

'I think it was the music,' said Justin bleakly. 'I remember her telling me once that her mother was very fond of the piano.'

'Then it was my fault?' Lucinda exclaimed.

Justin had been gazing into space, trying to imagine what nightmares Mary had seen, but now he turned his head and focused on Lucinda.

'No,' he said firmly. 'It wasn't the music, Miss Burleigh. It was what happened when the music stopped. Please don't worry that you did anything wrong.'

'You know her very well,' said Lucinda shyly.

'But not, perhaps, well enough,' Justin replied. 'Did Henry take a message to your mother?'

It was after midnight. Mary was sitting up in her room. The fire had been lit earlier, but she had done nothing to maintain it and it had nearly burnt out. She was wearing a borrowed nightgown, and a borrowed dressing-gown, and she had been brushing her hair with a borrowed brush—but now her hair was falling in disarray across her shoulders and her hands rested motionless in her lap.

Her eyes were blank as her thoughts roamed without discipline or direction over everything that had ever happened to her. She had made no effort to go downstairs again after her precipitate departure. She knew she must have alarmed her companions, but she had no strength left to reassure them. She didn't even have the strength left to get out of the chair and go to bed.

The door opened quietly and Justin came in. She turned her head and looked at him without surprise, but she didn't say anything. His eyes rested on her consideringly for a moment, then he went over to the fire and busied himself for several minutes in relighting it. It was very cold in the bedroom.

After that he rubbed his hands clean on his handkerchief and went over to Mary. He took the brush from her and held her chilly hands in a warm, strong grasp.

'If you're not going to attend to the fire, perhaps you should take to wearing your muff indoors,' he said, gently chiding.

She stared at him blankly, her eyes wide and desolate. He gave a muttered exclamation and swept her up in his arms, sitting down in the chair himself and holding her comfortingly on his lap, her head against his shoulder.

'It's over,' he said hoarsely. 'Don't you understand, my love? Alf is dead. Penrose is dead. You're safe here with me, and there's nothing left to hurt you.'

Mary started to cry. The ice which seemed to have encased her cracked and disintegrated in the fierce warmth of Justin's embrace. All her pent-up anxiety over Lucinda, her horror at shooting Samuel, and her fears about Justin while he'd been away from her, flooded out from her.

He held her tight, kissing her hair, murmuring reassurances. He rubbed her cold hands between his to bring life and warmth back into them. And at last, when the worst of her tears had abated, he said, 'Shush. I've only got one handkerchief, and you're going to have a sooty face if you dry your eyes with that.'

'I've had worse,' Mary replied unsteadily, blinking to clear her hazy vision. 'Thank you.'

She took it and wiped her eyes and blew her nose. Even now she couldn't help noticing what fine linen it was. There was a monogram embroidered in one corner. Another reminder of Justin's status.

She was so comfortable on his lap. She could have stayed within the shelter of his arms forever, but it still wasn't a dream she could give any credence to. With a supreme effort of will she struggled to get to her feet. His hold on her tightened, and for a moment she thought he wasn't going to permit her to do so—but then he released her.

She took a few steps away from him, suddenly feeling the chill of the room now that she was no longer close to him. Would she always feel cold when she wasn't near Justin?

'Mary.' He stood up. 'I wish you wouldn't keep turning away from me,' he said quietly. 'Is it that difficult to trust me?' He put his hand on her shoulder, looking down at her with a penetrating gaze, and she closed her eyes. He released her and took a couple of hasty paces away from her. Mary was aware of the familiar coiled, impatient energy within him.

'You said Samuel was dead?' she said questioningly. It was better to talk of something solid and practical rather than her muddled, undisciplined emotions.

'Yes. Come and sit down again.' He drew her back to the chair. Then he took the stool from in front of the dressing-table and went to sit next to her.

'Did I kill him?' Mary asked fearfully, wondering if she had injured Samuel more grievously than she'd realised.

'No,' Justin replied quickly. 'It wasn't a very serious wound—barely more than a scratch. I hope you'd have aimed nearer the heart if you'd been alone,' he added almost humorously.

'Yes,' Mary admitted, pain and reluctance in her eyes. 'I knew you were there so I didn't have to, but. . .'

'It's over. Don't think about it,' said Justin firmly, taking her hands again.

'So how did he die?' Mary asked. She thought she ought to withdraw her hands from Justin's grasp, but she couldn't quite bring herself to do so.

'I killed him,' he said grimly, his eyes briefly losing focus as he remembered the ugly scene on the road. 'I didn't mean to. . .but when I saw him charging at you like that. . .I must have hit him too hard. I didn't even realise at first. But when I bent down to see how badly he was hurt. . .'

Justin didn't attempt to finish his sentence, but his grip on Mary's hands tightened almost painfully, and she knew how disturbed he was by what had happened.

She shivered, remembering the look in Samuel's eyes when he'd tried to attack her, and the threats Lucinda said he'd made against her. 'I certainly earned his hatred, didn't I?' she whispered.

Justin's troubled expression cleared immediately. His attention focused once more on her. 'In the unlikely event that something like this ever happens again, you are *not* going to deal with it alone—or even at all,' he said categorically. 'I knew I should have sent you home before he came to Bath.'

A spark of indignation flared in Mary's eyes.

'You have no business sending me anywhere,' she said sharply, drawing her hands away from him. 'I'm quite capable of looking after myself. I don't need you—or any other rich protector,' she added hotly, remembering the way he'd been so reluctant to believe that she'd sold the Blue Boar. 'I still can't believe you thought it was more likely I'd run off with another man than that——'

'I'm sorry!' he interrupted. 'For God's sake, Mary, I didn't believe the rumour easily! Only when I'd spent months searching for you and I couldn't find you.' He got up and took a hasty turn around the room. 'It was better to believe that than that you were dead,' he said fiercely, over his shoulder. 'They were the only two alternatives open to me, and I couldn't bear to think——' He broke off. 'You knew where I was,' he said tautly. 'I knew you could find me if you wanted to. And you clearly didn't want to.'

'But. . .'

'I know.' Justin flung up a hand. 'Donald said!' His hand clenched into a fist, then he let his arm drop to his side, some of the tension easing out of him. 'Every time I feel particularly murderous towards Donald I remember that you probably wouldn't have survived without him,' he said almost conversationally.

'Oh, yes, I would,' said Mary flatly. 'I can survive without anyone if I have to. What did you do about Samuel?'

Justin turned his head and looked at her. It was there in her eyes, the fundamental core of steel which had enabled her to endure the appalling hardships and betrayals of her life. Loving her and trying to protect her were not enough. The years of bitter struggle had given her the right to demand respect for her capacity to survive—and she would not lightly relinquish her claim.

Justin took a deep breath.

'Yes,' he said slowly. 'I believe you would have done. Do you know how hard it is for me to accept that? I don't mean that I wish you had less courage or strength,' he added almost impatiently. 'But it is very hard for me to accept that you are also ruthlessly capable of surviving without me.'

Mary's breath caught in her throat at the expression of raw pain in his eyes. She tried to speak, but she couldn't say anything. He came back and sat down in front of her again, once more taking her hands in his.

'Have I told you since we met again how much I love you?' he asked quietly. 'Please don't keep turning away from me and shutting me out.'

Mary reached out and gently touched his cheek with her fingertips. She was suffused with a wondering, overwhelming sense of love for him. He closed his eyes and leant his face against her hand, catching hold of her wrist as he turned his head to kiss her palm. Her lips curved in a trembling smile, and she stroked his crisp, dark hair with her other hand.

'Oh, my love,' he murmured hoarsely, and she felt a pang of almost unbearable yearning for him. She wanted him to sweep her up in his arms but, after a moment, he gathered her hands in his and bent his head to kiss her fingers. She felt glorious warmth radiating out from the touch of his lips.

He looked up and met her gaze, gold flecks warming his hazel eyes as he smiled at her.

'I'm sorry I ever doubted you,' he said, his voice low and deep. 'And if I ever do have to deal with such an ugly situation again, I hope you are beside me—with your pistol in your hand. I think I need your protection as much as I hope you need mine.' His expression became almost rueful. 'Even after everything I knew about him, you were still more ready for Samuel this afternoon than I was,' he added.

'Not really,' Mary replied quickly. 'It's different for me, Justin. I've never been able to rely on my strength or speed, the way you can. Only on my wits. I've always known I can't take chances, so I've become over-cautious.' She smiled self-mockingly. 'The first thing I did last night after Samuel left was run down and make sure the front door was bolted,' she confessed.

Justin laughed softly. 'I'm glad to hear it,' he said. 'I hope I would have had the sense to do the same.'

'So what did you do about Samuel?' Mary asked, getting impatient. She was quite confident that Justin would have sorted things out satisfactorily, but she wanted to know *how*. 'And why didn't you tell me Samuel was dead before we left you on the road?' she added. 'You must have known by then.'

'I did,' said Justin, 'but I didn't want to cause you or Lucinda any more distress. I knew you'd be worried, and I thought you might insist on coming with me to see Sir Edward. All right!' Although she'd made no attempt to speak, he lifted his hand in a quick gesture which seemed both defensive and apologetic. 'I know you'd have been more than equal to the task—but it was better for Lucinda to be spared any more distress.'

'Oh, Justin, I wasn't complaining!' Mary exclaimed quickly, her voice not quite steady. 'I'm glad you didn't tell me. I wouldn't have wanted to speak to the magistrate any more than I imagine Lucinda did.'

'You may have to give him a statement tomorrow,' Justin warned her. 'But he'll come here. There won't be any difficulty.' He paused, his eyes dark with recollection. 'I told Sir Edward what happened,' he continued after a moment, 'and we got a statement from the postilion which confirmed my account. *He* was very anxious to dissociate himself from Samuel and Phelps. And Phelps himself was remarkably talkative when he realised what a precarious situation he was in. He told us things about Samuel which——'

'What things?' Mary prompted him softly, when Justin broke off.

'Apparently he killed a maidservant last year,' said Justin harshly. 'She was pregnant, and she went to him for protection. But her demands infuriated Samuel and he struck her down. Phelps is quite eager to show us where they disposed of her body. I don't think he realised how deeply he is incriminating himself—he's so keen to lay all the blame on his late master.'

'There really isn't going to be any problem for you about Samuel's death, is there?' Mary asked anxiously. 'I couldn't bear. . .'

'No, no,' Justin assured her hastily. 'As I mentioned, Sir Edward may need a statement from you and Lucinda—and Henry, of course. But Samuel's death was an accident, and even if it hadn't been I doubt if any action would be taken against me. Don't forget Samuel was in the process of abducting an heiress at the time he died. No jury would convict me for what happened.'

'They'd probably give you a medal,' Mary

replied firmly, trying not to let him see how upset she was on his behalf.

She knew that what had happened would not be easy for Justin to come to terms with. He could hardly help being relieved by Samuel's death, but she knew he would never be able to take pleasure or pride in being responsible for it. She thought bitterly that if she had aimed truer she would have spared him a great deal of pain.

'I'm sorry,' she said, instinctively voicing her thoughts. 'If I'd killed him on the road you wouldn't have had to. . .'

Justin looked up swiftly, and laid his fingers gently across her lips.

'You can't deny me any opportunity to demonstrate my ability to deal with a brutal world,' he said lightly. 'Between us we have managed to preserve Lucinda, and Penrose, relatively unharmed from Samuel's malice. I think we should be satisfied with that.'

'I am satisfied with it,' said Mary firmly.

'Good.' He stood up again, his movements once more restless and impatient.

He went over to the fireplace, staring down at the dancing flames. Mary saw that his hand resting on the mantelpiece had closed into a fist. After a moment he looked at her.

'I said I'd take you back to the Lazy Cat before we discussed this any further,' he said tautly, 'but I can't wait that long. You are going to marry me, aren't you?'

Mary stared at him. She'd wondered earlier

whether he'd asked her to marry him because he
felt he owed her a duty—or simply because he'd
been frustrated seven years ago. But she knew
now that that wasn't true. He was asking her
because he loved her. He had said so, and she
could feel his love for her as truly as she could feel
her love for him.

But it had never been that easy, even seven
years ago.

She thought of the austere, stately butler who
had greeted her on her arrival, and the footmen in
their magnificent livery. She thought of the lords
and ladies with whom Justin would be on familiar
terms. He must, she thought numbly, have met
the King! Yes, she remembered him describing
the corpulent George to her in the days when he'd
still been Regent. And Justin was certainly a
member of the House of Lords.

But she was only the landlady of a wayside inn.
Even if no one ever found out about her life in St
Giles, that fact alone would be enough to damn
her. She imagined the endless, polite charade that
her life would become, trying desperately to pretend that she was something she was not. Servants
were quick to judge their masters. How would
they feel about her if she became Justin's wife—
Lady Hawkridge?

Lady Hawkridge!

Hardly aware of what she was doing, she
pressed her hands against her cheeks.

'Are you thinking about my mistresses?' Justin
asked tensely. 'I couldn't lie to you when you

asked, Mary. I won't lie to you. But none of them meant anything to me.'

He came back to her and she stood up automatically.

'Why won't you answer?' he demanded impatiently, seizing her by the shoulders. 'For God's sake, Mary! Talk to me!'

She touched his cheek gently.

'I can't marry you,' she said sadly. 'I don't belong here.'

He took a hasty breath, and then chopped off what he'd been about to say. He bent his head and closed his eyes for a moment as if he was struggling to maintain his self-control, then he looked up and met her steady gaze.

'You belong with me,' he said harshly. 'Or I belong with you, if you prefer.'

'No.' Inside she felt as if her heart was breaking, but the familiar implacable expression had returned to her eyes. In her bitter anguish she was holding him more at bay than ever.

'Love isn't enough,' she said painfully. 'I don't know how to live in your world—and I don't think I want to. I would be a disgrace to you and to myself. No, wait!' She saw him start to speak. 'Justin, do you know what it is like to live with deception? To pretend to be something you're not—with the constant fear that one day you'll be found out? I do. I've done it for years. I cannot. . .' Her voice faltered.

'Are you telling me you're not fit to be my

wife?' Justin demanded gratingly. 'Don't you think I have a right to make that decision?'

'You have a right to ask me,' said Mary. 'I have the right. . .to refuse.'

She could see the hurt, thwarted, disbelieving look in his eyes, his fierce rejection of what she had said, and she was filled with bitter, agonising pain. But she was thinking of the day when her presence by Justin's side would bring shame to him. She could not endure that for his sake—or her own.

'You are the woman I love. You are the woman I want to marry. You are the woman I would be proud to claim as my wife,' said Justin categorically. 'You have spent the last week insisting you've lived a respectable life—why are you so determined to deny that now?'

'I don't deny it,' Mary said hardly. 'I have been a respectable landlady for seven years. An *innkeeper*, Justin. Can you imagine what your friends would say if they knew? And before that I was a thief's whore,' she continued harshly. 'You're not the first man who's laid hands on me, and not the first man who's made love to me—but I'm not a widow.'

She could see from the look in his eyes that she'd hurt him with her savage reminder of her past. She wanted to cry bitter tears of remorse for wounding him so badly. She wanted to put her arms around him and tell him that she didn't mean it. But she couldn't.

She stared at him with the same fierce, aloof,

implacable gaze she had used to keep the world at bay for over twelve years.

There were never any half-measures in her dealings with people. As Samuel had already discovered to his cost. When she had once made up her mind about a course of action, she never allowed herself the luxury of uncertainty—and she didn't indulge in it now.

'Do you seriously imagine I'm going to let you walk out on me again?' Justin demanded wildly. 'Do you think that after everything that's happened I'm just going to let you *go*? My God!' He shook her in his frustration. 'You know I love you. Do you think I care about your past? I'd still want you if you'd lived with a different man for every year we've been apart! Don't you understand that?'

'Don't.' Mary stretched her hands out to him imploringly and he released her so suddenly that she staggered and nearly overbalanced.

'I can only think of one good reason why you won't marry me,' he said, his voice cold and empty. 'And that's that you don't love me enough. And now I come to think about it you never have told me you love me. Ever. Not in St Giles. Not in Bath. And not tonight. Do you love me, Mary?'

She looked up briefly, but she couldn't meet his eyes. Nothing had ever hurt her as badly as this, because tonight she was hurting someone she loved. It was so much easier to endure suffering herself than to impose it upon the one person she cared about more than any other.

But she'd already set her course. Perhaps she'd done so all those years ago in Church Lane when she'd repeatedly told Justin that it would be a scandalous, unsuitable marriage—and Donald had quoted her own words back to her to destroy all her hopes of happiness.

And nothing had happened to change her mind. All she'd done was grow older and more conscious of the hazards of such a union. And now she'd even seen, and been daunted by, the splendour of Justin's world.

But he'd made it easier for her. He had handed her the one weapon with which she could end this bitter dispute forever. But she couldn't use it. She couldn't lie to him and say she didn't love him.

She lifted her chin to meet his eyes, not realising how chillingly cold and distant her gaze was because she was trying so hard not to let him see how much she was hurting.

'I'm here. Now,' she said. Without realising she was doing so, she glanced at the bed. 'Tomorrow I'll go home. But tonight. . .'

'Dear God!' Justin exclaimed, a stunned, horrified expression in his eyes. 'Are you so sick of me that you're prepared to sacrifice yourself to me to get rid of me?'

He took a step back, staring at her in shaken disbelief. Then he turned on his heel and strode out of the room.

For a moment after he'd gone, Mary continued to stand as cold and immobile as a pillar of ice. Then her face crumpled and she fell on her knees beside the bed, giving way to an outburst of tears as wild and despairing as the one with which she had responded to Donald's message all those years ago.

CHAPTER THIRTEEN

MARY didn't know how long she'd been huddled beside the bed, her face hot with tears, her hands clutching at the coverlet, when she felt a gentle touch on her shoulder.

'Don't,' Justin said. 'I can't bear it.'

He was on one knee beside her. She turned and flung herself into his arms.

'I'm sorry!' she wept. 'I'm sorry, I'm sorry!'

'Oh, my love,' he whispered unsteadily.

He gathered her against him, rocking slightly to ease the desperate flood of her tears. She'd thought that nothing could assuage the pain that had wounded her to the depth of her soul—but she'd also been afraid that she'd driven him away forever. She could feel the warmth of his body, and the rough texture of his waistcoat beneath her hand. She could hear the strong beat of his heart beneath her head.

He was still holding her when she'd done everything she could to force him away from her. He gave her back sweet for sour. No one else in her life had ever been so steadfast. Least of all those people from whom she'd had the most right to expect protection.

She lifted her head and he stroked her tear-stained cheek with gentle fingers, and then kissed her hot, swollen eyelids with the utmost tenderness.

'Why did you come back?' she whispered.

'Because I can't stay away,' he replied simply. 'Mary, you don't have to give me anything you don't want to. If you don't love me. . .' he paused, and she saw the pain in his eyes '. . .I can't force you to,' he finished with quiet agony. 'If you want to go back to the Lazy Cat I'll take you. But please don't shut me out of your life. I just. . . need to know you're safe. I'll always need to know you're safe.'

Fresh tears started in Mary's eyes, and she raised herself in his embrace, slipping her arms around his neck. Then she drew his head down to hers.

He kissed her, and she felt the yearning, hope and pain of his love for her in the way his lips caressed her mouth. She lifted herself a little more towards him, her lips parting in response to his gently questing tongue.

He drew back.

'Mary. . .?' he said questioningly.

'Take me to bed,' she told him softly.

'No.'

She saw the instant, uncompromising refusal in his eyes, and for a moment she was afraid that he no longer wanted her. But his arms tightened instinctively around her and she was reassured.

She looked down for a moment, trying to collect her emotions, then she lifted her head to meet his intent, searching gaze. She smiled unsteadily and touched his lips with slender, hesitant fingers.

'I can't talk to you,' she said helplessly. 'I can't *tell* you. . . Justin, I don't know what I think any more—or what I ought to do. You keep telling me not to turn away from you. Don't turn away from me.'

He stood up in one swift movement, carrying her with him. A brief, incoherent thought flickered through her mind that, even after all the exertions of the day, he still had energy to spare. Then he was laying her down on the bed.

He sat down beside her, his hand on her waist, and she felt a pulse of excitement begin to beat steadily through her.

'Are you sure?' he asked, looking deep into her eyes, doubt in his own. 'I haven't forgotten how distressed you were in the drawing-room in Queen Square yesterday. Mary, I never want to hurt you.'

She laid her hand on his arm. He'd discarded his coat long ago and she could feel the strong, firm warmth of his forearm beneath his fine linen sleeve.

'Is lust the same as love?' she asked, and saw a measure of illumination dawn in his eyes.

'No,' he said in a shaken, comprehending voice. 'No, my love, it isn't. But you already knew that. That's not really the question, is it?'

She hesitated, unsure of how to reply. Several of the candles had guttered out by now, and the light in the room was quite uncertain. He smiled and stroked her hair back from her face, touching her cheek with gentle fingers. She felt the breathless pulse of expectation within her begin to beat faster.

'Are you sure this is what you want?' he asked again.

She nodded, and then answered out loud, so that he could be in no doubt as to her response. 'Yes.'

He bent forward and kissed her. His lips were gentle and coaxing on hers, but she felt the barely contained force of desire within him, and her hands caught at his shoulders. Then she buried her fingers in his hair. She still wasn't sure whether the burning, desperate longing he aroused in her was shameful or joyous. But she knew it was what he wanted, and making Justin happy was more important to her than anything else. She had hurt him and spurned him and denied him—and she couldn't deny him any more. Nor could she deny herself. Whether she went back to the Lazy Cat or whether she stayed, they would still have had this night of love.

His lips became more demanding, his tongue probing deeper into her mouth, and fresh fires began to smoulder within her. She clung to him, raising her torso to press more closely against him. He slipped an arm beneath her shoulders and sat up, lifting her with him. Her head fell back as he kissed her throat. She shivered responsively, longing for the moment when she could feel his body more closely against hers.

He must have discarded his cravat with his coat. She'd hardly noticed before, but now she was grateful. She let her fingers slide tentatively beneath the open neck of his shirt, delighting in the firm play of the muscles in his chest and shoulders. She felt the shuddering response that jolted through him at her touch, and for an instant she was afraid that she had done something wrong. But then he found the fastenings of the dressing-gown and quickly slipped it back from her shoulders. Now all that separated her heated body from his questing hands was her borrowed nightdress.

He touched her breast very lightly through the material, and she gasped at the instant wave of pleasure that flooded over her. Her fingers dug into his shoulders, and she leant impatiently into his hand, her hair falling in wild abandon all around her. His other hand was warm on her back, urging her up. She curled her legs beneath her and he lifted her across on to his lap.

With his hand still on her breast and her arms around his neck she raised herself to kiss him. She felt his tongue sear across her burning lip, and his hand gently kneaded her swollen breast until she was conscious of nothing but the glorious, sensual delight claiming all her awareness.

She moaned softly, her eyes half closed and heavy with desire.

At last he drew back slightly and looked down at her, lying pliant and trembling in his arms. His breathing was quick and uneven, and she could feel the fierce thudding of his heart as he held her against him. She had a dim sense that he was fighting to maintain some semblance of control, and then he smiled wonderingly.

'When you decide to do something, you don't do it in half-measures, do you?' he asked. His voice was hoarse, but his tone was light, almost joking.

Shameful colour flooded Mary's body. She made a quick movement as if she intended to escape, and he tightened his hold on her.

'There is nothing you or I can do tonight, born of love, that would seem sinful in the eyes of heaven,' he said softly, his eyes holding hers in an infinitely tender gaze. 'Do you believe that, Mary?'

She stared at him in amazed wonder.

'How did you know?' she whispered disbelievingly.

'After all the lectures the rector's daughter must have had on the sins of the flesh?' he asked wryly. 'And I've never liked the sound of Lady Moorcock. Being thrown from the rectory straight into the hell of St Giles would confuse anyone's moral standards. I'm sorry, love,' he said regretfully. 'If I'd been paying more attention to what you were really feeling, instead of what I wanted you to feel, I might have served you better.'

'You've always served me well,' Mary replied unsteadily.

Her hand covered his where it still rested on her breast, and she smiled up into his eyes, shyly, but without any doubt. He gave a wordless exclamation and caught her hand in his, lifting it to press a fervent kiss on her palm. Warm ribbons of delight coursed up her arm and she turned more fully towards him, suddenly impatient of words.

He found the hem of her nightgown and slipped his hand beneath, his fingers sliding lightly and sensuously up her leg to her thigh. She caught her breath, clinging to him. His touch was causing waves of almost unbearable delight to flood through her, yet he was simultaneously arousing an unnamed and as yet unfulfilled longing to experience even greater pleasure.

She suddenly realised that part of his delay was caused by a wish not to hurt or frighten her.

'You can't hurt me,' she reminded him, half shy, half impatient.

He laughed unsteadily and laid his head between her breasts for a moment. She cradled him against her. She was vividly aware of his arousal, and the urgent, powerful desire he was rigidly controlling. She felt a rush of love and tenderness for him. His strength exhilarated her, but without his compassion and care it would have been worse than meaningless.

Then he caught the bottom of her nightgown and began to ride it up her legs. She lifted her hips and he eased it up to her waist and then over her head. She felt embarrassed and closed her eyes, turning her face into his shoulder, because she knew he was looking at her in the flickering candlelight. It didn't occur to her that she should

deny him the opportunity to do so. She knew—
none better—how much he lived through his eyes
and what he saw, but it was difficult to be naked
beneath his scrutiny.

He sighed, and her eyes flew open in
consternation.

'I don't suppose you'll ever let me sketch you
like this, will you?' he said sadly, and she saw the
loving, teasing light in his eyes. 'I told you,' he
reminded her, softly chiding, 'it always gives me
pleasure to look at you.'

'Justin!' She gasped with embarrassed indignation, and tried to huddle her arms across her
breasts. 'Why do you always know what I'm
thinking?'

'I don't. Only when you let me. And you're not
trying very hard to shut me out right now, are
you?'

He smiled at her. Then she saw his expression
change. His hazel eyes began to burn with intense,
urgent longing. Not just for her body. She knew
he wanted more than that. But she caught his
shoulders and lifted herself up against him, pressing a kiss against his mouth.

He responded hungrily. His hands moved
urgently against her naked back. The desire which
he had aroused in her earlier began to throb even
more insistently through her body. She wanted to
feel his touch on every part of her. She wanted to
see and touch him as he was seeing and touching
her. She tugged impatiently at his shirt.

He turned with her still in his arms, and then

she uttered a soft sound of protest as she found herself lying alone across the bed. He stood up and swiftly discarded his clothes, then he pulled back the covers and lifted her so that she was inside the bed rather than on top of it. A second later he had joined her between the crisp linen sheets.

She was lying on her back. He was lying beside her, on his side, and they were touching for the whole length of their bodies. The fire in the hearth had long since died down again, and Justin hadn't pulled the covers very high, but Mary wasn't cold.

Her hair was spread wildly across the pillow, and her skin glowed with eager excitement. Justin gently nudged her legs apart with his knee, and she felt a surge of satisfaction and expectation.

His hand cupped her breast and he rubbed her nipple gently with his thumb. She arched her back, thrusting herself against him, and he leant down to brush her aching flesh with his lips. She caught her breath as she was pushed to another level of pleasure and longing. His lips closed around her nipple, and she felt the soft rasp of his tongue against the hard, sensitive peaks of her breasts.

She gave a soft moan, half in yearning, half in protest at the experience of so much pleasure, and he lifted himself up until he was poised above her. She parted her legs willingly—eagerly—and raised her hips to meet his deep thrust.

A feeling of overwhelming satisfaction and contentment filled her as he entered her, but she had no time to reflect upon it before he began to urge her to new heights of ecstasy. Her hands clutched at his back, clenching and relaxing in an involuntary rhythm which echoed the rhythm of their bodies. She had surrendered all her control to Justin. She had been swept away from her familiar bearings, and everything she knew which gave her security, but she was not afraid, and she did not try to claw her way back to rational normality.

Her world had exploded. Her body was no longer a mundane, earthly vessel for her soul. It had become a glorious means by which she could give and receive love. A physical expression of every passionate, tender feeling she had ever had for Justin.

She seemed to hover on the edge of a blinding revelation. Then Justin raised her to the last, culminating moment of ecstasy, and an unbelievable warmth and contentment filled her.

There was no hasty separation. Justin withdrew slowly. But he slipped his arm beneath her and took her with him, so that she lay with her head resting on his shoulder, her leg resting casually across his.

Her hand drifted across his muscular chest. She was thinking, incongruously enough, of Bill Crawford. The cracksman had only been five years older than Justin when she'd known him, but his wiry body had been scarred and coarsened by the life he'd led. He'd seemed very alien and unattractive to Mary—but then she'd only been fifteen at the time.

'Bill Crawford?' said Justin softly.

She lifted her head in surprise and looked down at him.

'What?'

'Aren't you making a comparison?' he asked, a crooked, self-deprecating smile on his lips. He pushed her wildly tangled hair back as it fell over her face and on to his.

'But this wasn't the first time for us!' Mary exclaimed, disconcerted. 'Why. . .?'

'The last and only time we made love you weren't there,' said Justin quietly. 'You gave yourself to me so wearily. As if your body was nothing more than a means of silencing my importunities. I loved you so much. It was one of the most soul-destroying experiences of my life. I promised myself I'd never repeat it unless. . .'

'It was different this time, wasn't it?' said Mary, her heart aching for the hurt she had unknowingly inflicted upon him.

He smiled tenderly.

'You were here, weren't you?' he said softly.

She nodded, and her hair fell forward again, tickling his nose. He blew at it in mock-exasperation and she giggled, settling down to rest once more with her head on his shoulder.

Then she sat up again.

'If you knew I was thinking about Bill Crawford, you must have been thinking about Bernadette,' she said accusingly.

'No,' he denied immediately. 'Well. . .' He hesitated. 'Not Bernadette, exactly. The question you mentioned earlier, about the difference between love and lust.' He sighed. 'If I could undo. . .'

Mary laid her fingers across his lips.

'Whatever happens, we must never talk about the past to be undone,' she warned softly. 'There's too much that should have been different.'

'Whatever happens?' Justin repeated sharply. A question sprang into his eyes, but he didn't voice it.

Mary was grateful. Some things she still didn't know the answer to. Justin loved her, she loved him, but that didn't mean she was any more suitable to be his wife now than she had been two hours ago. She needed time to think. She needed time to get used to the idea that for the first time in her life she really did have someone who would never betray her.

'Who taught you to shoot?' Justin asked idly.

Mary blinked, the question was so unexpected. Then she raised her head and looked at him, and an almost mischievous smile spread across her face.

'I know,' he declared, just before she could speak.

'Bill Crawford,' they said in unison.

Mary laughed and nestled down beside Justin again. They were cooler now, and he reached down to pull the covers over them. Only two candles were still burning, and neither would last much longer.

'I've never heard you speak badly of him,' said Justin quietly. 'For all you described it to me as a

practical bargain, I think you were fond of him—
and it wasn't pain you were afraid of in my arms.'

'He was never unkind to me,' said Mary slowly,
looking back across the years. 'You're right. He
gave me no pleasure, but he gave me no pain
either. I think he cared about me. And he was the
only one who never made me promises he could
not keep. He gave me the pistol and he taught me
to use it because he said he might not always be
there to protect me. He said I should know how
to protect myself.'

'He showed a better understanding of you, and
your situation, than I always have,' said Justin
sadly. 'And his gift is still protecting you ten years
later. You've never had anything of mine to
comfort you in my absence.'

Mary's hand moved on his chest as she instinctively began to touch the ring on her third finger
with her thumb. As soon as she realised what she
was doing she stilled the gesture. She wondered if
Justin had noticed. If he had, he didn't comment.

'You must go to sleep,' he said almost regretfully. 'There isn't much of the night left.'

'No.' Mary felt a moment of panic. The night
was passing and tomorrow she would have so
many decisions to make. She was suddenly very
afraid, and full of desperate longing that this
beautiful interlude need never come to an end.

Justin stroked her back reassuringly and she
realised that her distress had communicated itself
to him.

'Tomorrow's just another day,' he said softly.

'You don't have to make any decisions. You don't have to do anything but sit in a sunny spot in the garden and watch the blackbirds eat last year's apples. Mrs Marlowe's fond of blackbirds. She says they sing sweeter than any other kind. But for myself, I'm not so sure. They seem a fussy bird to me, always clucking anxiously in the hedgerows. I prefer the storm bird—the missel-thrush that sings in the teeth of even the worst winter gales. I've seen her many times in the park, singing as if her life depended on never giving way to the storm—perhaps it does.'

Tears glistened in Mary's eyes. She knew he was telling her far more than he was saying. But she kept her head down on his shoulder so that he wouldn't see how deeply his words had affected her.

'What about Lucinda?' she reminded him unsteadily.

'We'll wait for word from Bath before we do anything,' Justin replied. 'She told me that she wrote in her letter to her mother that she was quite well, unhurt and safe, but that she couldn't return to Bath until she knew what had been done about Samuel. She thought she might be needed as a witness, or to give a statement. She's a brave girl.'

'Did you tell her about Samuel?' Mary asked.

'Yes.'

She felt Justin's muscles tense beneath her and she moved her hand instinctively in a reassuring caress. His hand captured hers, holding it in a warm, strong grasp.

'I think she was relieved,' he said after a few seconds, 'although she inevitably found it distressing. I'm afraid she may have a few nightmares before she can put the whole thing behind her completely.'

'Will you have nightmares?' Mary asked, thinking how much more unpleasant his involvement in Samuel's death had been.

'I don't know yet,' he replied quietly, his hand gentle on her hair, and suddenly she knew he wasn't talking about Samuel. 'Go to sleep, love. You need a certain amount of energy, even to watch the blackbirds.'

Mary closed her eyes, still feeling his light touch on her hair. They had made a tacit agreement not to discuss the subject which was uppermost in both their minds. But the issue of whether Mary would marry Justin still lay unresolved between them.

She knew how much he wanted that, and she knew what it would do to him if she refused. But the decision was ultimately hers. He had acknowledged as much when he'd come back into the room what seemed a lifetime ago and found her weeping on the floor by the bed.

But he'd said that he needed to know that she was safe. And as she listened to his quiet breathing beneath her head she knew that she needed to know at least that much about him also. But she didn't have to marry him to ensure that. He could visit her sometimes at the Lazy Cat. Perhaps even stay at the inn. And she would have the comfort of seeing him, without the anguish and fear of bringing shame to him.

And he would have. . .what? An opportunity to see her but not to touch her? It would destroy him, just as surely as it would destroy her. She sighed, and felt Justin's hand pause for a moment in its soothing caress. An arrangement like that would be even more disastrous for their love than the strains that would be imposed on their marriage by malicious scandal. They had to be together, or apart. There could be no half-measures between them.

Which left one, final possibility. She had declared so vehemently that she would never be his mistress. Yet it was also true that seven years ago she had tried to persuade him that it was the only possible relationship between them.

As his mistress, her past could never be used as a weapon against him. He would be free to live his normal life and she would have the satisfaction of knowing that he was free to do so.

And their children would be nameless bastards.

There was no way out. No way that didn't involve hurting someone. She didn't know the answer to his question. She was tired and confused, and she could see only calamity whichever way she turned.

She was drifting through a succession of uneasy dreams, half awake, half asleep, when he gently lifted her away from him and slipped out of the bed. She was aware of him going, and a silent cry of loss filled her. But she was still only half awake and she made no move to stop him.

He dressed in silence and went out of the room before any of the servants were stirring.

bed. She was aware of him going, and a silent cry of loss filled her. But she was still only half awake and she made no move to stop him.

He dressed in silence and went out of the room before any

CHAPTER FOURTEEN

MARY woke after a few hours of fitful sleep. No one had come to disturb her. She wondered if Justin had given orders to that effect. If he had, she could only be grateful. She was still naked between the fine linen sheets. She had never before in her life slept naked.

She rolled over, taking almost guilty pleasure in the caress of the linen against her skin. It took no effort of the imagination for her to remember what it had been like when Justin had shared the bed with her. Her body glowed with the remembered feel of him—and the desire to feel his ardent touch again.

She could not feel ashamed of that. She remembered Lady Moorcock's tight-lipped, elliptical comments—and then she remembered Sir Richard Moorcock. A reprehensible smile flitted across her lips. If she'd been married to Sir Richard she might have felt the same way as Lady Moorcock.

Then she thought about St Paul and the many exhortations in his epistles to practise the virtue of celibacy—his repeated warnings that it was better to be celibate than to marry, but better to marry than to burn in hell.

As a child she had never really understood the significance of those admonishments. Now she did, and she could not accept them. She was more than a suffering soul struggling to be free of the unclean, sensuous demands of her body. Her heart, her mind and her body could be as united in love as they had always been in her determination to survive.

She had never flinched from forcing her body to undertake the hard, back-breaking work of building up the Lazy Cat into a successful business. Why should she hesitate to use it now to give pleasure to herself and the man she loved?

She smiled up at the canopy of the bed. One uncertainty, at least, had finally been resolved for her. She had learnt a great deal about herself—and the meaning of love—these last few days. Was she ready to take the great gamble of marrying Justin?

Half an hour later she walked down the grand, sweeping staircase, trying not to look as nervous as she felt. It was ironic that in some ways she had been less worried at the thought of confronting Samuel than she was at the possibility of meeting Dibley again. But she'd always had the option of shooting Samuel. She could hardly do that to the butler if he upset her.

A footman sprang to open the door to the breakfast-room for her, and she sailed past with a courteous smile, trying to look as if expressionless young men in magnificent livery had been opening doors for her all her life.

Lucinda was sitting at the table alone. She smiled when she saw Mary, but there was a worried question in her eyes. Mary glanced around, but they were alone.

'I'm so sorry I rushed out like that last night,' she said seriously, and with a certain amount of embarrassment. 'After all you'd been through yesterday, it was hardly fair. . . But my mother used——'

'Please don't,' said Lucinda quickly as Mary stumbled over the words. 'Please don't feel you need to apologise—or explain. Not unless you really want to. And not after everything you've done for me. Would you like some coffee?' she added, picking up the coffee-pot.

'Yes, thank you.' Mary sat down, looking round in puzzlement. 'Where. . .?'

'Lord Hawkridge sent all the servants away,' Lucinda explained blithely. 'I told him last night how uncomfortable they'd made us feel at dinner.'

'You did?' said Mary faintly.

'I didn't think he'd mind,' Lucinda said, passing her a cup. 'He's never been at all grand.'

'What did he say?' Mary asked.

'He laughed and apologised and said he only kept such a large household to satisfy Dibley's notions of baronial splendour,' Lucinda replied. 'He said that, since Dibley had been butler here before *he'd* even been born, he felt he owed it to him—especially as he spent so much of the rest of his time setting things in an uproar by *not* behaving conventionally. Lord Hawkridge, I mean. I shouldn't think Dibley's ever done anything unconventional in his life. Mind you. . .' she paused thoughtfully '. . .when I met him this morning, when Lord Hawkridge was with me, I thought perhaps he wasn't as austere as he likes to appear.'

Mary was watching Lucinda, a curious half-smile in her eyes.

'You're very observant,' she said.

'I must develop my skills,' said Lucinda serenely. 'Lord Hawkridge says that it's very important to learn to see things truly if you want to produce an accurate likeness.'

'Lord Hawkridge has been practising those skills all his life,' said Mary quietly. 'I'm sorry,' she added a few moments later, the distracted expression clearing from her eyes. 'I haven't asked you how *you* are this morning. Did you sleep well?'

'I had some bad dreams,' Lucinda admitted, her eyes clouding. 'I'll be glad to go home—even to Cousin Emma. But I spoke to his lordship, and he said it would be best if we wait for Henry to come back. Just in case Mama has decided to come here. I begged her not to do so in my letter, but it would be dreadful if she did and we missed each other on the road.'

'I'm sure Henry will be back very soon,' said Mary reassuringly. 'He'll have ridden hard all the way to Bath. And I'm sure he knows you're just as anxious to hear from your mother as she will have been to know you're safe.'

Lucinda smiled. 'Do you really think he had an uncle with a woodwormy leg?' she asked.

'I think he may have embellished his story slightly,' Mary replied. 'I embellished mine—well, actually I made it up completely,' she confessed.

'I thought you did.' A twinkle danced in Lucinda's eyes. 'You were trying to distract me. Ma'am, you couldn't. . .you couldn't teach me how to shoot, could you?'

Mary choked on her coffee.

'I hope you'll never have any reason to need to know how!' she exclaimed.

'Oh, so do I,' Lucinda agreed fervently. 'But it does seem a useful accomplishment to possess.'

'I haven't got my pistol any more,' said Mary. 'Justin took it away from me yesterday. But I'll see what I can do.'

It suddenly occurred to her to wonder where he was. She glanced around almost as if she expected him to appear beside her, a puzzled, uncertain expression in her eyes.

'He said he was going to sketch the blackbirds in the kitchen garden,' Lucinda told her, buttering another slice of toast. 'Are you sure you wouldn't like something to eat, ma'am?'

'No—no, thank you,' said Mary vaguely. 'I'm not hungry. The coffee is fine. I really think you ought to stop calling me ma'am,' she added. 'I'm beginning to feel like an octogenarian dowager! My name's Mary.'

'Thank you!' Lucinda replied warmly. 'You know, I almost think it was worth being abducted if it meant I got to meet you and Lord Hawkridge,' she said reflectively. 'Oh, for heaven's sake go and look at his sketches,' she added with impatient affection. 'It was bad enough having breakfast with one distracted companion; two in less than half an hour is excessive!'

Justin was sitting in the sheltered lee of the kitchen garden wall. The wind was keen, but the sun was bright, and it was warm on the stone bench.

He was sketching the birds as they pecked at last year's rotting apples which Mrs Marlowe had thrown out to them. Mary paused for a moment, watching. There was a missel-thrush among the blackbirds. Its pale brown plumage was drab and unexciting beside the glossy blackbirds, but she too had heard it singing in the winter storms.

She had seen it, but she had never given it a second's thought. Justin had not only seen it, he had remembered it. Perhaps he would always see more than most of his fellow men.

Then the wind caught her skirts, alarming the birds, and Justin looked up. When he saw her he smiled, and her heart turned over at the love and affection in his gold-flecked eyes. She glanced down at his sketch, trying to find some inner balance before she spoke to him.

'"To see a World in a Grain of Sand",' she quoted, '"And a Heaven in a Wild Flower". I've always wondered what the world looks like to you.'

He laid aside his sketchbook and took her hand, drawing her to sit down beside him.

'The trick is learning to see the world through

your eyes,' he said almost humorously. 'I've been trying to understand why you're so determined to resist me.'

'I. . .'

'No, let me speak.' He smiled into her doubting eyes with loving certainty. 'I think, after all the years of fending for yourself, it must be difficult to surrender even a limited degree of control over your life to someone else. And marriage means so much more than that, doesn't it?'

She caught her breath, her eyes fixed in wonder on his face, because she hadn't expected him to understand that aspect of her reluctance.

'You can't go on running the Lazy Cat,' said Justin reasonably. 'But you can keep it if you like. And I'll never expect you to stop thinking for yourself—I'm not interested in a wife who's nothing more than an ornament in my drawing-room.'

He saw the renewed doubt in her eyes and reached out to cup her cheek gently in the palm of his hand.

'But that's the real problem, isn't it?' he said softly. 'You don't think you're fit to be an ornament in my drawing-room, or anywhere else.'

Mary caught his wrist in her hand.

'We can't change the past,' she whispered desperately.

'We don't have to. Do you really think I care what anyone else thinks?' he asked. He spoke quietly, but there was a fierce undercurrent of passion in his voice. 'I don't give a damn about the rest of the world, Mary. They can say what they like about us behind our backs—but if I ever hear anyone abuse you in my presence they'll rue the day they learnt to speak.'

Mary's heart was beating with wild, all-consuming happiness. She could hear the throbbing sincerity in his declaration; she knew he meant every word he said.

'You asked me if I knew what it was like to live a lie, all the time in fear that you might be found out,' he continued, his voice strong and uncompromising. 'And you're right, I don't know. But it doesn't matter. Because I'm not asking you to live a lie. You don't have to pretend to be anything you're not. All I'm asking is for you to be my wife, with all the love and courage at your disposal—as I will try to be your husband with all my heart and soul.'

Mary bent her head because the burning intensity of his love-filled gaze was almost too much to bear. She was too full of emotion to speak. She couldn't deny him now. He deserved nothing less from her than the same commitment with which he had pledged himself to her.

'I can only think of one reason for you not to marry me,' said Justin more quietly. 'And that is that you don't love me. Give me your hand. No, the left one.'

She smiled unsteadily and gave it to him, letting him slip the ring from her finger. Then she watched, her eyes locked on his face, as he held it up to look at it. He was still holding her hand in his, and when the pressure of his fingers on hers suddenly became almost painful in the fierce surge of his relief she knew that he had recognised the inscription.

Ruth 1 v 16. He quoted it from memory in a soft, confident voice.

'Intreat me not to leave thee, or to return from following after thee: for whither thou goest, I will go; and where thou lodgest, I will lodge: thy people shall be my people, and thy God my God: Where thou diest, will I die, and there will I be buried: the Lord do so to me, and more also, if ought but death part thee and me.'

He let his hand fall, and turned to meet Mary's glistening, tear-filled eyes, love and understanding blazing in his own eyes.

'Donald didn't want me to take it,' said Mary unsteadily, because now she really had no more secrets from Justin. 'But it was more respectable to be a widow than a spinster. And I said if I was going to be anyone's widow it would be yours.'

'You're not going to be my widow, you're going to be my wife!' Justin declared triumphantly.

He pulled her into his arms, or perhaps she threw herself there. Her arms were locked around him. His head bent protectively and possessively over hers. He rubbed his cheek against her hair, and she felt his hold on her tighten until she could scarcely breathe. At that moment she knew there was only one power on earth that would ever part them again.

Just for one agonising instant the dreadful possibility of losing Justin gripped her heart. She had lost too much already, and she knew better than anyone the uncertainties of life.

Then she put the fear aside. It was not worthy of her love. If God willed it, they would share decades of happiness together. But if, by some dreadful fate, it was not to be, then their love would protect and comfort them. Nothing, not even the shadowy presence of suffering or death, could change that.

Justin released his hold on her slightly, and lifted her head with one hand beneath her chin to look deep into her eyes.

'Tell me!' he said insistently.

'I love you,' she replied, without hesitancy or doubt. 'I have always loved you. I always will.'

His expression was transfigured, his burning eyes swam before her face, and then he kissed her.

Some time later, when Mary was leaning quietly against Justin's shoulder, his arm firmly around her waist, they heard the drumming of distant hoofbeats on the other side of the wall. She looked at Justin, startled, and he shook his head.

'I don't know,' he said. 'It might be Henry, but I doubt he'd be coming quite so urgently—unless something's wrong in Bath.'

He stood up and went to a gate in the wall. Mary went with him, her hand still resting in his.

'Well, well,' he murmured in amusement.

'What is it?' she demanded impatiently.

'Look.' He drew her to stand in front of him, his arm around her, and bent to kiss her hair as she gazed across the expanse of park beyond towards the road.

'But who. . .?' Mary watched the distant, hastening horseman with narrowed eyes. He looked familiar, but she was sure it wasn't Henry.

'Peter King,' said Justin helpfully.

Mary gasped and turned round to look up at him in amazement. But before she had time to speak he slipped one hand behind her head and kissed her parted lips, his other hand pressing warmly into the small of her back. Her arms instinctively slid around his neck, and for a long, timeless moment she was lost in his embrace.

At last he drew back, laughing softly.

'The sooner we get that ring back on your finger the better, I think,' he said humorously. 'What I was going to say, before you drove every other thought out of my head by looking at me so beguilingly, was that he'll have to follow the road round to get to the front of the house. So we have a bit of time in hand. Except that I don't think it's either of us he's riding so urgently to see.'

'Nor do I,' Mary agreed. 'I wonder if Lucinda will be pleased to see him?'

'Oh, I think so,' said Justin, grinning. 'We had an interesting though typically allusive conversation last night which seemed to touch on the subject of how a young man might feel if a lady he had a high regard for had just been abducted.'

'You did, did you?' said Mary with a certain amount of resigned amusement in her voice. 'Now I come to think about it, this isn't the first time Lucinda has confided in you. How on earth do you always manage to get people to talk to you?'

'I don't. Always.' There was a flicker of remembered torment in his eyes, and Mary knew what he was thinking.

'I'm sorry,' she whispered. 'Justin, if I'd had more faith in your love. . .if I hadn't been so sure I wasn't suitable. . . I wouldn't have been so ready to believe Donald all those years ago. I could have spared you so much pain.'

He smiled down at her tenderly. 'But we aren't going to talk of things to be undone,' he reminded her softly. 'And if I had once thought to go and claim the ring, I would have found out that you'd already done so—and then I'd never have given up my search. But I didn't even remember it when I came back to London and couldn't find you. And later, when I did, I couldn't bear the thought of having the ring without also having you.'

Mary slipped her arms around his neck and drew his head down to hers, kissing him with all the love and passion at her disposal.

Eventually he dragged his lips away from hers.

'I am *not* going to make love to you in the vegetable patch,' he said firmly. His breathing was ragged, but there was a hint of amusement in his eyes.

'Are you going to make us wait until we're married?' Mary asked, a laughing, almost brazen twinkle in her own eyes. 'I seem to remember you making some such decree last time.'

'Last time was different,' he pointed out, but there was no condemnation in his voice—only love. 'And no, I don't think I could—even if I wanted to. We'll have to get a special licence.' He kissed her quickly and stepped away from her. 'Come and sit down again,' he said. 'We'd better give Lucinda some time to greet her beau before we go in. If she needs us, she knows where to find us.'

When they returned to the bench, Mary picked up the discarded sketchbook, flipping idly through the pages.

'Do your servants know about me?' she asked, recalling her fears of the previous evening.

'No,' he said reassuringly. 'Only Henry.'

'Henry?' She looked at him swiftly.

'He doesn't know everything,' said Justin, answering her unspoken question. 'But it was when I was looking for you that I found him. He's been with me ever since.' He grinned. 'He's expressed his approval of you in the strongest possible terms,' he added. 'He'll never forgive either of us if we don't get married.'

'I wouldn't want to disappoint Henry,' said Mary teasingly. 'Does. . .is there anyone else who knows?' she asked hesitantly.

'None of the servants in this house—or any other,' Justin told her, drawing her back within the security of his arm. 'And nobody else. I've never had much inclination to talk about you. You've always been too important to me.'

'Oh, Justin.' She turned impulsively towards him. 'I do love you.'

He kissed her. And then reluctantly drew back.

'I was going to offer to be your mistress,' she confessed after a moment. 'But then. . .'

'You thought about the children,' he said for her, smiling crookedly.

'How on earth did you know?' she demanded, amazed. There was no possible way he could have guessed that. They'd never discussed the issue of children. 'Can you read my mind?'

'No, but I'm learning how it works,' he said affectionately. 'You can endure almost any shame or hardship for yourself, but you can't bear to inflict it on those you love. And you will love our children.'

'Yes.' Tears sparkled in Mary's eyes. 'You've second-guessed me at every turn,' she said, feeling overwhelming love and tenderness for him.

'Do you mind?'

'No.' She took a deep breath, remembering all the women who had gone before her. There was something she needed to know, but she wasn't sure how to ask it.

'What is it?' he asked, seeing the change in her expression. 'Mary?' he added as she hesitated.

'Do you have any children?' she asked in a rush,

her voice sounding rather harsh in her distress at asking such a question.

He held her gaze with his for a long moment. She saw the troubled look in his eyes and realised he was caught between the need to be honest with her and the fear of hurting her. She felt a wave of sickening anxiety sweep over her. If Justin had children, he would be a good father to them, whether or not they had been born in wedlock. Was there someone else in his life who had a claim on his heart?

'One. Perhaps,' he said at last.

'Perhaps?' Relief was hammering through her body, but she tried not to show how much the question had mattered to her.

'His mother claimed he was mine, but I don't think she was in a position to know for certain,' he explained. 'Certainly as the boy has grown older he has never looked like me.'

'Do you. . .see him often?' Mary asked.

'No, not often.' Justin held her hands in his, as if he was aware of how difficult she was finding this revelation. 'His mother didn't want him. I took him and put him in the care of a good couple who've brought him up as their own. He knows me only as a friend of the family. And no one but his parents know he is not their child. They'd already got two daughters, and their only son was stillborn. I've known them all my life.'

He frowned, his eyes losing focus as he looked back on what had happened. 'It was very. . . strange,' he said at last. 'Something which to me was a source of shame and distress brought them great happiness. I've never really been able to resolve my feelings on the matter. I only know that it made me more careful in future.'

He met Mary's gaze and smiled, and she knew that his thoughts had returned to the present.

'It was before I knew you,' he said. 'The lad's ten years old now. And after that. . . Well, if you must know, I think some of the women I've had in my keeping have often been disappointed in the demands I've made upon them,' he admitted, half laughingly, half reluctantly. 'I won't be at all surprised if I get back to London to discover that Bernadette has already found someone to replace me.'

'Justin!' Mary exclaimed.

She tried to sound shocked, and certainly she was relieved. But all the same her first, reprehensible thought was that she couldn't imagine how any woman could leave Justin for another man.

He smiled lopsidedly. 'The truth is,' he said, 'that all I ever really wanted was to lie with love. But the only time I lay with you. . .'

'I never meant to hurt you,' Mary said urgently, seizing his hand impulsively.

'I know.' He squeezed her hand warmly. 'And then I lost you, and I was angry as well as hurt, hence the succession of mistresses—but it never really worked. At first, perhaps. But in the end they became more ornamental than functional. Bernadette's probably had fewer demands made upon her than the average vicar's wife. Although she is extremely ornamental,' he added wickedly.

'What does she look like?' Mary asked jealously.

'Fast,' said Justin, grinning. 'But she has no heart——' he laid his hand gently on Mary's breast, and she felt an instant leaping response '—so she isn't beautiful. Or perhaps she would be if she was with the right man.'

'I see,' Mary murmured, determined not to ask the question that was hovering on her lips.

'Yes, you're beautiful,' he said instantly, smiling teasingly at her. 'I wonder how many times I'll have to tell you before you believe me?'

'But you love me,' Mary pointed out, though she was warm with happiness at his words. 'And you said. . .'

'I can still, with difficulty, look at you objectively,' said Justin with mock-severity. 'Or do you suppose my powers of observation, as well as my heart, are completely overwhelmed by you? I'll prove it to you if you like,' he added, picking up the sketchbook again.

She smiled, making no objection when he started to draw her. She knew he would do so many times in the years to come, and she was no longer afraid of what he might see. She leant back comfortably against the sun-warmed wall and looked out thoughtfully across the kitchen garden. She had always been fond of gardening and, although she knew there would be an army of servants to take care of the grounds, she hoped that perhaps she would be allowed a small corner for herself.

Then she laughed inwardly at the absurdity of the thought—and finally, almost unexpectedly, surrendered to the glorious, swelling certainty that she had come home. She was suddenly filled with such joyous energy that she wanted to leap up and run before the wind like a hare, but she kept her feet tucked demurely beneath her and her hands folded modestly in her lap. If she moved now, she would spoil the picture, and she was aware that Justin was working with swift, intense concentration on his sketch.

At last he laid down his pen. She flexed her arms luxuriously at her release, and reached out for the sketchbook.

'May I see it?'

'Of course.'

He was about to put it into her hand, when he glanced past her and smiled. She turned and saw Lucinda and Peter coming slowly towards them. Lucinda's hand was resting demurely on Peter's arm, but there was an indefinable air of happiness about them which was very revealing.

'It seems to have been a satisfactory morning all round,' Justin murmured, letting Mary take the sketchbook.

She glanced down, and saw herself as Justin had seen her. Her head uplifted, poised for whatever lay ahead. Behind her the tempest still raged. But before her, already casting a glow upon her cheek, the summer sunshine was bringing warmth and happiness.

'You've survived the storms, the dark and the shadows,' Justin said to her softly. 'Now it's your turn to come out into the light. Or perhaps I should say it's *our* turn. Because wherever you go, and whatever you do, I will be with you. Forever.'

LEGACY of LOVE

Coming next month

TO WIN THE LADY
Mary Nichols
Regency England

When Major Richard Baverstock, heir to Viscount Dullingham, returned from the Wars, he knew he must marry and set up his nursery. Having met Miss Georgiana Paget in her role as owner of Rowan Park Stud, he was surprised how well she turned out for a season in town. But it was her younger sister, Felicity, whom Georgie was intent upon firing off, and when the matrons linked him with Felicity Richard didn't object. It took the wager of racing, like Dick Turpin, from London to York, for Richard to know where his heart lay—but how could he now, in honour, withdraw his suit?

MACKENNA'S PROMISE
Elizabeth Lane
East Africa 1899

Meg MacKenna had come to find her husband for only one reason: to get a divorce. She needed her freedom if she was to marry kindly old Arthur and provide for her daughter's future.

Cameron MacKenna hadn't seen his wife for four years, and he'd never seen his daughter Jenny. Suddenly he was afraid he would never see either of them alive again. Slave traders had taken his little girl, and Meg had set off alone across the plains of Kenya to find her. But even if Cameron could rescue his wife and child, could he bear to see them return home to another man?

A years supply of Mills & Boon romances — absolutely free!

Would you like to win a years supply of heartwarming and passionate romances? Well, you can and they're FREE! All you have to do is complete the word puzzle below and send it to us by 29th February 1996. The first 5 correct entries picked out of the bag after that date will win a years supply of Mills & Boon romances (six books every month—worth over £100). What could be easier?

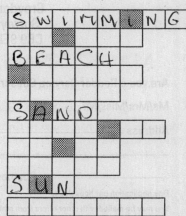

GMWIMSIN

| S | W | I | M | M | I | N | G |

NNSAUT

ACEHB

| B | E | A | C | H |

EMSUR

ANCOE

DNSA

| S | A | N | D |

RTOISTU

THEOL

ATYCH

NSU

| S | U | N |

MYSTERY DESTINATION

Please turn over for details on how to enter →